Small Town Secrets

An Alex Taylor Novel

ANDREW G. NELSON

Cover Design Copyright © 2014 by Huntzman Enterprises
Cover Photo Copyright © 2014 by Canstock Photo Contributors
2009 Disorderly, 2010 Piedmont Photo, 2012 Mocker

Huntzman Enterprises
2007 N 600 E Rd, Edinburg, IL. 62531

First Edition: August 2014

ISBN-10: 099112975X
ISBN-13: 978-0-9911297-5-1

Printed in the United States of America
1 3 5 7 9 10 8 6 4 2

DEDICATION

To God, through whom all things are possible.

For my wife Nancy; without your love, support and constant encouragement this book would never have been possible. Thank you for always believing in me.

And to the men and women of the New York City Police Department, and our brothers and sisters in law enforcement everywhere, who put themselves in harm's way each and every day. God bless the sheepdogs. - *Fidelis Ad Mortem*

Romans 8:28

Other books by Andrew G. Nelson

The James Maguire Series

PERFECT PAWN

QUEEN'S GAMBIT

They all like to pretend that they're so much different from the folks in the big cities, but they're not. They have white washed houses with picket fences and everyone smiles and waves when you walk by. They talk about the virtues of faith, family and community. But their words ring hollow.

At the end of the day, when they close their doors and shut their blinds, they hide the same deep, dark secrets that everyone has. You see, you can change the location, but you can't change what is in a person's heart.

Small Town Secrets - *Anonymous*

CHAPTER ONE

Alex Taylor awoke to a stream of bright sunlight coming in through the half closed plastic blinds, of the living room window, in the small efficiency apartment in Penobscot, New Hampshire.

It was a sleepy little community, nestled among the rugged mountain ranges in the northern part of the state. It had a regular population of fewer than ten thousand residents, but those numbers had swollen to nearly fifteen thousand, now that summer had arrived, due to its location on Lake Moriah.

The lake was renowned for its bass fishing, hosting both state and national championships every year. Its proximity to Northern New Hampshire University also ensured that it was a summer mecca for students.

The small room smelled of stale cigarettes and whiskey, both of which presently occupied a space on the oak end table that doubled as a night stand when the sleeper couch was open. Directly under the front window an old wall mounted air conditioning unit struggled to keep the interior of the room cool, even as the late July temperatures outside steadily gained traction on the thermometer.

Even at six a.m. it was brutally hot and humid.

The apartment itself was located up on the second floor and was smaller than most of the other units. However, beggars couldn't be choosers, especially at this time of the year. Finding an available house or apartment in Penobscot wasn't exactly an easy affair. It depended more on who you knew or, more importantly, how you were related to them.

The sleeper couch occupied the majority of the front of the room and was positioned directly across from where an old

1

twenty-seven inch color TV sat on a *faux* oak entertainment center. A small kitchenette took up the other half. It came furnished with a 1950's era chrome and Formica topped table along with two matching chairs with red vinyl seats. The bathroom was in the back, next to the rear door which led out onto a small wrought iron patio. It would be a couple of months before sitting outside would be a viable option.

Taylor rolled over and sat up with a groan, fighting the urge to go back to sleep. It would be a futile attempt as the alarm on the cell phone would be going off in a few minutes anyway. Still, it didn't make it any easier to get up.

The half-finished bottle of scotch sitting next to the glass tumbler was far too appealing a target to pass up.

"Hair of the dog," Taylor said and knocked back the freshly poured shot.

The feel of the cool liquid on the back of the throat quickly turned into a warming sensation. It felt good, in that old familiar sort of way. Taylor then reached over to grab the pack of cigarettes, tapping one out and lighting it, before drawing in the first breath deeply.

Alex sat on the edge of the bed, letting the combination of the morning sun; whiskey and a cigarette achieve the process of waking up.

As appealing as the thought was of staying in bed, or finishing off the remainder of the bottle for that matter, this was an important new day. As if on cue, the cell phone began to chirp its exceedingly annoying alarm ring tone.

Alex crushed out the remains of the cigarette then got up and headed across the room, flipping the switch on the coffee maker, before going to the bathroom.

The apartment itself might have been uncomfortably small, but it did have one thing going for it, water pressure. Taylor stood under the spray, feeling the stinging sensation of the hot water.

After delaying the inevitable as long as possible it was time to turn the water off. Taylor stepped out of the shower and stood in front of the mirror which was now shrouded in moisture. There was a threadbare washcloth on the counter which Alex used to wipe away the condensation and stood there looking into the mirror.

At thirty-seven years of age Alex Taylor was far from old, but the carefree days of youthful indiscretion were now only distant memories. Still, age had certainly been kind. This was a fact that took on much more significance when one considered the battle scars borne from having spent over a decade and a half in the rough and tumble world of law enforcement.

Taylor had started with the NYPD in 1995, spending most of that time as a police officer in Brooklyn North, one of the toughest proving grounds in New York City. Hell, for that matter, Brooklyn North was one of the toughest proving grounds in the entire United States. It was one of those places where you either survived or you were simply chewed up and spit out. It tested the mettle of the strongest men, let alone a lanky, wide eyed girl from the well-manicured lawns and white picket fences of suburban Long Island.

From her first day on patrol she had made a promise to herself that she would never back down, never show fear. In the thirteen years she spent on patrol she had amassed nearly six hundred arrests, and had been decorated countless times, including being awarded the Combat Cross, the NYPD's 2nd highest medal, for a shootout at a bank robbery. In fact, she was so tenacious that she earned the nickname *La Diabla Rubia*, or the blonde devil, from the local street thugs.

The bank robbery incident, coupled with her stellar arrest history, had also earned her the coveted gold shield of a detective. However, her career as a detective was fairly short lived as she passed the sergeant's exam and was promoted less than a year later.

Over the course of her career, Alex had seen many good cops broken by the unrelenting torrent of poverty, crime, apathy and death. It was difficult thing to endure day after day.

Most cops lived out on the Island, or in upstate New York, and commuted in daily. If you listened to the plethora of community activists and organizers you would think that they were an invading army, out of touch with the needs of the residents. The truth was that they were most often just trying to provide their families with a better environment.

Too often the constant stress of having to live in two different worlds begins to take its toll. It becomes very difficult for a husband or a wife to work in a world where life is cheap, and just surviving is a challenge, then hang up their uniform at the end of the shift and switch it all off. Then they get in the car and go home to hear how *tough* junior's day at school was, because the bus was running fifteen minutes late, or their spouse got yelled at by their boss. Whether they wanted to admit it or not, many often began to associate more with work than home.

As a result, some lost their marriages, some their sobriety, and some their lives.

She had endured the struggles as well. After several failed romances, the bottle seemed to be a more stable relationship to her. Besides, the bottle was never jealous. It never complained that you didn't spend enough time together, and it never threatened that it was going to leave you.

That elicited a laugh.

No, the booze never threatened to leave you, did it? she thought.

Alex dried off, wrapping the towel around her wet hair, and walked out of the bathroom. The strong aroma of coffee now filled the small apartment. She poured herself a cup of coffee into a cobalt blue mug, which bore a gold replica of her old detective's shield.

She walked into the living room, setting the coffee mug onto the table in front of her, before taking a seat on the couch. She reached over, removing a cigarette out of the pack and lit it up. In a way, she knew that the drinking and smoking would most likely be the death of her. Yet she couldn't seem to find the strength to quit. In response, she worked out daily, hoping to at least delay the process till she could find the will to one day kick her bad habits.

She looked at the packing boxes that lined the far wall of the small apartment. Inside were all her personal belongings. It was the remnants of a career which had ended well before its time.

"So this is it?" she said out loud. "Sixteen years in the trenches and now you've been relegated to *Podunk*, U.S.A."

The words belied the truth she knew deep inside. No one had *relegated* her to this place; she had drunk her way here. Alex's evaluations had always been stellar, yet everyone knew what lurked right beneath the surface. Or as one lieutenant so poignantly stated, "She doesn't have a drinking problem, she has a *stopping* problem."

In the end, it was a calculated move. Retire with dignity, and forge a new path for yourself, or dig in and wait for them to fire you. She still had friends and they looked out for her. It was about four months before her old partner called and gave her a number.

"They're looking for a chief of police in Penobscot. I told them to expect your call. They are highly interested in you Alex."

"Where the hell is Penobscot?"

"New Hampshire, up near the Canadian border."

"You're fucking joking?"

"Consider it purgatory, with a pine tree scent."

"I don't know," she replied. "What the hell am I going to do there?"

"You're going to do your time, round off your resume, and hope the fresh country air brings you to your senses."

The last part was abundantly clear to her. She needed to get her head out of the bottle.

It had been a gutsy move on his part she knew. Putting yourself out on a limb for a drunk wasn't the sort of thing that made you very popular; certainly not in the circles that he currently enjoyed, but James Maguire was not your typical person.

The two of them had been partners a life time ago when they had worked in the 73rd Precinct. He'd come in as a rookie, and she had drawn the short straw according to her squad sergeant. At first she detested the thought of having to work with a rookie. In a place as tough as the Seven-Three, you didn't get a second chance out in the street because your partner was a newbie.

After all, this was Brownsville, home to everyone from Murder Inc. to Mike Tyson.

The cops are surrounded every day by people hardened by life's adversities. It's hard to maintain the façade of being a tough guy when the 17 year old they're acting tough with already has a notch or two carved into the grip of the gun they caught him with.

But it didn't take long for her to figure out that he was different than the others, including the veteran cops. It seemed as if even the truly hardened criminals respected him, as if they inherently knew he was the *real deal*.

Yet Maguire never acted tough and no one seemed willing to test him. In fact, in all the years that they had worked together she had only seen him lose his patience with one person. He had taken the man into the next room and closed the door. Alex had fully expected to see the man come back out a little worse for wear. However, when the two men did finally return, the previously belligerent man bore no marks, but was as docile as a church mouse. All Maguire would tell her was that they had a *conversation*, and that the man had a sudden *epiphany*. In retrospect, she realized that he did appear to be about two shades paler than when he had gone back into the room.

Being his partner, she had seen both sides of Maguire. He had the most amazing blue eyes and a smile that would light up a room. Everyone seemed to gravitate toward him. But she had seen the other side too, saw the eyes go in a flash from happy and vibrant to cold and dark, the same eyes she had seen in those stone cold killers they had often locked up. Together they made an unstoppable team. Losing him as a partner was the single worst day of her life. It was then that her social drinking became vocational drinking. Both of them knew it, and she felt Maguire still blamed himself.

And that was precisely the reason why she was currently taking up residence in beautiful downtown Penobscot, New Hampshire.

Alex crushed out the cigarette, took a last sip of the now lukewarm coffee, and went to finish getting ready. At the last minute she pulled her hair back into a pony tail, opting to avoid the fight with the oppressively humid weather they had been experiencing over the last few days.

The previous chief, Charlie Parker, had moved up through the ranks and had worn a uniform till the day he died. Coming in as an outsider, Alex thought it best to forego such familiarities, at least until she knew that she'd be sticking around a while.

She selected a black business suit with a blue dress shirt and flat black dress shoes. She threaded the black belt through the loops, stopping for a moment to slide the end through the black holster containing the Smith & Wesson, Model 5946, 9mm pistol.

When she was done, she grabbed her jacket from the kitchen chair, along with a pair of sunglasses from the counter. Alex then headed out the door and into the blazing morning sun.

CHAPTER TWO

Penobscot was one of those idyllic communities that you routinely see pictured in heartwarming holiday movies on cable movie channels. The town itself was founded in 1814 and would be celebrating its bicentennial next year. Despite the progress over the last two hundred years, it still managed to hold onto its *old world* charm.

Like most small towns, it was built from the middle out. City hall was a three story red brick building that sat in the middle of an expansive, perfectly manicured, lawn and was surrounded by a dozen or so mature oak trees. The front of the building had four large white columns that supported the intricately detailed portico. In the center was a wide granite stone staircase that led up to a front entrance that featured two oversized oak doors.

Alex walked up the stairs and stepped inside. It was like walking back in time. The center of the building was a rotunda design that allowed each of the floors above to look down at the intricate tile inlaid floor which featured the state seal of New Hampshire. From the first floor, where she was currently standing, guests could look up to the stained glass ceiling. It was all quite impressive.

Alex checked the building directory and found that the city manager, as the mayor was referred to here, was located up on the third floor. She still hadn't located a gym in the town so she decided to make up for it by taking the staircase. She located the office at the far end of the building. The door was partially closed and she knocked on the polished oak door jamb.

"Come in," a voice called from the other side.

She opened the door and stepped into the room. Behind an antique oak desk sat Sheldon Abbott. It was only the second time the two had met, the first being when he had interviewed her in Concord about the job.

Abbott was a short, overweight man, who waddled a bit when he walked. He was in his late fifties she guessed, and seemed to dress a bit on the eccentric side. Today he wore a pale blue dress shirt, with a dark blue bow tie and navy Docker pants. A white poplin sport coat hung on the coat rack just inside the doorway.

"Alex, how are you?" he asked, getting up and extending his hand across the desk to shake hers. "Please have a seat."

"I'm doing well sir," she replied and sat down in one of the maroon leather wing back chairs that faced the desk.

"Please, call me Sheldon. We don't stand on ceremony here. Are you ready for your first day as chief?"

"As ready as I'll ever be I guess," she replied.

"I, for one, think you are going to do an exemplary job," Abbott said.

The title was so odd to her and she still struggled with it. To Alex Taylor, chiefs occupied a different plateau, far above her pay grade. They were someone you generally only saw when things went wrong or you were in trouble.

"I appreciate your confidence in me."

"This has been a long time coming," Abbott said. "I think the Department will benefit from having an outsider as chief especially one with your experience and capabilities. It can close the chapter on the old and move ahead into the future."

"I will certainly do my best."

"Just remember, I have an open door policy here, Alex. Just let me know whatever it is that you need."

"I'll remember that," Alex replied.

She suddenly felt very uncomfortable. As if this was all some sort of big joke and they were going to pull the rug out from under her. She'd been only slightly intimidated when she had first made sergeant, but running a squad of officers was entirely different from being in charge of an entire department. She felt a sense of panic gripping her. Deep down inside she just wanted to get up, run out of the building, and head back to the safety of the apartment.

You should have had one more drink, she thought.

"Well, I guess we should go and make this official then," Abbott replied. "The members of the city council are in the conference room next door waiting for you to take the oath of office. Shall we join them?"

"After you, sir," Alex replied and stood up.

They walked across the hall and into the conference room. On the far side of the room sat a long wooden table, behind which sat the four men and two women of the Penobscot City Council. There were about two dozen wooden benches, which reminded her of church pews, in the room which was used for public meetings. About a half dozen people sat in them today waiting for the spectacle to unfold.

Abbott motioned for Alex to take a seat in the first row and then walked around the table to take his place in the middle.

The special meeting was called to order and they all stood, reciting the Pledge of Allegiance. When they were done everyone sat except for Abbott.

"I want to thank everyone for taking the time out of their busy schedules to attend today's special meeting for the swearing-in of Penobscot's newest police chief," Abbott said. "Even though the city council and I believe in the capabilities and professionalism of our police department, we also believe that it is in the best interests of our city to avail ourselves of the best people we can. Alex Taylor is a decorated veteran law enforcement officer with nearly twenty years of experience. She has served as a patrol officer, detective and sergeant and was one of the brave heroes who responded to the World Trade Center attack on September 11th, 2001."

Alex felt herself squirm in the seat. She felt as if the eyes of everyone gathered in the room were staring deep into her soul, seeing the real her. She waited for someone to call out that he had forgotten to mention she was a drunk as well.

The words never came.

A moment later, Sheldon Abbott asked her to stand and raise her right hand. She took the oath of office and he shook her hand again, then handed her the large gold badge that read: Chief of Police – Penobscot, N.H.

Then Alex and the city council members all posed for photos taken by the photographer sent over from the local paper. One by one the council members, then the attendees, shook hands and welcomed her. After they were done, all but Sheldon Abbott left, returning to their full time jobs elsewhere in the community.

"Would you like me to walk you down to your new office?" Abbott asked.

"No, I'll be fine," she replied.

"Well, if there is anything you need, you know how to find me.

"I will. Thank you."

"Congratulations, Alex, I know you'll do great."

Alex shook hands with Abbott and headed back down the staircase to the first floor.

The Penobscot Police Department occupied the entire left side of the first floor of the building, along with most of the basement, which housed the Department's jail and evidence and supply rooms.

Alex took a deep breath and stepped inside.

It wasn't quite Mayberry, but it was a lifetime away from New York City.

Which was a good thing, she supposed.

Just inside the front door was a waist high wood partition wall, complete with swinging door. This acted as a buffer between the entrance and the squad room just beyond. Two old wooden benches sat across from one another in the makeshift waiting room.

The squad room was an open floor plan design, with a half dozen desks scattered around the middle. Several large square support pillars were spaced evenly throughout the room.

God, I wish I had the Murphy's Oil contract for this place, she thought.

"May I help you," said one of the uniformed officers sitting at the desk closest to her.

"Hi, I'm Alex Taylor. I'm the new chief," she replied and walked through the gate.

The officer got to his feet with an expression that ran the gamut somewhere between confusion and fear. It wasn't the first time that Alex, short for Alexandria, had been mistaken for a man's name. Judging from the looks she got from the other two cops present in the room, it would appear that Sheldon Abbott had gotten a good laugh at their expense.

"Sorry, sir,... Uh,... I mean, ma'am," the officer said in a panic stricken voice.

"No problem," she replied. "And you are?"

"Officer Hutchinson, ma'am, Chris Hutchinson."

"Nice to meet you," she said and shook the man's hand.

The other two officers looked at one another and cautiously approached.

"I'm Steven Harper," the first replied.

"Abby Simpson," said the other.

"Nice to meet all of you," Alex replied. "Can someone point out where my office is and, more importantly, where the coffee pot is?"

"I can show you both," Hutchinson replied.

Taylor followed him to the back of the squad room to a large office that featured oak wainscoting along with glass windows inset along the top which allowed the occupant to look out into the squad room. The door also had a glass pane with the word "Chief of Police" stenciled in gold and black lettering.

"The coffee pot is right across the squad room, Chief," Hutchinson said. "Can I get you a cup?"

"That would be great, Chris," Alex replied.

"Actually, everyone just calls me Hutch, ma'am."

"Okay, Hutch, you can call me Alex."

"Yes, Chief, uh, I mean.... Alex."

"We can work on that," she said with a smile.

She stepped into the office and removed the suit jacket, hanging it up on the old fashioned coat rack that sat just inside the doorway.

The office looked like it had been transplanted from some old 1940's detective movie. Which when she thought about it was kind of ironic because it was most likely the inspiration for the movie version in the first place.

The desk sat in the center of the room, an old banker's lamp sitting off to one side and a phone on the other. Behind it were several windows that looked out onto a corner of the square. One of the windows held an oversize window air conditioner. It was one of the noisy, old fashioned ones that actually worked and made the room cold. Two old wooden filing cabinets sat in the corner along with a bookcase. She noticed a door ajar and peeked in to find her very own bathroom.

This job is getting better by the moment, she thought. *I guess there are perks that come along with being chief.*

"Here's your coffee, Chief," Hutch said as he set the mug down on the desk. "I mean, Alex."

"Thank you, Hutch."

"If you don't mind can I just stick with chief?"

"Whatever works best for you, Hutch."

"Inside the desk you'll find a gun and the keys for the chief's car that's parked out front in the spot marked *chief*."

"That should make it easy to find," she replied.

Hutch didn't seem to pick-up on the humor.

"Anything else I can do for you, Chief?"

"No, I think I'm good right now," Alex replied. "Wait; there is something that you can do for me. Can you give me a list of all the open investigations we have."

"Open investigations? This is Penobscot."

Alex looked at him quizzically.

"We've got nothing open?" she asked.

"The last case I remember was when the Kutcher boys went out and played boxball."

"Boxball?" Alex asked.

"Yeah, you know when you drive down the street and hit mailboxes with a baseball bat."

"Seriously?"

"Hand to God," Hutch replied, raising his right hand up.

"Boxball," Alex repeated, letting the word trail off. "*Who'da thunk it?*"

It was just after six when she pulled the chain on the desk lamp, turning it off.

By the end of day one she had managed to meet seven of her ten officers. A few had come in on their off time to gawk at their new *female* chief. Most of them seemed friendly enough, although a bit cautious. That was to be expected. She'd been on both sides of the fence before. New playground, new rules and she would have to prove herself all over again, more so being a woman. There were an additional six part time officers during the summer, but they mostly worked only weekends and special events.

In addition to her officers, a number of the various city agency heads dropped by to greet the new chief, although to Alex it felt like they were only interested in seeing the new oddity.

She reached into the desk drawer, removing the car keys, before getting up. She left the gun in the drawer as she was accustomed to carrying her own. She put her jacket on, and closed the office door, before walking out into the squad room. Officer Bobby Willis, who worked the four by twelve shift, sat at one of the desks. He pecked away at the keyboard, as he put the finishing touches on a missing wallet report.

"Good night. Bobby," Alex said as she walked through the gate.

"Night, Chief," the man called out as he continued to stare intently at the keys searching for the right letter.

Alex stepped outside and into the sultry evening air.

That's what they called it in Penobscot, sultry. In Brooklyn they just called it *hot and fucking humid*. Another thing she would have to get used to.

The chief's car turned out to be quite nice. It was a black, unmarked, Dodge Charger. She got inside and immediately cranked up the air conditioning. As she drove home, she stopped off at *The Bamboo Garden*, a local Chinese takeout joint, and picked up her dinner. She still hadn't mastered cooking anything; other than boiling water on the electric hot plate back at the apartment.

When she got home, she immediately undressed, swapping out the business suit for an oversized gray sweat shirt. The front depicted an old whitewashed fort with a grim reaper peering out over the edge. The top read '73rd Pct - Fort Zinderneuf' and on the bottom, under the fort, was the legend 'Everybody does his duty at Zinderneuf, dead or alive!'

She put some ice in a glass and poured a healthy dose of whiskey over it. She grabbed the Chinese food container before heading over to the couch and curled up on it. Alex located the cable news channel and began to catch up on what was going on in the rest of the world. Unlike Penobscot, the world beyond remained completely *un*-idyllic.

When she was done eating she got up and threw out the container then refilled the glass. She had just sat back on the couch and lit a cigarette when the cell phone on the table next to her began vibrating.

"Hey, Chief Taylor," said the voice on the other end.

"I hope you were standing and saluting when you said that," Alex said with a laugh.

"Don't make me have to come up there and show you how to be a cop again," Maguire replied. "How was your first day?"

"It was quiet in the beginning," Alex explained. "But then after lunch things got really quiet."

"It figures that you'd find yourself a cushy little gig out in the country."

"Yeah, thanks to you. You know I never did get a chance to really thank you."

"It's okay, Alex," he replied. "Just don't let me down."

"Have I ever?" she said with a mischievous tone in her voice that she knew he would hear.

"You know what I mean."

"I do, and I won't screw this up. I promise you."

"Good, that's what I wanted to hear," he replied. "You call me if you need anything, or even if you just want to vent. Okay?"

"I will," Alex said.

"Good, now get to bed early. You've got a department to run."

"Goodnight, James."

"Night, Alex" he said.

Alex heard the call disconnect. She laid the phone back on the end table and took another drink.

She missed him, missed his strength and reassurance. For all the years they had been partners she had never had any doubts, any fears. She always knew he had her back and she trusted him implicitly. And then he was gone, transferred to the Street Crime Unit.

After his 'going away' party, they had spent the night at his house boat, which he kept moored in the Shinnecock Bay on Long

Island. They sat up on the party deck drinking and waiting for the sun to come up. He'd gone downstairs to get another bottle, and she had finally made up her mind that when he got back she was going to tell him how she felt about him. She desperately wanted to explain to him that now, since they were no longer partners, she wanted more. It was the closest she had ever come to telling him how she truly felt, and now there was no going back. She had waited, watching for him to return.

When she awoke the next day on the couch, she realized that she had passed out the night before. Her head ached and the alcohol induced bravery she had felt earlier was long gone. It had been her last chance, and she had let it slip away.

She picked up the glass and swirled the whiskey around inside before taking a sip. The news had transitioned over to an opinion show, and the talking head was going on about some *new* scandal in Washington. No one even got upset anymore. They just simply accepted that it was politics as usual and stopped keeping track of them.

Alex reached over and took another drag on the cigarette before crushing it in the ashtray. She then picked up the remote and turned the television off; she wasn't in the mood to listen. Besides, her thoughts had already turned to something different, something much more intimate.

She propped her feet up on the coffee table then reached over and turned off the lamp.

CHAPTER THREE

Alex looked up from the pillow as if caught in some strange dream. She was just about to lay her head back down, chalking it up to a nightmare, when that thought was interrupted by the buzzing of the cell phone on the night table.

She reached up and turned on the lamp as she grabbed the phone.

"Hello," she managed to say.

"Chief Taylor?"

"Who is this?"

"It's Officer Glenn Albright, ma'am," said the voice on the other end. "We've got a problem."

"Geez what time is it?"

"Just after five o'clock."

"Albright, this had better be really important."

Alex sat up in the bed and reached for the pack of cigarettes.

"Yes, ma'am, we have a body."

That got her attention. Alex took a long drag on the cigarette.

"Where?"

"Over at Cedar Cove," he said. "Down by the marina."

"Albright, pretend I'm brand new and that I don't have a clue as to where it is you're talking about."

"It's okay, Hutch is coming on duty. He is going to swing by in about fifteen minutes and pick you up."

"Ok, thanks. I'll see you in a little bit."

She ended the call and swung her legs over the side of the bed and sat there for a moment. She took a drag on the cigarette and let the cobwebs clear from her head.

A body? she thought. *Here in Penobscot?*

Was it some sort of crazy initiation for the new chief? For the love of God they had better hope not.

Alex got up and made her way to the bathroom, splashing some cold water on her face. There really wasn't enough time to get ready so she just rushed through it as best as she could. She ransacked the boxes till she found the right one, pulling out a pair of jeans and a blue denim dress shirt that had a gold NYPD sergeant's badge embroidered on the left pocket.

She was just finishing putting on her hiking boots when she heard a knock on the door. She got up and answered it. Chris Hutchinson stood on the landing.

"Be right with you, Hutch," she said. She walked back into the apartment, grabbing the cigarettes and lighter, then put them in her pocket before picking up a ball cap with the lettering NYPD across the front. She put it on and pulled her pony tail through the opening in the back.

"Guess it might be time for a new hat," she said and walked out the door, closing it as she left. "Please tell me you guys have a coffee shop open around here?"

"We got a Dunkin' Donuts. Would that help?"

"Oh yeah, we really need to hit that on the way."

A few minutes later, caffeine fix resolved, they were on their way toward the Cedar Cove Marina on Lake Moriah.

It was one of about a dozen marinas on the lake, but by far the largest and most popular with area fisherman. It had several trailer ramps from which they could launch their boats.

As they pulled up, Alex spotted two marked patrol cars along with an ambulance and a rescue truck from the Penobscot Fire Department. She also saw a small fishing boat tied up at the dock next to the fire department's small Zodiac boat.

Everyone was milling around waiting for some sort of direction.

"What do we have?" asked Taylor.

"Two fishermen were heading out and got their prop snagged on some rope, Chief," Albright told her. "One of them went into the water to try and free it, at which time he found the rope tied to a body. The fire rescue guys went out and recovered it."

"Are those the fishermen over there?"

"Yeah, they are pretty shaken up," replied Henry Daniels, the other midnight shift officer.

Taylor walked down the dock to the fire boat and climbed on board. The sun was just beginning to creep up over the mountains in the distance.

"Anyone call the medical examiner?"

"Yes, ma'am, he's on his way."

"We have any camera and crime scene collection equipment?" she asked.

"I do," Albright replied. "It's in the back of my car."

"Go get it and have Hutch come back down with you."

Alex continued to examine the body. She was a young girl, probably in her late teens. It was hard to tell precisely how old. The water hadn't been kind to the body. She was wearing jean shorts and a tee shirt, so she'd most likely gone in within the last several weeks. The body was wrapped tightly with yellow nylon marine rope. One end of the rope was secured around two large cinderblocks. The other end was lying loose off to the side, with its edge frayed.

Must have come loose and floated up to the top where the propeller grabbed it, she thought.

Albright returned a moment later with the camera and a large black bag.

"I want you to take as many photos as you can, every angle, front, back, sides, top to bottom," Alex said. "When you've taken all the wide shots you can stomach, then start taking close-ups: face, hands, legs, clothing, knots on the rope, all of it. If you can't remember if you took the shot, take it again. Remember, nothing is inconsequential. We'll only have this body like this for so long, so I don't want to miss anything."

Alex rummaged through the bag until she found a plastic collection jar. She climbed back up onto the dock and looked out over the water.

"Hutch, I want you to take one of those guys back to the office. Get him some coffee, a pen and a piece of paper then have him write a detailed statement. We need everything he remembers from the time he got up till the time they called us. Send the other one down to me."

"Sure thing, Chief," he said and jogged back up the ramp.

A moment later one of the fishermen came walking toward her.

"You wanted to see me, Chief?" the man said, glancing over at Albright who was snapping away with the camera.

He moved away slowly toward the opposite edge of the dock. He was clearly disturbed by the body of the young woman.

"Yes," Alex replied. "And your name is?"

"Morgan, Danny Morgan," the man replied. "That's my neighbor Riley Brooks."

"Well, Mr. Morgan, I'd appreciate it if you could take me out to where you found the body," Alex said.

"Ok," the man replied, stepping off the deck and onto his boat.

Alex followed Morgan on board. The man released the ropes that held it to the dock and fired up the engine. Fifteen minutes later they were idling in the water about thirty yards from shore.

"So this is where it happened?"

"Yes, ma'am, give or take a few feet. I remember it because of that tree lying in the water over there."

"Tell me what you recall happening?"

"We were just trolling along at this point when we snagged the line. I killed the engine then Riley went into the water to try and free it. Next thing I knew he shot out of the water like he'd seen a ghost. I guess in a way he did. We called 911 and just waited out here till the fire guys came out in their boat. They were the ones who went in and cut the line loose."

Alex looked around. There wasn't anything in sight. It would have been the perfect place to dispose of the body. She took out her cell phone and began taking photos of the whole 360 degrees. When she was done she scrolled through the apps, pulling up the GPS one and copied down the coordinates. She then leaned over the side of the boat, took a water sample in the evidence collection jar and sealed it up.

"How often do you come out here?" she asked.

"This was our first trip this season," the man replied. "Riley and I just got back from the Gulf of Mexico, spent two months working on retrofitting an oil platform down there. Thought we could get some fishing in before all the yahoos started showing up for the regional bass tournament."

"When did you guys get back?"

"Last Wednesday," the man replied.

"Okay, Mr. Morgan, I'm done here. We can head back into the dock. But I'm going to need you to come into the station to make out a report.'

"That's fine. I don't feel much like fishing anymore."

By the time they returned to the marina the medical examiner had arrived and was beginning to conduct a preliminary examination of the body. Danny Morgan quickly secured the boat. He wasted no time heading back up the dock and away from the body.

Alex waited till he was out of earshot before saying anything.

"What do you think, Doc?" asked Alex.

"I'm going to go out on a limb and say it was most likely not as a result of accidental or natural causes."

"I was sort of leaning that way myself."

"So you're the new chief of police?" he asked.

"Alex Taylor," she replied.

"Peter Bates, medical examiner and general practitioner," he replied. "Depending on the time of day, and not necessarily in that particular order."

"I'll try to remember that if I ever have to make an appointment to see you."

Alex wasn't sure what she had expected him to look like. Somewhere in her mind she had envisioned someone older, more mature, maybe a country doctor, with graying hair and a bow-tie.

Peter Bates didn't even come close to that mental image. He was in his early thirties, with wavy brown hair and an infectious smile. He stood about six feet tall and appeared to be in pretty decent shape.

"Heck of a first day for you."

"Eh, it's not my first rodeo," Alex replied. "How long do you think she's been in the water?"

"Wish I could say. Judging from the clothing I'd say not that long, but I assume you've already deduced that."

Alex nodded.

"What are the odds we'll get the tests back reasonably quick?"

"Slim to none," he replied. "That is unless you've got some juice at the State Police Crime Lab."

"No, not really," she replied. "But I can make some calls to a few folks above my pay grade and see if they can be more persuasive. I did collect a water sample from the scene to ship with the body."

Alex handed the jar to him.

"I'll get the body back and do my best to give you some preliminary stuff as quickly as possible."

"I'd really appreciate that, Doc," Alex said and turned to head back up the dock.

"Hey, Chief," he called out.

Alex turned and looked back at the man. "Yeah?"

"Can you let the ambulance guys know I'm just about done and to bring the stretcher down here?"

"Will do," she said and headed back up the ramp.

Peter Bates continued to watch her walk away. He had to admit that it was a much better view then watching old Charlie Parker.

When she got to the parking lot she walked over to where Albright was talking to the fire and ambulance crews.

"The doc's ready for you guys," she said.

The EMT's began to wheel the stretcher down the dock.

"Glenn, I need you to take me and Mr. Morgan back to the station," she said.

CHAPTER FOUR

Alex walked in and headed toward her office as Officer Albright ushered Dan Morgan into one of the back interview rooms. Hutch got up and walked over to the coffee pot, pouring a cup of coffee for her and brought it in.

"Thought you could use this," he said.

"You're a lifesaver," she replied.

"What do we have so far?"

"The first fisherman is done with his written statement. I'll give the other guy a pen and paper to begin his."

"And what did our first guy say?"

"Just that they had recently returned from working down in the Gulf of Mexico and were looking to get some fishing in before the crowds started arriving. They'd been out on the water only a few minutes when they snagged the line."

"What's your gut feeling about him?"

"I'm not a detective, but I get the feeling he's telling the truth," he replied. "He seems genuinely shaken up by it all. I'll check to see if there are any glaring differences in the two statements."

"Good answer," she said. "Normally people who kill their victims don't call the police. Plus, I think she's been in the water a lot longer than they've been home. We'll just have to confirm that part of the story. Where are we at with the victim?"

"Abby pulled the old missing person reports and the alerts we get from local departments. It looks like our victim could possibly be Susan Waltham."

"What's the story with that?"

"She's a seventeen year old local who went missing several weeks ago," Hutch explained. "According to the report the parents claimed that they'd been having some problems with her recently. She stormed out of the house and told them she was going to live with people who really cared about her. Parents figured they would give her a few days to cool off, but when they couldn't get in touch with her they notified the police."

"That's it?"

"Yeah, it's kind of slim. Here's the whole report," Hutch said and handed Alex the folder.

Alex read through the narrative. Hutch was right. It was slim, and that was being generous. She scanned down at the bottom of the page, but it was unsigned.

"Who took the report?"

"Chief Parker did," Hutch replied. "I was working when the call came in. Sheldon Abbott called, said he needed to speak with the chief. Next thing I know he came back bitching and moaning about wasting his time about some teenage kid who got pissed off at her parents and ran away."

"Why would Sheldon Abbott call?"

"I think he and the Waltham's are friends. I've seen them at a lot of the big social functions here in town."

"Ok, let me interview Riley Brooks and we can take a ride over to speak with them."

After the interview was completed Alex was convinced that the two men had nothing to do with the death.

Brooks' story was the same as Morgan had told her earlier, with the exception that Brooks had explained how he'd gone over the side to free the prop and had come almost face to face with the dead girl. She could see that there was real fear in his eyes when he recounted that part of the story. It wasn't something you could fake.

Still, she'd follow-up with their employer to get the exact dates that they had been working and when they departed the rig. She thanked both men for their cooperation, and Albright gave them a ride back to the marina.

"Hutch, you ready?"

"Sure thing, Chief," he replied.

The ride took them out of the town proper and into the rural section of Penobscot. It was a very posh area of town, where the nearest houses were often a quarter of a mile or more away from one another.

Hutch pulled the patrol car off Miller Road and headed down a long, tree lined driveway that Alex guessed was at least a half a mile long.

Kevin and Rebecca Waltham lived in an old, Plantation style house, with a half dozen white pillars in the front and contrasting black shutters on the windows. The driveway made its way around a large circular garden in the front, complete with a pond and water fountain.

It was all quite impressive and very refined.

Alex wondered if what she would find inside would be equally impressive and refined.

"So, Hutch, what can you tell me about the Waltham's?"

"They are an old Penobscot family," the man replied. "Kevin Waltham owns several companies, mostly construction related. His wife, Rebecca, is the chairperson for the Penobscot Women's Auxiliary. They basically run all of the social events here in town. I think they are also on the board of the yacht club."

"Yacht club?"

"Yeah, the yacht club pretty much runs Lake Moriah with an iron fist. Last year they successfully petitioned the city council to enact an ordinance which limits all sport and recreational craft to the northernmost part of the lake. They claimed all the jet skiers and party boats were disrupting the aquatic life. They even got themselves a professor from Dartmouth to back them up."

"I bet that went over well."

"Not really. The northern half of the lake is pretty rough. No beaches and very limited access to ramps or docks. A lot of the locals were really pissed off about it. The only exemption is for the fishing tournaments. The city wouldn't bite the hand that feeds them."

Hutch pulled up to the front of the house and they both got out. As they approached the front door, it opened and a woman stepped out onto the porch.

"May I help you?" the woman asked.

"I'm Chief Taylor, this is Officer Hutchinson. Are you Mrs. Waltham?"

"I am," the woman replied. "What's this about?"

"I'd like to talk to you about your daughter, Susan. May we come in?"

"Yes, please do."

Rebecca Waltham led them into a large sitting room, just off the front entry. She was an attractive woman in her mid-forties with long auburn hair, pulled back in a tight bun, and emerald green eyes. She wore a white pinstriped long sleeved dress shirt with dark gray slacks and black heels.

"I hope we're not interrupting anything?"

"No, not all," she replied. "What can I do for Penobscot's finest?"

"We're following up on the report you filed about your daughter's disappearance," Alex said. "Is Mr. Waltham home?"

"No, he's not. He's at work."

"Well, perhaps you can help me. Being new to Penobscot, I'm trying to follow-up on some open cases and make sure we haven't missed anything."

"I appreciate your interest Chief Taylor, but I'm not sure what else I can tell you that we didn't already tell Chief Parker."

"Why don't you just start from the beginning?"

"Well, please have a seat then," Rebecca Waltham said, motioning to the love seat in the middle of the room as she took the seat opposite from them.

"We had been having problems with Susan for several months," she began. "We have two older children and Susan is our baby. At first we thought it was just the age, but she became more disruptive, more argumentative. It made no sense to us; it was as if she was arguing just to provoke us."

"Had she met anyone new?" Alex asked.

"Not that we were aware of. She was always a good student, never any problems. We know all her friends and their families. We were quite honestly ill prepared for all of this."

"Kids don't come with manuals," Alex said. "And each one is different."

"Sadly, that is very true," Rebecca replied. "Anyway, we were making plans for the upcoming Lake Moriah Regatta when Susan burst into the study to tell us that she was through with living a lie. She said that she was leaving to be with someone who really cared about her and her feelings."

"So she went to stay with one of her friend's families?" Alex asked.

"I'm afraid that was our original assumption as well," Rebecca explained. "So we were not overly concerned. Kevin and I felt that letting her go would defuse the situation and that she would return in a few days. When we didn't hear from her, or any of her friend's parents, we began to get worried. So we started to call around. After we had exhausted every attempt to contact those whom we knew, we finally reached out to Sheldon Abbot, who had Chief Parker come out and speak to us."

"How long had you been noticing the change in her behavior?"

"I'd have to say five, maybe six weeks, at the most. It seemed the closer we got to summer vacation, the worse it actually became. We were dreading the thought of her being home and acting this way."

"Did she have any plans for the summer?"

"Yes, she did. She was supposed to start work the next week at the yacht club, as a lifeguard for the children's summer pool camp program."

"So, according to the report, the last time you actually saw Susan was May 5th?"

"Yes, it was just before school ended."

"Do you have a recent photo of Susan?"

"Yes, I do," Rebecca replied. "Wait one moment and I'll get it for you."

The woman got up and walked out of the room. Alex stood up and looked around. It was clear that the Waltham's enjoyed the finer things and loved having them on display. The house was impeccably arranged and had more of a 'show house' feel rather than an actual home. It looked like one of those houses you see in a magazine.

She wondered if this same level of perfection also carried over to their children as well.

Just then Rebecca returned holding a photo and handed it to Alex.

"This is her high school yearbook photo. It was taken just a few months back."

Alex stared at the beautiful girl in the photo. She had brown hair and eyes, with a vibrant smile that made you genuinely believe she was a normal, happy seventeen year old.

"Thank you," Alex said. "We'll get this scanned in to the file and return it back to you."

"That's ok, you can keep that one. I have more," Rebecca replied. "So tell me, Chief Taylor, do you have any leads?"

"Nothing at this time, but I promise to keep you updated as we move along."

"I got the feeling that Chief Parker didn't seem very interested in pursuing this. I think he considered Susan just another typical runaway."

"Well, in the end that may very well be the case, Mrs. Waltham," Alex said. "But we need to find Susan first before we just file this case away. Would you mind if I looked in her room?"

"No, not at all. Susan's room is at the top of the staircase. Make a left and it's the first door on the left."

"Hutch, can you get a list of Susan's friends from Mrs. Waltham, please?"

"Sure, Chief," Hutch replied.

Alex made her way out of the sitting room and back out into the foyer. To her left, was an oversized wooden staircase that led up to a second floor landing. She made her way up the stairs and located the room.

The bedroom was just as impressive as the rest of the house.

It had old polished wood floors that provided a stark visual contrast to the white wood wainscoting and pastel blue walls. A coffered white ceiling, with a fan that hung silently in the middle, completed the look. There were several large windows that allowed daylight to stream inside, filling the room with both light as well as a gentle breeze. In the center sat an intricately carved four poster bed. A matching dresser sat on one side of the room, while a reading chair and small table sat on the opposite side. Across from the bed was a patio door that led out to the 2nd floor balcony.

The room would have been quite at home in one of those glossy pictorial magazines on refined living, but it certainly didn't look to be the bedroom of a seventeen year old girl.

Alex opened the dresser drawer and began to look around. Everything was folded neatly. She felt around, trying to feel for anything out of place without disturbing too much. When she was done she peered under the mattress and around the reading table searching for even the slightest clue.

As she began to leave the room she noticed it, the thin outline in the wall of a hidden door. Actually, it was more of a *discrete* door rather than actually hidden.

At one time this room probably had a much more vibrant and detailed wallpaper scheme that would have made it much more difficult for the casual observer to see.

Alex pressed it gently and felt it pop open. She pulled the door back and stepped inside.

It had most likely originally been intended to be a decent sized walk-in closet. But now it had been arranged much differently. A book case was on one side, filled to overflowing, and a large number of books also sat scattered on the floor along with some discarded articles of clothing. On the opposite side of the bookcase was a small desk that had more books laid on it, along with an assortment of papers. A standing lamp with an adjustable head stood next to it along with a chair. The wall above the desk held a collage of personal photos, drawings, and miscellaneous clippings.

Alex sat down in the chair and looked around; taking the scene in. This was Susan Waltham's private space. This was where she retreated to, where she planned. She glanced over at the desk. There was a small manila envelope sitting in the middle with her first name written on it along with a small heart that had been doodled on it in red ink. It bore the printed return address of the Penobscot High School District.

Alex opened the envelope. It was empty.

She looked back up at the wall above the desk. There were a number of photos showing Susan goofing around and posing with some of her girlfriends. She opened the center drawer of the desk and peered inside. There were a bunch of papers inside as well; most of it looked like old homework assignments, along with several other photos. She was just about to close the drawer when she felt something hard at the bottom. She pulled the papers out to reveal, another hardcover book.

The girl certainly loved to read, Alex thought.

She removed the book and held it in her hand opening it up and reading the title. She laid it down on the desk, on top of the others, and got up and started to leave the room.

She stopped in the doorway and looked back at the desk. Something wasn't right.

It was an odd colored book. It had a blue cloth spine with an almost neon green cover. It stood out starkly against the glossy dust cover graphics of all the other hardcover books scattered around the room. She walked back and began to examine the other books on the shelves. It took her a minute, but she finally found the missing dust cover on the second to last shelf in the corner. She pulled the book off the shelf and opened it up to reveal the handwritten notes of Susan Waltham's diary.

As she leafed through the book she discovered another small manila envelope. She peered inside and discovered that it contained more photos, and these were not suitable for display.

Alex opened her shirt and slid the book into the small of her back and buttoned it back up. Then she left the room, shutting the door behind her.

When she arrived back downstairs, Hutch and Rebecca Waltham were standing in the entryway.

"Find anything useful?" Rebecca asked.

"No, unfortunately," she replied. "Although it seemed that Susan put the closet to good use."

There was no reason to pretend that she hadn't found the room. In fact it would have looked more suspicious if she had tried to avoid it.

"Ah yes, the closet," Rebecca replied. "That was Susan's sanctuary. We told her she could do anything she wanted in there as long as she kept the bedroom itself looking presentable. She always had her head buried in one book or another."

"Well, thank you for indulging me. I am sure it is hard for you to keep going over this."

"No, thank you, Chief Taylor," Rebecca said. "I appreciate the fact that you are taking this matter seriously."

"Well, if you can think of anything else, please do not hesitate to call me."

As Alex was walking out the door she turned back around. "Oh, I do have one more question, if you don't mind."

"No, please ask."

"Did Susan have a boyfriend?"

"She did, but it ended rather abruptly sometime in April. He was a senior and planning on going away to school. You don't think that has anything to do with it, do you?"

"I'm sure it doesn't," Alex replied. "But I always like to err on the side of caution. Do you remember his name?"

"Yes, Paul, Paul Bollinger."

"Ok, we'll look into it," she said. "Just in case I have any other questions, is there a better number I can reach you at?"

"Yes, let me give you my cell phone number," Waltham replied.

Alex watched as the woman walked over and wrote the number down on a writing pad and handed it to her.

"Call me anytime, day or night, Chief."

"Thank you again for your time, Mrs. Waltham," she said.

Alex and Hutch walked down the stairs and got back in the patrol car. As they drove down the driveway, Hutch was the first to speak.

"Well, that was a bust."

Alex began unbuttoning her shirt.

"Chief!" cried Hutch.

"Calm down there, junior," Alex said as she reached inside and pulled the book out. She laid it on her lap and re-buttoned the shirt.

"What the heck is that?" Hutch asked, a perplexed look on his face, as he tried to process what just happened.

"That is Susan Waltham's diary," she replied as she opened the book up.

"Is that legal?"

"Depends," replied Alex.

"On what?"

"On who it is in these photos," she said, holding up one of the pictures showing a man and young girl having sex.

"Oh crap," replied Hutch.

"Yeah, that's pretty much the same conclusion I came to as well," Alex said. "I don't need to remind you, Hutch, that this stays between us for the time being."

"Yes, ma'am, I understand."

CHAPTER FIVE

All cities have secrets and Penobscot was no different. In fact, the only real difference was the potential fallout. Secrets in big cities only held any real significance if those involved were either high profile celebrities or politicians. People there loved scandals that brought down the elite of society. In small towns, people took what they could get.

Alex sat in her office, with the door closed.

When she got back to the office she had carefully removed all of the photos and duplicated them on the small printer / scanner in her office. She then put them back in the original envelope and deposited them into a plastic security envelope, which she then locked away inside one of the filing cabinets. When she was finished with the photos she did the same for the diary.

She felt better having the originals safely secured. It was only the beginning of the investigation, and she had no idea where it would lead. No sense in getting a case thrown out because the chain of custody was screwed up.

Spread out on the desk in front of her now were the digital copies. There was a total of thirty-six of them which showed different girls and men. The majority of them where grainy, and it was a bit difficult to see who it actually was. But there were a few of them that were quite clear and would leave no question as to who the participants were.

It would have been a much easier job if Alex happened to know the people who lived in Penobscot. She had a steep learning curve ahead of her.

She looked up at the old Seth Thomas office clock that hung just above the door. It was just after five. Alex gathered up the photo copies of the pictures and the diary, then put them into a canvas bag. She gathered up the rest of her stuff and headed out the door, shutting it behind her.

"Hey, Abby, can you drop me off at my place?"

"Sure, Chief," Abby replied.

"I just need to stop off at that Chinese takeout place over on Main."

"Is that taking the place of home cooking these days?" Simpson asked.

"Actually, my idea of home cooking is frozen dinners and a microwave. I tried to cook from scratch before; mostly it involved smoke detectors and fire extinguishers."

"Well, normally it is fairly quiet here, so maybe you'll have more time to hone your skills," Abby said with a laugh.

"I'm not sure what your definition of 'fairly quiet' is, but it's been a helluva second day on the job so far," she said with a laugh. "But in terms of cooking, I just don't ever envision myself becoming proficient in the kitchen. Maybe I just need to find a guy who has some cooking skills."

"Not to say anything bad about the men in this town, but after a few dates you might find that frozen dinners and microwaves aren't really all that bad."

"That's a reoccurring theme in my life," Alex replied.

A half hour later Alex walked into the apartment, tossing the canvas bag onto the coffee table, before heading to the kitchen with the takeout, which she placed on the counter.

She walked into the bathroom and undressed, swapping the jeans and denim shirt for the sweatshirt she had discarded earlier that morning. It felt good to be able to get back into the apartment and relax.

Alex went back to the kitchen and poured herself a drink, grabbing the container of chicken lo mein. She took everything back to the couch, where she turned on the television and began to eat.

Watching the local news in places like Penobscot was sort of like watching minor league baseball. They knew what they were doing, most of the time, but it came across as the *unpolished* version that she had grown accustomed to in the New York City market. Maybe if she stayed here long enough she'd have to invest in cable.

When she was done, she got up and went to the kitchen, tossing the container in the garbage and got a refill on her drink. She then went back to the couch, turning off the TV and lighting up a cigarette, before picking up the cell phone and making the call.

"Did you quit yet?" Maguire asked.

"I'm saving that for Friday, smartass. I need your help."

"Whatcha got?"

"A body," she replied. "Looks like a homicide."

"Are you drunk?"

"I wish," she said. "No I'm being quite serious. Young girl, recovered from the lake up here this morning. She went out for a swim with a couple of cinder blocks tied to her."

"Outstanding," Maguire said. "Investigators?"

"Oh yeah, full complement. Me, myself and I. Geez, James, the last murder they had here was back in 1973."

"Well, the good news is, no one is going to expect much from you. Are the state people coming in?"

"No, no point. The crime scene was in the middle of the lake. We handled all the primary stuff in-house. They'll do the toxicology stuff and get back to us."

"What do you need from me?"

"You know anyone up here who might be able to expedite the labs for me?"

"Yeah, I do, one of the guys on the governor's security detail. I'll call him and see if he can bump your swimmer up on the list."

"Thanks, James," Alex said.

She picked up her glass and took a sip, feeling the effects of the drink a bit quickly. Alex loved hearing his voice. It made her feel as if she really wasn't so isolated in the world. Besides that she had always thought it was sexy. It'd been a long day. She took a drag on the cigarette.

"You need anything else, Alex?"

"Yes," she said, before realizing her thoughts had drifted off to a completely different topic. "Uh, I mean, yeah, there is something else."

"Okay, so what else do you have?"

"My victim matches the description of a missing local girl," Alex said. "Went out to speak with the parents today, did a follow-up interview with the mother. She let me go through the missing girl's room and I found something, something a bit disturbing to be honest."

"What was it?"

"I found her diary hidden as a novel in a book case. I sort of borrowed it. Inside were some photos, James. Most of them consisted of what appeared to be young girls having sex with older men."

"Borrowed? As in you took it without permission?" he asked. "Forget I asked that. Don't answer. Are they locals in the pics?"

"I think so. I mean yes, at least a couple that I know even in my short time here."

"What does the diary say?"

"I haven't had a chance to read it yet. I brought it home for some light reading tonight."

"Anyone else know you have it?"

"Just one of my cops. Seems like a solid enough kid, but he hasn't read the diary or seen all of the photos."

"I think it's best to compartmentalize this for now. Who have you recognized?"

"For one the guy who hired me, Sheldon Abbott, and I am pretty sure the chief I replaced."

"Are we talking kiddie sex?"

"I won't know till I positively identify all the girls in the photos, but the consent law is sixteen here so I don't think so."

"Married guys?"

"Abbott is. At least I assume so from the wedding ring. Not sure about the old chief."

"Keep it *close-hold*, Alex. Remember, you're the outsider. Everyone else is on the inside until you prove otherwise. Unless you're certain you can trust them with your life, don't let them in on what you know. Follow the leads, wherever they go. Right now those photos are like an insurance policy. Keep them safe. Read the diary and let me know what else you glean from it."

"I will, and thanks."

"Remember what you told me the first night we worked together?"

"You're buying dinner rookie?"

"Besides that," Maguire said with a laugh. "You said, and I quote, '*They threw you into the deep end of the pool kid, sink or swim, the choice is up to you*'."

"Karma's a bitch, isn't she?"

"You'll do fine. I'll reach out to my contact tomorrow and let you know what happens."

"Thank you."

"Call me if you need anything else."

"I will," Alex said and ended the call.

The cigarette in the ashtray had gone out and she lit another one. She leaned back in the couch and took a long drag on the cigarette as she examined the small room.

"Thirty-seven years old and living in an over glorified box," she said to no one in particular.

She reached over and picked up the glass, raising it up in a mock toast to herself.

"Congratulations, Alexandria Taylor, you're a sexually frustrated drunk, stuck out in the middle of nowhere. Oh, how the mighty have fallen."

She took a drink, then set it back down on the end table and took another drag on the cigarette. She stared at the diary that sat on the coffee table in front of her.

"Ok, let's see how dysfunctional this place really is," she said and picked the book up.

It was nearly one in the morning when she finally finished. It was Penobscot's very own version of *Peyton Place* as seen through the eyes of Susan Waltham, who was herself no angel.

In a way, Alex was glad that she had found the diary and taken it. To say that Susan was a wild child would have been a gross understatement. She'd been having sex since she had turned sixteen, first with boys, and then crossing over to girls about six months ago. It seemed as if Susan was quite happy to play on both sides of the fence, and she also took pleasure in documenting each encounter.

In addition she also seemed to enjoy documenting the goings-on in the town as she saw them. The girl, it seemed, was very observant. If Sheldon Abbott was indeed one of the men in the photos, he needn't be too concerned. His wife was apparently too absorbed in her own dalliances to have noticed his infidelity. According to Ms. Waltham, Ericka Abbott, who sat on the school board, was romantically involved with both the hunky young gym teacher, as well as her gardener. Alex wondered how she had gotten some of the juicier details she wrote about. There were several other people that she specifically mentioned, but Alex didn't recognize the names.

The first mention of the photos was dated this past January. She wrote about an envelope that had been secretly placed in her locker. As she read along, the entries went on to describe some of the photos and who was depicted. Alex pulled out the envelope and laid the scans on the coffee table. She took out a piece of paper and began recording the dates and names. As the diary progressed, it became evident that there were more photos that she had written about than the ones Alex had actually found. It seemed that Susan had been getting other envelopes on a fairly regular basis.

For the most part Susan had treated it as a game, commentating on both the girls and the men in quite graphic terms. In fact, one of the entries alluded to a missing photo that must have involved another woman. It was clear that someone else was feeding her the information. The only question was who?

Then in April, things became real. An entry dated April 13th chronicled her breakup with Paul Bollinger. Apparently he'd gotten everything he wanted or needed from her and moved onto his next conquest, someone she identified as Lisa Putnam. It was clear that Susan had thought he was the *one*.

He wasn't.

"They rarely are," Alex said, as she continued reading.

To add insult to injury, apparently the next round of photographs contained an image of Kevin Waltham with one of Susan's friends. The diary entry was clearly angry, and Susan pulled no punches, either at her father or her friend.

Was that the catalyst? Is that when things in the Waltham home had changed? she wondered.

Alex laid the diary down on the coffee table and lit another cigarette. She got up and walked over to the kitchen to refill her drink. She sat back down on the couch, staring up at the ceiling.

It was clear that someone else was taking the photos and sending them to her in the manila envelopes with her name on them. The diary entry said that they appeared in her locker. It had to be someone at the school or at least someone who had access to the school.

A teacher? Perhaps another student? It was a potentially long list, but what was the purpose?

The photo of her father had not come until much later. Was that true or was the person feeding her the photos, staging things to their liking?

It was late. She was tired, and she felt kind of dirty, like some voyeuristic peeping-tom looking in through a window.

She took one last drag on the cigarette and crushed it out. Then she washed it back with a final drink and turned off the light. Tomorrow would be here much too quickly.

CHAPTER SIX

It was just after seven when Alex walked into the office carrying a box of donuts. She tossed them onto the counter next to the coffee pot and poured herself a much needed cup.

"Feeding the stereotype aren't ya, Chief?" Hutch asked.

"It's *cop food,* Hutch. Learn to embrace it," she replied. "Anything back on our CUPPI?

"Guppie?" repeated Hutch.

"Sorry, my bad," Alex replied. "No, it's CUPPI not a guppie. It's old NYPD jargon. It stands for *circumstances undetermined pending police investigation.* Basically it's a death requiring additional investigation as to cause and or identity."

"Oh no, nothing yet," he replied. "You did have a call from a Captain Blackshear from the state police. I left his number on your desk."

"Thanks," she said and headed off to her office.

She sat down and picked up the phone, calling the number on the piece of paper.

"Major Crimes, Blackshear," the man said tersely.

"Captain, this is Chief Alex Taylor from the Penobscot PD."

"Hi there, Chief," the man said, his tone softening. "How are they treating you up there?"

"I was having a good run, up until we found the body," she said. "And please, it's Alex."

"I'd imagine that is a mood buster. You can call me Tom. I got a call from the governor's office telling me to help you in any way I can. So what can I do for you, Alex?"

"Give me something more to go on than just a kid dressed in summer clothes, floating at the bottom of a lake. The body was sent out for pathology, and I'm hoping we might be able get some help doing a DNA match for a missing local."

"I heard about that one, tied up with cinder blocks right?"

"That's the one," Alex replied.

"Let me look into it and I will get back to you as quick as I can. Do you have anything we can run a test against?

"I'll get it for you today."

"Sounds like a plan. If you need anything else, you have my number."

"Thanks, Tom, I really appreciate it."

Alex hung up the phone and sat back in the chair, propping her feet up on the desk.

She had to figure out a discreet way to get a DNA sample without raising any flags. Gossip tended to spread quickly through small towns, like a California wildfire in August.

She took a sip of coffee and closed her eyes.

"Break time already?"

She looked up as Sheldon Abbott stepped into her office.

"When I was a rookie cop I would make the sign of the cross and tell my sergeant I was just praying. Truth is it was a long night."

Abbott sat down in the chair across from the desk.

"I heard. Do you have anything new?"

"Not for a few more days at the very least. I've got a phone call in to the state police; they are going to expedite it for us, but testing takes time."

"Any leads?"

"Just an open missing person case at this point," Alex said.

"Do you think it's Susan Waltham?"

"Truth is, it is just a guess at this point. I don't want to look much harder until I have a firm direction to go in. I'm not a big fan of speculating, and I don't want to cause a family any more grief than they have already been through."

"Well, if there is anything you need, just let me know," Abbott said. "Sometimes the locals might not be as open as they should be with someone not from around here, even if they are the chief of police."

"Thanks," Alex said. "I'll certainly let you know if I need any assistance."

"Okay," he said. "I will leave you alone now to do your police work."

Sheldon Abbott got up and walked out of the office. Alex stared after him for a moment, trying to reconcile the man who had hired her for this position and the one she had seen in the photo the day before.

"Small towns," she muttered.

She got up and closed the door. She walked over to the window and opened it wide before she turned to the filing cabinet and unlocked it. She withdrew the personnel folders from inside then brought them over to the desk and sat down. Reaching into her shirt pocket she withdrew the cigarette pack then took one out and lit it. There was probably some local ordinance prohibiting it, but she didn't really care.

Maguire was right. She needed to know who the players were and who she could trust. The first few days were always a *feeling out* period, but she needed to know everything she could in as short a time as possible. As very good as she might be, she knew that she was going to need help at some point.

Much to her chagrin, she found that the personnel folders were basically worthless.

The majority of the officers were all hired locally. Only one officer on the midnight shift and another, who covered the 6:00 p.m. to 2:00 a.m., were from outside Penobscot. Other than that, they contained only pedigree information and the occasional training slip.

Charlie Parker it seemed was not apparently too big on maintaining any real records.

She'd have to do it the old fashioned way. Interviewing each of them, until she could begin filling in all the missing blanks.

Alex took a long drag on the cigarette and set the last of the folders on the pile at the edge of the desk. She swiveled in the chair and stared out the window, looking at the activity on the street outside.

What other secrets did Penobscot hold? she wondered.

She was roused from her thoughtful contemplation by a knock on the door.

"Come in."

"Chief, I just sent Hutch out on a domestic over at the Lion's Head Pub. It doesn't have the greatest reputation."

"Ok, Abby, I'll take a ride over. I was just going to go out for lunch anyway."

"You smoke?" Abby asked.

"Yeah, but only when I'm stressed."

"Uh huh, me too," Abby replied with a laugh.

"I got the impression you were a serious fitness buff?"

"Oh I am, I just started smoking when I was young and haven't been able to quit. I get ragged about it a lot, but then again Schwarzenegger smokes cigars."

"Feel free to join me when the door's closed."

"Thanks, I don't always have a relief to sneak outside."

Alex got up and headed out of the office. She'd gotten about halfway to the main door when she turned around.

"Abby, where's the Lion's Head exactly?"

"Open your computer terminal; you'll see it on the GPS display."

"Thank you," she said and headed out to the car.

The Lion's Head was the local *bucket of blood*. Most of the time, trouble was relegated to either the evening shift or the weekends. However, on occasion there were the local drunks who diverted their attention away from their drinks for a moment to quarrel and bicker with one another. Today it was a domestic dispute between two regulars.

Hutch's patrol car was already parked outside when she arrived. She got out of the car and headed into the bar.

It was your typical local bar with an overly dark interior that had very few windows. The ones it did have hadn't been cleaned since the bar was first opened. The air smelled from old beer and cigarettes.

As Alex's eyes adjusted, she saw a bartender serving a drink to a customer. She counted about a half dozen people sitting at the bar. The man looked up at Alex and pointed toward the back of the place, near a pool table.

She looked in that direction and saw Hutch standing between a pair of large, clearly intoxicated, patrons. He was playing the losing part of referee as the verbal argument began to turn physical.

In the corner, an old jukebox was playing some country song a bit too loud, which only seemed to add to the sense of chaos.

Alex walked up and tapped him on the shoulder. "What do we have?"

"Mrs. Robertson has decided that it is time for them to leave, and Mr. Robertson is *declining* at this time."

"Who the hell is this?" asked Gary Robertson, slurring his words.

"I'm Chief Taylor," Alex replied. "Mrs. Robertson, why don't you come over here and talk to me?"

"Hey," Gary Robertson cried out. "I'll talk to you gorgeous."

He attempted to physically brush past Hutch, who pushed him backward. "Take it easy, Mr. Robertson."

"Fuck you, sport," Robertson said.

The man slammed his hands into Hutch's chest and knocked him into the bar.

Alex closed the distance between the two of them and drove her right forearm up into Gary Robertson's face, knocking him backward where he crashed over a table and landed on the floor.

Seeing her husband get hit, snapped Lucille Robertson out of the alcohol induced anger she previously had against him, and she redirected it at the *blonde bimbo* who had just hit him.

Alex turned around just in time to see Lucille cock her arm back to sucker punch her from behind. Fortunately for Alex, drunks do not have the greatest coordination in the world. She was able to side step the punch and caught the woman's arm as it went by. In one fluid movement she jerked it behind her back and drove the woman down to the floor. A moment later the woman was handcuffed and screaming like a banshee.

With that problem resolved Alex turned her attention back to the husband who had regained his wits and was now rolling around on the floor fighting with Hutch.

As the two men grappled with each other, Alex waited for just the right moment before jumping on the husband's back. She wrapped her left arm tightly around his neck, gripping her left wrist with her free hand, and held on tightly. The man stopped his assault on Hutch and reached up frantically, desperately trying to pry her arm free. Within seconds the fight began draining away from him as he struggled to maintain consciousness. Alex jerked him to the side, pulling his body free from Hutch, who scrambled to his feet and managed to cuff him as Alex released her hold on the man.

"Get off him, you fucking bitch," screamed Lucille. "I'm gonna sue all of you fuckers."

Alex pushed herself up off the floor and sat down with her back against the bar, to catch her breath. She looked down the bar at the other patrons who had been sitting on their stools watching the fight. She reached out her hand and gave them the *thumbs up* sign. They all turned their heads away and went back to their drinks.

A moment later Hutch sat down next to her.

"God, don't you just love police work," she said with a laugh.

"If you say so," he replied.

The husband and wife were transported back to the station and processed. Each ending up in adjoining cells where they continued the dispute they had started nearly two hours earlier. Fortunately there were no other prisoners being held at the time, and the sound of the argument didn't carry upstairs.

Eventually the two intoxicated love birds lost interest in verbally abusing each other and passed out on their respective bunks.

As Hutch was finishing up the paperwork on the two arrests, Alex grabbed a cup of coffee and sat down at her desk. She pulled out the Susan Waltham missing person folder and began going over it again.

The initial report was slim to say the least. It was almost as if Charlie Parker didn't take it seriously. From everything she had heard about Parker, he was a well-liked, affable man, who seemed to have been a decent cop. But the report just covered the basic *who, what, when, where, why* and *how* questions that cops are taught to ask and the details on the why question were essentially glossed over.

Alex thought back to the personnel folders she had read. Did Parker just have an aversion to doing any paperwork, or was he less inclined to take it seriously for another reason, like the one depicted in the photo?

Obviously something had change in Susan's little world to make her leave. The question that really needed to be answered was why.

Alex began to look at the notes she had made. Everything seemed to point back to the diary and the photos.

The photos had been coming in for a while, and, from what Alex had read, Susan seemed to enjoy them. It must have been something about the mystery and intrigue of who would be seen in the next group and with whom.

She flipped the page on the legal pad and began to make more notes about the things she actually knew.

Susan had seemed to enjoy a normal, albeit very sexually active, life. In January she had begun to receive photos of locals, including some prominent ones and friends of hers, engaged in illicit sex acts. She had also been documenting the sexual activities of others. Was this based on the missing photos or her own personal observations? One of the missing photos apparently showed her father. So where were the missing photos?

Alex pulled the scanned photos out of the envelope and looked over them, comparing them to the notes she had made regarding the identities. She knew she had Sheldon Abbott, Charlie Parker, as well as several others, including the bank president, one of the local attorneys, and the head of the yacht club. So far she had identified about fifteen of the girls. Some of whom Susan had indicated as being either her classmates or those who had just recently graduated.

She pulled up the original report and looked at the date it was taken, May 9th. She remembered Rebecca Waltham mentioning that it was right before school ended.

What if Susan hadn't emptied her locker yet, she wondered.

Alex closed up the folder, stuck it in the filing cabinet and locked it up.

"Hutch, got a minute?" she asked.

"Sure thing," he replied.

He picked up several of the papers that were lying on his desk and made his way over to Alex's office.

"I'm done with the arrest reports," he said. "I figured you'd want to review them."

"Toss them in the inbox, and I'll go over them later," Alex said. "I have a question. What if I wanted to take a look in the high school, how would we do that?"

"I guess you could just take a ride over and use the key we have," Hutch said.

"We have a key?"

"Sure, we make routine inspections during the summer to make sure no one is messing around inside," he explained. "One year a bunch of kids got in and were using the indoor pool as a hangout all summer long. Left quite a mess, if you know what I mean."

"Maybe it's time we do an inspection. You know, show me the ropes."

"Ok, I'll go grab the keys."

Penobscot High School was a two story, red brick, building that sat on the northern edge of the city. It had a pretty solid sports program which had allowed the local school board the ability to add on some amenities. School sports were apparently a really big thing up here. Where people would normally bitch and moan about money being spent on anything else, the sports teams got a free pass. In fact, the booster program had been so successful that over the course of the last few years they had raised enough funding for an annex that featured an Olympic size indoor pool, along with a comprehensive weight room.

Hutch pulled the patrol car up to the main office door, and he and Alex went inside.

"The building is divided up into two sections," Hutch explained. "The freshman and sophomores are on the left side, the juniors and seniors on the right. They thought it would be a good idea to keep the new kids separated from the older ones. It puts less stress on their delicate psyches or some other bullshit like that."

"That would make me more interested in the right side," Alex said.

They walked down the long, dark hallway, their footsteps echoing off the stone walls.

It had an eerie quality to it, like something out of a B-movie horror flick. She laughed at the mental image of some masked terror emerging from one of the classrooms holding a carving knife, only to get lit up by a hail of bullets from her and Hutch's weapons.

That wouldn't end so well for old Jason now would it? she thought.

Toward the end, dozens of lockers lined each side of the hallway. Each one had a last name and first initial stenciled on the top.

Alex scanned them as they walked along, looking for Susan Waltham's name.

"You know, while we are here I think I'm going to check out the pool and the gym." Hutch said. "I don't think anyone has done it this week."

"I'll look around here," replied Alex. "We can check the other side when you're done."

"Sounds like a plan. I'll meet you back here."

Alex pulled out the small tactical light she carried in the belt pouch, next to the extra magazine for her firearm, and began scanning the lockers in earnest. Susan Waltham's locker was not on the first floor so she made her way upstairs and began to search the next group of lockers. She found it about halfway down the hallway, a broken lock dangling from it.

She put on a pair of gloves and opened the door, but it was pretty clear that someone had already ransacked it.

Inside were piles of loose paperwork and a couple of text books. A few photos were taped to the interior of the locker door. There was a brush lying at the bottom of the locker, and this she removed, placing it in a plastic evidence bag.

It wasn't what Alex had hoped to find. She scanned the interior with the flashlight one more time, flipping through everything. And then she came upon it, a hard copy of John Steinbeck's *The Grapes of Wrath,* and it was missing the dust jacket. She picked the book up and flipped through it. There were no library markings inside. It was a private purchase book.

Alex tossed the book back inside the locker and closed the door. She'd have to find a way to get back into Susan Waltham's closet and see if Susan had put the cover to better use.

She met back up with Hutch back on the first floor.

"Find what you were looking for?" he asked.

"Maybe," she replied. "How often did you say they check the school?"

We're supposed to do it on a regular basis, but it really depends on what's going on."

"So there really isn't a fixed schedule is there?"

"No, more like if you have free time take a look."

"How well do they check?"

"Depends on who's doing the checking."

"Sounds exactly like the way it's done back in New York," she replied. "You feel like getting some coffee?"

"Sure, I could use a cup."

They hit the local Dunkin' Donuts and grabbed two large coffees before driving over to the lake. They parked the patrol car down by the marina that had started this mystery.

"Tell me something about you, Hutch," Alex said as she pulled back the tab on the coffee container and took a sip.

"What do you want to know?" he asked.

"Well, I looked at your folder. It says you were born and raised here. Went to the local community college and got an associate's degree in criminal justice. Then you joined the Department and have been here ever since. Tell me something I don't know."

"I like to fish," Hutch replied.

Alex reached into her pocket and took out the cigarette pack. "You mind?"

"No, go ahead."

Alex lit up the cigarette and took a drag.

"Fishing huh? Is that what you do in your spare time?"

"I wish. A year ago I bought a fixer-upper. Now all that spare time goes toward fixing one problem or another."

"Is there anyone around to help you?"

"Nope, just my sister," he replied. "But I don't think that's who you were asking about. There's no girlfriend, fiancé or wife.

It's been my experience that they don't mix well with fishing, hunting or house repairs. Maybe one day when I'm done having fun."

"Smart man," she said. "So what do you think about Penobscot?"

"Small town," he replied. "Probably less problems than in a big city, but only because the population is smaller I think. We have the same issues, even if the city board doesn't want to believe it."

"What do you think about them?"

"Eh, I'm not really good with politics. I try to keep my mouth shut."

Alex read his face; clearly he wasn't a big fan.

"Who hired you? Charlie Parker?"

"No, I came in under Chief Bennett. He was only here about a year and then died in an accident."

Alex looked out the window and took another drag on the cigarette.

Penobscot didn't seem to have much luck with their police chiefs, she thought.

The last chief, Charlie Parker, had died of a heart attack back in May. He was out walking his dog near the high school when he keeled over. It was about an hour before anyone began to worry, and by the time they found the body he was already gone.

"So how do you like being a cop in a small town?"

"I like police work, but sometimes I wish I was somewhere else. There's too much politics around here for me. It seems that everyone is related to someone, and you never know who you just might piss off."

"How so?" Alex asked.

It wasn't that she didn't know, but she wanted to hear his take on things in Penobscot. Getting to know the players was easier when the cops told you who they believed were off limits.

"Try writing a moving violation for starters," Hutch said. "No problem if they are out-of-towners, but just try and stop a connected local. They'll tell you up front not to bother, because they know so and so. It's pretty damn frustrating."

"How did that sit with Parker?"

"Chief Parker was here from cop to chief. I guess he just grew to accept it and never really made an issue. Guess if he did they wouldn't have made him chief."

Alex gazed out the passenger window, staring out across the lake, and took a drag on the cigarette. When she was done she flicked it out the window, reached up for the coffee cup on the dash board and took a drink.

"So who do I not want to offend?" she asked.

"Well, I'd start with the people who hired you. Sheldon Abbott pretty much runs everything here. He's been the manager for as long as I can remember. The other members just agree to whatever he wants, because they know they can't get reelected without him. I guess it's okay though, because everything seems to run smoothly around here. He has his fingers in just about everything in Penobscot. So, if you do write someone local, you can probably expect a visit from him."

"Well, like you said, *small towns.*"

"Isn't that the truth?"

"Here's the thing," she said, "I don't do politics well. If you write someone you think really needs to be written, you come to me and I'll make sure it sticks. They hired me, and, until they fire me, they can't tell me how to run my shop."

"I appreciate that," Hutch replied.

"Hey, while we are out and about, why don't we swing by the Waltham house again? I'd like to see when Mr. Waltham is going to be around."

"Ok, you gonna steal another book?"

"I might," Alex replied, staring at him. "Does it bother you?"

"No, ma'am,' Hutch said. "You're the chief of police."

She smiled and took another sip of coffee.

As the patrol car pulled up, Alex noticed a gray sport utility vehicle parked on a small service driveway back toward the rear of the house. They walked up on the porch and rang the bell. It took a few moments before Rebecca Waltham answered the front door.

"Chief Taylor," she said. "I didn't expect to see you back so soon."

"I just realized that when we spoke yesterday I never did ask when would be a good time to chat with your husband."

"Kevin?" she asked. "Oh you didn't have to come all the way out here for that. I feel bad actually. He's out of town for a few weeks on business."

"Oh, it was no bother. We just happened to be out in the area," Alex said. "Actually, I think I may have left my pen up in Susan's room yesterday. Would you mind if I took a look?"

Rebecca Waltham stared back at the staircase. "Uh, no, be my guest."

"Thank you," Alex replied. "It was a present from my old partner, and I'd hate to think I lost it already. I'll just be a minute."

Alex made her way up the stairs. As she turned to go into Susan's room she heard the unmistakable sound of the lock on a door clicking shut from further down the hallway.

She walked straight into the closet and began scanning the books on the shelf. She found *The Grapes of Wrath* up on the top shelf and pulled it down and looked inside. It was a second handwritten journal, but about half way through the remaining pages had been glued together and a pocket carved out. Secreted inside this pocket was another stack of photos.

Alex slipped it under the polo shirt she was wearing and headed back out of the room, holding her cell phone to her ear and made her way down the stairs.

"No, we are across town," she said into the phone. "We'll be there shortly. Tell them to wait for us. Wait hold on for a moment..."

Alex cupped the phone in her hand and looked at Rebecca as she approached her. "Didn't find it, but we have to go." As she passed by, she shifted her body around so that she was walking out almost backward. "If you see it, it's a blue steel pen, little gold badge on the top."

"Okay, I will keep an eye out for it," Rebecca said and closed the door.

Alex put the phone back to her ear and made her way to the car with Hutch in tow. They got back in and she put the phone back into the holder.

"So where are we going?" Hutch asked quizzically, as he drove down the driveway.

"Back to the office," She replied.

"But I thought...." his voice trailed off, as he watched her reach behind her back and toss the book up onto the dash.

"Seriously?"

"I know, I have a problem," Alex replied. "I'm gonna start going to a twelve-step program soon."

"What if you had gotten caught?"

"Rebecca Waltham was much too concerned with getting us out of the house to be focused on anything else."

"What makes you say that?"

"Didn't you see the car parked in the back?"

"Yeah, I just thought it was hers."

"Hutch, the house Rebecca Waltham lives in is worth *beaucoup* money, and you honestly think she drives around in a twenty year old Jeep?"

"I hadn't thought about that," Hutch replied.

"Well, did you notice that when she answered the door her skirt was pulled to the side?"

"Uh, no actually, I didn't."

"Hutch, put on your investigative cap," she chided him "As meticulous as Rebecca Waltham is about her appearance, I don't imagine that was a conscious mistake. I think we interrupted something. Besides, when I went upstairs I got the impression that someone else was on the second floor. I just wish I could have gotten the license plate."

"Want to go back?"

"No, I've already pushed my luck as far as I am willing to at this moment. Head back to the office."

"So are you going to tell me what is in that book?"

Alex gazed out the window at the dense forest that lined the road they were driving down. It was so incredibly different than what she was used to back in New York City.

The majestic scenery was so beautiful and tranquil. It was as if God had carved out a space and left it pure and unblemished. It could easily captivate a person and make them forget that the folks that inhabited this area did not unfortunately share those same virtues.

"Small town secrets, Hutch," she replied. "Small town secrets."

CHAPTER SEVEN

Alex walked out of city hall and ran to her car, tossing the bag, containing the newest book, onto the passenger seat. She got in and ran a hand through her hair, brushing the wet strands away from her face. She looked at herself in the rear view mirror.

"Well don't you look just like a drowned rat?"

A summer storm had come in unexpectedly, providing a much needed cooling off for the area. From outside the sound of thunder reverberated through the car. She started the car up and headed home. She thought about stopping off to pick up dinner, but decided against it. She was tired and just wanted to get home and change into something more comfortable. Tonight she'd have to raid the limited food supply in the pantry and conjure something up.

Eventually you are going to have to go shopping, she thought.

Alex felt restless. It was as if the book sitting beside her was calling out to her. At this point, all she knew was that she wanted a drink and to curl up on the couch to see what latest revelations would jump out.

Was this how Susan Waltham had felt each time a new envelope had arrived?

She thought back to the locker at the school. Clearly someone had searched it, but now the question was who? Could it have been the same person who put the photos inside originally? No, they obviously knew the combination; otherwise Susan would have mentioned her locker being broken into. Someone else had to be looking for something.

This had all the makings of being one of those cases where, for every door you closed, two more opened.

By the time she got to the apartment, the rain had stopped and the oppressive humidity had returned with a vengeance. She walked inside the apartment and was immediately hit by a blast of cold air. She tossed the bag onto the coffee table and walked into the kitchen. The glass was patiently waiting for her. She put some ice into it and then poured the whiskey in, watching the golden liquid envelope the ice. Alex held the glass up to the light, watching as the cubes inside cracked and shattered.

She took a sip and placed the glass down on the counter. It felt good to be home, it had been a long day. She lit a cigarette and took a long drag. She suddenly became aware of the cold chill that had seemed to sneak up on her, and she felt her body shiver.

Alex went into the bathroom, grabbed a towel and dried her hair off. When she was done she got undressed, tossed the clothes into the hamper in the corner, and put on the oversized cotton robe that was hanging behind the door. Immediately she felt her body beginning to warm up. She made a mental note that she'd have to do the laundry soon.

Alex walked back to the kitchen. She picked up the drink and cigarettes then sat down on the couch. She opened up the bag on the coffee table and removed the book she had just gotten from Susan Waltham's closet.

Alex took a deep breath and began reading.

This book seemed to be dedicated strictly to documenting the story behind the mysterious photos.

The first entry was dated January 9th - *I am so scared. We returned back to school today after the Christmas recess. It started off as a great day, but after 1st period I went to my locker to get my history text book and inside I found a school envelope with my name on it. I opened it and there was a photo of me and Paul at the motel we went to. I don't know what to do.*

Alex opened the other journal and thumbed through the pages. She remembered seeing an entry that mentioned a trip.

December 28th – *For Christmas Paul got us tickets to go see the matinee performance of The Lion King in Concord. I can't wait to go. It might be the closest I ever get to Broadway.*

Concord was only about a three hour drive. It certainly didn't merit an overnight stay. Was that just a ruse to get away?

Alex reached back into the bag and removed the envelope that contained the newest photo scans. Again she had copied the originals carefully and then secured them in the office along with the others. She hadn't had the chance to scan the newest book yet. She would have to do that tomorrow. Besides, since it never actually left her possession, there really wasn't an issue with the chain of custody.

She began flipping through the photos, like a deck of cards, until she found the right one. There was no denying who was in the photo. It showed Susan Waltham on the bed, looking forward, and Paul Bollinger behind her, in *flagrante delicto*.

The next entry in the second journal was dated January 19th.

I got another envelope today. This one said, "you're not the only one" on the cover, and boy was that right. There were six more photos but no more of me and Paul, thank God. I don't know who's doing this, or why they chose to send them to me, but I can't believe who is in the photos. Three of the photos show Kim Collins, the head cheerleader, and they clearly show why she is the head cheerleader. Another two showed Pam from my history class with some old dude. I didn't recognize the last girl. She might have already graduated, but I think she was with my math teacher, Mr. Armstrong, or Mr. Phillips, the physics teacher. They have the same receding hairline so it is hard to tell.

The subsequent entries continued to document the latest arrivals. The delivery times were staggered, probably to avoid a discernable pattern, but it averaged out to about one every two weeks. As new envelopes came in, the original fear that had gripped Susan had given way to anticipation. It became a big thrill to see who was going to be depicted in the next round. In all there were a total of eighty-nine photos between the two books. Some showed the same people together multiple times, while others showed them with someone new.

The thrill seemed to last for Susan right up until the last envelope arrived on April 30th, which, coincidentally, was also the last entry.

I cannot fucking believe that piece of shit. He sits down there having dinner with my mother and me, and all the while he has been fucking that little whore Paige. That little bitch has the nerve to call me her friend while she's fucking my father. I should invite her over right now; ask her to come help me with homework. When she comes I could reintroduce her to my father and say, "you remember Paige don't you dad? You should, you had your dick inside her." I bet that would go over big. Wonder how mommy dearest would handle the thought of dear old dad balls deep inside that slut. Hell, maybe she'd get off and stop being so fucking uptight about her perfect little house. I've got to get the hell out of here, away from these fucking losers once and for all before I lose my fucking mind and become like them.

Alex reached over to grab the glass and took a drink. She then lit up another cigarette and took a deep breath, exhaling slowly.

"So the last entry comes just two weeks after Bollinger breaks up with you," Alex said, giving voice to the thoughts running around in her head. "Talk about perfect timing. You hadn't even recovered from your *broken heart,* and then you get hit with that. No wonder you went bat shit."

She leaned back against the couch and stared at the ceiling, letting all the information she had just digested swirl around in her head.

"So you get pissed off after getting the last envelope on April 30th," Alex said to the ceiling. "You're already angry, then you fly into a rage at seeing daddy and your friend. But, judging by the other entries, things were not all picture perfect in the household to begin with. So why is it that you don't actually leave until May 5th, nearly a week later?"

Alex rubbed her eyes and took another drag on her cigarette.

"None of this makes any sense. You're not offended by any of this stuff; in fact it actually gets you turned on. Then you get the photo that really does piss you off. I get that, but you don't fly out in a rage. You wait till the following week to leave, and then, when you do, you leave behind the journals and photos you took such great lengths to hide. So what happened during those next few days? You obviously didn't intend to leave for good; you just needed to get away for a few days. So where did you go? What am I missing?"

She got up, grabbing her glass and headed off to the kitchen to pour another drink. She took a sip and then topped it off before returning to the couch. Alex took another drag on her cigarette and began to blow smoke rings in the air as she struggled with the puzzle unfolding in her mind.

Alex looked down at the books and the pile of photos on the coffee table. She grabbed them and started leafing through them again.

There is a lead here damnit, she thought. *You just have to find it.*

Alex knew that there was something she had missed.

"Start from the beginning," she told herself.

She took the first photo, the one of Susan, and stared at it. They weren't the greatest quality photos, but as she looked through them, she began to see a pattern emerge. She had gotten so focused on trying to identify the people that she had missed it. The people changed, but the characteristics of the room became more consistent.

Alex reached down and picked up the second journal and reread the journal entry. "…..*there was a photo inside of me and Paul at the motel.*"

"Gotcha."

CHAPTER EIGHT

Alex walked in at just after eight in the morning carrying a large coffee and still wearing her sunglasses. It had been a very long night, and she was feeling the after affects.

"Morning, Chief," Steve Harper said. "You got a call from Doc Bates. I left a note on your desk."

"Thanks, Steve," she replied as she made her way to her office. "Is Hutch on patrol?"

"Yeah, why, you need anything?"

"No, just trying to get the personnel schedule straight in my head."

She hung up her jacket, closed the blinds and took off her glasses before sitting down in her chair.

In the center of her desk blotter was a yellow sticky note. It had Peter Bates' name and number on it. She picked up the desk phone and dialed the number.

"Penobscot Primary Care, this is Angela. How may I help you?"

"Hi, this is Chief Taylor. Is Dr. Bates available?"

"Please hold while I check for you, Chief."

A moment later he picked up.

"Hey, Alex, how are things by you?"

"Quiet, but the day just started," she said. "You got something for me?"

"Your girl was alive when she went into the water."

"Fuck."

"That about sums it up as well as anything I guess. She had some other injuries, but nothing serious enough that would have caused her death prior to getting chucked into the lake. There was something else though, Alex."

"What was that, Doc?"

"She was pregnant."

"*Sonofabitch*," Alex said.

"Yeah, I'm sorry.

"Not your fault," she replied. "We live in a cruel world."

"I guess you're right," Bates replied. "You have a lot more experience than I do. Other than that, she was in her late teens, and the body was probably in the water between five and six weeks. We'll have to wait for the toxicology report to come back from the state police to determine whether there were any drugs or alcohol in her system. I'm sending you over the autopsy report this afternoon."

"Sounds good, Doc, I'll talk to you later."

Alex hung up the phone and took a sip of her coffee. She got up and walked out into the squad room.

"Hey, Steve, I got a question for you."

"What do you need, Chief?"

"How many motels or hotels do we have here in Penobscot and the surrounding area?"

"Why? Place your staying at now not going well? Hutch's sister is a real estate agent."

"No, it's working out okay so far. Although, I guess I might have to start making some phone calls to find something a bit more permanent. Just curious where everyone stays during the fishing season."

"Well, we have two here in town, Route 38 Inn and the Hampshire B&B. Just outside of town there is a Howard Johnson's and a Motel 6. Then along the edge of the lake there are three local places, the Cedar Edge Cabins, the Wallingford Inn and the Lake View Cottages."

"Do we have any issues there during the fishing tournaments?"

"Not really," Harper replied. "Occasionally you'll get the drunk and disorderlies over at the lake ones. That's normally where the fishermen stay. They have ample parking for the boats, and all three have ramps to launch them from. Sometimes the contestants will clash with the locals, usually over a broad,... uh... I mean a woman."

Alex laughed.

"Don't worry, Steve; I know the difference between the two. Do we have addresses on those places?"

"I think they are all listed," he said

Harper got up and walked over to the book shelf near the back of the squad room. He searched through the shelves until he located the local phone book and thumbed through the pages until he found the listing.

"Yep, got them right here," he said. "I'll make you a copy."

"Thanks, Steve," Alex replied and headed back into her office.

She closed the door, opened one of the windows and lit a cigarette.

Harper knocked on the door and entered the office.

"Here you go, Chief," he said and handed her the paper.

"Thank you," she replied.

Alex walked over to the back wall of the office where a large pin map of Penobscot and the surrounding area was mounted to the wall. The unused pins lay in a tray on a small shelf under the map. She looked at the addresses in the phone listings and found them on the map, pressing in small red pins to mark their locations. She then put a green pin into the lake where the body was discovered.

The Route 38 Inn was inside the town near the western edge and was the farthest from the lake. The Hampshire B&B was right in the center of town, just two blocks over from city hall. She'd take a ride by, but she didn't believe either of them to be the places depicted in the photos.

Neither location was conducive to sneaking off for sex romps. Some nosey neighbor would have noticed the well connected clientele showing up along with a bunch of young girls. Neither place was discreet enough of a location to carry on such extracurricular activities.

The same was true for the national chains. These sat opposite from one another, just off the main road that led into town from the south. They tended to have more modern interiors as well, something that was definitely not present in any of the photos she had seen.

That pretty much left the three lake locations as her primary targets. They were spaced out along the western edge of the lake, each probably about a mile or two away from one another. The Wallingford Inn was the closest to town while the Cedar Edge Cabins was the farthest away, just southeast of Northern New Hampshire University.

She would have to make a point of visiting them under the pretense of doing a courtesy call before the fishing tournament season got underway. It shouldn't be too hard to poke around and get a tour. She'd just say that she had family looking to come up for a visit.

Alex stared at the small green pin in the lake. All three of the lake locations were in the general vicinity, and she had a gut feeling that at least one of them was somehow related.

Cops didn't believe in coincidences.

Alex sat back down at the desk. She removed a pen and piece of paper from the drawer then began writing some notes. She needed to stop off at the store and pick up a few office supplies.

She would need several large sheets of foam board to paste the photos on. Alex was sure there was a pattern to be found in them, but she needed it to be in some semblance of order to see it. Laying the photos out would allow her to put each of the names she had identified next to them. She would also need a separate board to list the names on, to see how they were all connected to one another.

She would also have to stop by the clerk's office. She needed to get a smaller version of the wall map so that she could see if any patterns emerged with the known participants and where they lived and worked.

Sometimes it all came down to just connecting the dots.

Alex was just about to light another cigarette when she heard a knock on her door. She looked up and saw a man standing on the other side of the door in a dark blue suit.

"Come in," she said.

The man opened the door and stepped inside.

"Hi," he said, extending his hand to her. "I'm Scott Nichols, I'm the County Attorney."

"Hi, Scott, I'm Alex Taylor. Please have a seat."

"Welcome to Penobscot, Alex," the man said as he sat down in one of the seats in front of the desk. "I bet this is a far cry from New York City?"

"Thank you," she replied. "It is a bit quieter, but when the folks here wave to you they tend to use all of their fingers, so that's been a refreshing change."

"I bet it would be."

"So what brings you up from Belkin?" Alex asked.

"Well, I figured I would just pop in and say hello. I also wanted to let you know how things went with your two love birds, Gary and Lucille Robertson."

"Oh, I bet they were none too pleased."

"That's an understatement," he said. "I believe they claimed that you tried to kill Mr. Robertson."

"That demon alcohol will really mess with your mind if you let it."

"Indeed," Nichols replied. "Anyway, as they seem to be back in love with one another, the domestic violence charges were dropped to time served. For the assault on you and Officer Hutchinson they were ordered to pay a two hundred and fifty dollar fine. In addition, they will both have probation for six months."

"Wow, I'm impressed," she said. "Call me jaded, but I actually didn't expect any of the charges to last."

"It's an election year," Nichols replied. "Judge Andrews is our associate judge. He's up for re-election, and it's a contested race."

"So we have a potential hanging judge for at least a few months longer."

"Yeah, I don't expect it to last either way. His opponent is a bleeding heart defense attorney who cut his teeth down in Concorde before moving up north where the election competition isn't as fierce."

"Lovely."

"Yeah, so in the future you might want to exercise some restraint on the choke holds."

"I'd hate to see the Department's ammunition costs increase, but I'll see what I can do."

"Sounds like you have a plan," Nichols said and stood up. "It was a pleasure to meet you, Alex."

"Same here, Scott."

He reached into his pocket withdrawing a business card which he then handed to her.

"If there is anything I can do for you, don't hesitate to give me a call."

"Thanks, I'd give you mine, but I'm all out of napkins at the moment. I really do need to find the printer in town."

"No problem, I'll get one on my next trip."

Alex watched as the man walked out the door.

What was it about attorneys that made you instinctively want to reach for the hand sanitizer? she thought.

Alex got up, grabbing her jacket off the coat rack and walked back out into the squad room.

"I'm going out for a bit, Steve; call me if you need anything."

"Will do, Chief," Harper replied.

She stopped at the door and turned around.

"Steve, do we have a library close by?"

"Yeah, we only have one," he said. "Make a right on Main Street and go three blocks down. It's on the left hand side of the street."

"Thanks, I'll see you in a bit," Alex said and walked out the door.

CHAPTER NINE

The Penobscot Memorial Library was an impressive looking building. That was because it had been the First National Bank of Penobscot in its prior life.

The exterior still bore the hallmark look of strength and stability that was once a common look for early twentieth century financial buildings. A wide stone staircase led the way up to the entrance which was flanked by two large pillars.

Alex made her way up the stairs and walked inside. The interior was completely different. Gone were the tiled floors and oak teller windows that had once filled the main room. Now book shelves lined the walls and were used to create aisles through the cavernous space.

In the center of the room was a large reception station at which a young woman sat, sorting through books. She looked up as Alex entered the library.

"Hi, can I help you?"

"I hope so. I'm Chief Taylor. I was hoping to speak with the librarian."

"You found her," the woman replied. "I'm Sara Bonetti. I'm the librarian."

"I'm so sorry," Alex replied.

"Oh, don't be. I'm not sure what the typical librarian type looks like, but I was told a long time ago by some of the regulars that I didn't look it."

"I'd say that old thoughts and ideas are slow to change in small towns, but I'm new myself so I don't have an excuse. Maybe Penobscot being an old town I expected the librarian to reflect it as well."

"Oh, it did until I took over. Mrs. McBride was 82 when she retired. In fact, if the stairs out front hadn't been so steep she probably would have hung around a lot longer."

"I guess they may say that about me some day, as well," Alex replied.

The woman laughed.

"So what can I help you with today, Chief?"

"I was hoping you might have the high school yearbooks for the past few years available."

"I do actually," Sara replied. "They're not part of the regular library stock, but we maintain all the books and papers for the town historical society here. We have them going back to 1951 when they first produced them. Before that there were just class photos. What years were you looking for?"

"How about the last five?"

"Sure, follow me."

Alex followed Sara downstairs into a large room with a wrought iron security door.

"This used to be the old safe deposit box repository. It still has the working climate controls, so we store our more sensitive documents and books down here. You'd be surprised what people donate to libraries."

"Really? Anything valuable?"

Bonetti turned and pointed to a book contained in a glass box.

"That's a May 1936, first edition, *Gone With the Wind* by Margaret Mitchell."

"How much is it worth?"

"In that condition I'd say ten thousand minimum, more, if you found the right buyer at the right time."

"Wow, I don't think I've spent ten percent of that on every book I ever purchased, combined."

"Me neither," Sara replied. "Librarians may love books, but the job rarely pays enough to be able to afford them. Do you like to read?"

"I do," Alex said. "But I rarely have the time anymore."

"What genre?"

"Everything, anything," she answered. "I grew up as a sci-fi nerd. If it had a ship that could take me anywhere other than where I was at I loved it. I'd have to say Frank Herbert's *Dune* was my favorite. Then as I got older I got hooked up in political / mystery type books."

"Well, we do have a book club here. Meetings are at six o'clock every third Wednesday of the month. If you're free, drop in and check it out."

"I just might do that."

"Do you need these for anything official?"

"Actually, I do."

"No problem," Sara said. "I'll just sign them out to you. This way, if anyone should ask, they will know where they are at."

The two women headed back up the stairs.

"I appreciate your help, Sara," Alex said. "I'll get these back to you as soon as possible."

"Take your time. No one has ever asked to see one of them as long as I have been here."

As Alex made her way out to the car it had started to rain again. She tossed the books into the front passenger seat of the car and ran around to the driver's side.

She made her way over to the office supply store near the southern end of town. By the time she arrived, the rain had stopped and the sun was back out shining brightly.

Weather up here has more friggen' personalities than a schizophrenic, she thought.

Alex returned to the car a short time later with a dozen large foam boards, a package of fine tip markers in assorted colors, glue sticks, a can of spray adhesive and pins which she proceeded to place into the trunk.

When she got back into the car, she opened the laptop computer and turned it on. After it had booted up she logged on and pulled the photocopy of the phone directory out of her jacket pocket. She began typing in the addresses of the various hotels.

She started with the two major ones, Howard Johnson's and a Motel 6, since they were on this end of town. At both locations she spoke to the managers, telling them that she just wanted to speak with them about the upcoming tournament season to see if there was anything they needed.

They seemed quite happy to have a visit from the chief law enforcement officer. Both managers were more than willing to give her a tour of their rooms and facilities, as well as discuss what their upcoming reservations looked like.

Alex had been right that these two were not contenders. Both establishments had undergone major renovations within the last six years. The rooms were all brightly lit and had a modern design.

When she was done, she stopped by the Route 38 Inn. At first glance Alex had thought that the Route 38 Inn might have some potential. When she had first pulled up to the location, it felt like she had been teleported from the present day back into the 1950's. There was a separate main building for check in, but all the guest rooms were attached to one another in a curved, half-moon shape around the fenced in pool in the front. Unfortunately, her excitement had ended abruptly when the manager had opened the door to show one off one of the recently renovated rooms.

The Hampshire B&B had exactly the opposite problem. It had embraced its Victorian charm. In fact, it was furnished with so many antique pieces that you would have to be blind not to notice them in photos. At one point Alex sat down on one of the vintage beds and listened to the springs squeak. There would have been no way to conceal the activity depicted in the photos with these accommodations. On top of all the rest, this place was so out in the open that there was no way someone could have ever hoped to not be seen going into the location.

When she was done she checked her watch. It was already nearly four. Alex decided that the other locations would have to wait till the next day. She wanted fresh eyes when she looked at the others. She didn't want to have to worry about missing a critical piece of evidence because she had been rushing.

She pulled into her spot and headed back inside city hall, stopping off at the City Clerk's Office first and picking up a smaller version of the city map. On her way back she was stopped several times by folks wanting to chat with the *new* chief. They were all very nice, but Alex couldn't shake the feeling that she was like the new attraction at the carnival.

By the time she made it back to her office, it was already four-thirty, and the evening shift had come on.

"Evening, Chief," Bobby Willis said as she walked in.

"Hi, Bobby," Alex replied.

"Is there anything going on out there?"

"Nope, pretty much the usual," Willis answered. "That's going to change soon enough though. The Regatta signals the beginning of our busy period, and then we go right into the tournament season."

"When is that?"

"The Regatta will kick off in two weeks. We should start seeing a lot of folks beginning to arrive in the next week or so. The actual race is on a Sunday, but the Waltham's will be hosting their annual Regatta *Gala* the day before. Anyone who is someone or wants to be someone goes to it."

"Lovely," Alex replied sarcastically. "Who covers the lake during the event?"

"Us and the State Police," he replied. "One of the reserve officers has his own boat and acts as sort of a Marine Patrol on the weekends from July 4th through Labor Day."

Alex walked over to the coffee pot and poured a cup. She then took a seat across from Willis.

"Does everyone usually play nice?"

"Yeah, we hardly have any problems on the water. The state boys take a pretty hard line on horse play on the water. It had been pretty wild at one time, and the folks upstairs," Willis explained, pointing his finger toward the ceiling conspiratorially, "would pressure the old chief into not doing anything. Guess it finally torqued him off enough that an *anonymous* call got placed. That next year the troopers came out. They wrote dozens of citations, and that pretty much ended it."

"I generally prefer handling things in-house, but sometimes having an outsider come in isn't always such a bad thing."

"Yep, sometimes it's hard to deal with all the political crap that goes on here. Abbott pretty much has a stranglehold on things here, but we get decent enough raises and new cars every once in awhile, so I guess it could be worse."

"So I have heard," Alex remarked. "Has it always been that way?"

"Pretty much," Willis replied. "To be honest you're the first outsider for as long as I can remember. In fact, no one could remember a time in recent history when the chief hadn't come up through the ranks. Not saying that them hiring you was a bad thing."

"Trust me, I understand."

"We were all shocked when Abbott announced that he had hired a replacement for Chief Parker."

"It is kind of unusual," she replied, taking a sip of the coffee. "Had he considered anyone from here?"

"I don't think so. Chief Parker had nearly thirty years in before he died. Then there was Michael Williams. He was a sergeant here, but he butted heads with Abbott over something and retired earlier this year. He moved out west someplace, California I think. Matt Christianson, who works the midnight shift, has the most seniority now. He's been on now for twelve years. Everyone else has less than ten years."

"I guess it could be worse," she said. "They could have brought in a civilian who had no law enforcement experience."

"That's kind of what we were afraid of. A lot of names had been rumored, and then, out of the blue, Abbott announced that he had hired you. We were nervous about it, but at the same time relieved that a few of the people mentioned didn't get the job."

"Hopefully, you'll still feel that way as time goes on."

"Well, to be honest, when Charlie Parker got promoted he rarely walked out of that office, except to maybe grab lunch or go on one of his *errands*. So you going out to help Hutch the other day sent a pretty positive message to everyone."

"I'm not really happy unless I'm in the middle of things."

"That's something we are not used to. We've always sort of had to take care of each other and hoped we did the right thing."

"I've known a lot of supervisors in my time. Some were good. Very few were great ones. A lot more were just incompetent, but thrown into the mix were enough jackasses to make you regret ever becoming a cop. By the time I got promoted to sergeant I knew everything about what not to do. I won't ask anyone to do anything I wouldn't do or haven't done. The day I can't get out of that office to help out, is the day I hang up my gun belt and retire."

"So what was it like in New York City?"

"Sort of like here, just a little busier."

"I don't believe that. I bet it was a lot busier."

"Yeah, but in a way it was easier," she replied, reaching into her pocket for the pack of cigarettes. "We never worried about having enough backup. If you needed help it was coming and would be there in seconds, not minutes."

She began to light the cigarette and realized that she was out in the main room. She flipped the cover of the Zippo lighter shut.

"Oh don't worry," Willis replied. "Chief Parker smoked cigars out here. I doubt they'd even smell a cigarette. Besides, half the city heads smoke in their offices."

He reached inside the desk, pulling out an ashtray and handed it to her.

"We started keeping those handy so that the Chief wouldn't flick his ashes in half empty coffee cups."

"*Gracias.*"

"So, did you ever shoot anyone?"

"Yeah, I have," Alex replied.

The answer elicited a shocked look from Willis.

"Oh shit, I'm sorry, Chief," he said when he regained his composure. "I was just trying to be funny. I figured you guys from New York get asked that all the time."

"That's okay. It's ancient history. My partner and I got into a gun fight when we interrupted a bank robbery. It just so happened that we were driving down the block at the same time as the call for the alarm came over the radio. We pulled up across the street just as they were coming out the door."

"What did it feel like?"

"Weird," she replied. "It was almost as if time began to slow down from the minute we saw them. I remember being afraid that I wasn't moving fast enough as I was getting out of the car. Your peripheral vision begins to go pretty quickly. You start focusing only on the threat, and you have to force yourself to scan, because you might miss something. I remember that I couldn't hear very clearly, as if the sounds all around me were muffled. Then, all of a sudden, I could hear this roaring sound that turned out to be the blood rushing in my head. Next thing I know I see this shotgun come up and all hell broke loose."

"Wow. That must have been some scary shit."

"Actually that part wasn't scary," Alex replied, taking a drag on the cigarette. "The scary part was trying to reload and approaching the car after they disappeared from view. I was afraid they were going to pop up someplace I didn't expect, and I was going to get shot. When we finally were able to move around the cars, they were both lying on the sidewalk."

"Dead?"

"Yep."

"Wow....," Willis replied. "Did it bother you?"

"Not really. They wanted to get away and were willing to shoot us to accomplish that. They caused all of it by aiming their guns at us. My partner and I were just better shots than they were."

"I don't think I've known anyone that was in a shooting before."

"It's not something that I recommend to anyone," she replied, crushing the cigarette out in the ashtray.

"What advice would you give someone who found themselves in that position?"

"To quote Wyatt Earp, 'Fast is fine, but accuracy is final. You must learn to be slow, in a hurry'."

"I think I'll just pray that I don't find myself in that position."

"How often do you guys qualify?"

"Qualify for what?"

Alex was taken aback by the comment.

"With your service weapons," she replied.

"Chief Parker wasn't big on that. Said we didn't have the time or the money to waste on something we were most likely never going to use."

"Are you shitting me?"

"No, ma'am."

"When did you shoot last?"

96

"Last summer with my handgun, but that was on my own time, with some of the other guys, for bragging rights. Other than that, most of us hunt so we are pretty good with a long gun."

"That's going to change starting tomorrow," Alex replied. "I'm not going to a funeral because you guys didn't get the training you deserve."

"I didn't mean to cause any problems, Chief."

"You didn't, Bobby. I just don't want to see any of you guys get hurt because you weren't given the right tools for the job. But we will begin to fix all of that."

"Yes, ma'am."

Alex got up from the chair.

"You mind if I take this with me?"

"No, we got about a dozen hidden around here."

"Thanks," she replied. "I'll see you tomorrow."

"Have a good night, Chief."

"You too, Bobby."

Alex dropped the ash tray off in her office before heading out the door.

How the fuck do you not train your people, she thought.

Tomorrow she was going to have to go through all those folders and see when the last time any of them had received any training after the academy.

On the way home she stopped by *The Bamboo Garden* to grab some dinner.

"Hello, Chief Taylor," Peggy Lee said, from behind the counter.

"I must be eating here too much if you know my name already."

"No, you can never eat here too much," the woman said. "You want your usual?"

"Sure, why not."

Peggy Lee shot a stream of rapid fire Cantonese to the man working in the kitchen behind her. As Alex watched, the man tossed in a bunch of ingredients into the wok, working it like a conductor in front of an orchestra. It was almost mesmerizing to watch.

"So how you like Penobscot?"

Alex diverted her attention from the cook back to the woman.

"Huh? Oh yeah, it's really nice," she replied. "Quiet."

"Yes, quiet," Lee repeated. "But then not so quiet when you learn when to listen."

"What do you mean?"

"Lots of people come in here. Like to talk. You don't say much. You listen. You learn a lot."

"You're a very smart woman."

"I know. That's why I live in Penobscot now and not in Bushwick anymore," she said, with a smile.

"Small world isn't it?"

"Very small world," she replied.

"So what do you hear, Mrs. Lee?"

"Oh, lots of things. People still not sure of you. Some not so happy a woman in charge."

"If only I had a quarter for every time I heard that," Alex replied.

"Some think you don't know what you're doing. They think they hired you because you're a pretty woman. I laugh, they fools. They don't know what it takes to survive in Brooklyn," she said as she bagged up the order and passed it to Alex.

"How much do I owe you, Mrs. Lee?"

"This one *on the arm*. You be careful, Chief. You listen."

"I'll do that," Alex said, stuffing a ten dollar bill into the 'tip' jar on the counter. "Have a good night."

It was nearly seven by the time Alex got home, unloaded the car then finally collapsed on the couch with her take-out and scotch. Spread out on the coffee table were the yearbooks, diaries and photos.

"I really need to find a hobby," she said.

Alex stuck her fork into the container and swirled it around, gathering up some of the noodles.

So now I'm known as the chicken lo mein Chief by the takeout lady? she thought. *I guess it could always be worse. It could be the bartender that has the name for me.*

After dinner she dumped the container in the garbage, got a refill on her drink and lit a cigarette before sitting back down on the couch. She took each of the photos and sprayed the backs with adhesive before sticking them onto the foam boards. A half hour later she had all the photos posted and had begun to list the names she knew next to each of them.

Alex spread the boards out across the living room, and it became readily apparent that what she knew paled in comparison to what she didn't know. By eleven o'clock she had only managed to identify about seventy people in the photos, leaving more than a hundred unidentified. It was becoming clear that she was going to need someone more familiar with the locals to identify everyone.

She knocked back the last of her drink and refilled it from the bottle she had moved to the coffee table. She lit another cigarette and leaned back against the couch, staring at the boards in front of her.

The majority of the men were all older. There were some young men, like Susan's boyfriend Paul, but they were the exception. Most appeared to be in their forties and above, while the girls appeared to be in their late teens or early twenties, at the oldest.

In addition to Sheldon Abbott, and the other men she had previously identified, she was able to identify two city council members, the highway commissioner, along with two high school teachers. The list was growing longer by the day and read like a *Who's Who of Penobscot*.

It was obvious to her that this was a sex ring, but was the person taking the pictures part of it or taking advantage of it?

Probably taking advantage of it, she thought.

Anyone running this would never jeopardize a good thing, by letting photos surface. Which meant that whoever was doing it was most likely in jeopardy. Did they stop taking the photos by their own choice, or did someone find out, and was there another body floating around in the lake?

Alex picked up her glass and finished the drink, setting it back down on the table.

Was the girl in the lake part of all this? Was it Susan Waltham? Or was she someone else in one of the photos? At this point she had to assume that they could be related.

She rubbed her eyes and looked back at the empty glass sitting on the table. Sadly, she couldn't even get a decent buzz from the stuff anymore. She took another drag off the cigarette and crushed it out in the ashtray.

She was tired and her head hurt. The rest of this would wait till tomorrow. Alex reached down and grabbed one of the pillows off the floor and laid it down on the end of the couch. She didn't even have the energy to open the bed. She stretched out and pulled the comforter down on top of her.

God, I need to find a place with a real bed, she thought.

CHAPTER TEN

It was around six thirty when Alex came through the front door of the station.

She'd had a terrible night's sleep and finally gave up trying around five thirty. Just because she had gotten up early, didn't mean that she wasn't exhausted, or hung over for that matter.

"Morning, Chief," Paul Murphy said, as Alex walked into the office.

Murphy was one of the late tour officers that had popped in earlier in the week to meet the new boss.

"It is that, Paul," she replied.

"Hey, at least I didn't add 'good' to it."

"That is true. You have any plans today?"

"Nothing that I know of," Murphy replied. "You need me to do something?"

"Yeah, actually I do," Alex said. "You want some overtime?"

"Sure."

Alex walked into her office and returned a moment later holding the plastic security envelope containing the brush she had taken from Susan Waltham's locker.

"Can you run this down to Captain Blackshear, at the State Police Major Crimes Unit for me? I'll call ahead so that he knows to expect you."

"Yes, ma'am."

"When do you want me to leave?"

"You can head out now," Alex said. "I'll watch the fort till the day shift comes in."

"Works for me," Murphy replied. He grabbed the envelope and headed out the door.

Alex grabbed a cup of coffee and headed off to her office. She picked up the phone and called the number for Blackshear, getting his voice mail.

"Hey, Tom, it's Alex Taylor. I'm sending that brush down to you this morning for comparison to the DOA. If you have any questions give me a call back. Thanks."

She hung up the phone and took a sip of coffee, enjoying the relative quiet that she knew wouldn't last long.

Alex got up and walked over to the filing cabinet and pulled out the folders containing the training record.

Over the next half hour she went through the records trying to make sense of what Charlie Parker had been doing. It wasn't giving her the warm fuzzies.

As she went through the firearms qualification log, it appeared that either Bobby Willis was a bald-faced liar or that Charlie Parker was a thief. The files indicated that every member of the Department had qualified at least twice a year, and in some cases three times a year, for the last decade. According to the records, the last qualification had been held in April and the second shoot was tentatively scheduled for September.

There were also a series of handwritten receipts attached to each log for ammunition purchases from a Mountain View Sporting Goods in Belkin. Each receipt was for two thousand rounds of .9mm ammunition, with the prices rising with each recent order.

There was nothing overtly wrong with the receipts, other than the last order was dated from May of this year, and yet she had not seen any boxes of unused ammunition in the firearms locker in the basement.

Ten minutes later she heard the front door open and Hutch strolled into the office.

"Morning, Chief," he said, as he walked by her office.

"Morning, Hutch," she replied.

A few minutes later Abby Simpson came in.

Alex grabbed her coffee mug and walked out into the squad room to get a refill.

"Is there anything going on today, Chief?" Abby asked.

"Yeah," Alex replied. "I need you to track down a company called Mountain View Sporting Goods in Belkin for me. Get a quote for two thousand rounds of Winchester 115 grain, jacketed hollow point, .9mm ammunition. Then get another half dozen quotes from other vendors. Have each of them send a fax on their letterhead."

"Okay," Abby replied. "Is there a problem?"

"Nope, just need to get everyone qualified, and we are out of ammo. When you have them all take the low bid and do an official purchase order for them."

"I'll have it done for you by this afternoon."

"Thanks," Alex replied as she headed back to her office, closing the door and opening the window.

What other mysteries am I going to uncover around here? she wondered, as she lit up her cigarette.

Alex set those thoughts aside for the moment. She had other pressing matters, like the lake homicide and the potential sex ring, to focus on.

She needed to get out and look at those lakeside motels this morning. Those were her best shot as far as this being something local. If they didn't pan out she'd have to begin expanding outward toward the adjoining towns. There was always the potential, however remote, that the location could be a private residence, but after examining all the photos she was convinced that an older style motel was the prime suspect.

Alex finished the last of her coffee and crushed the cigarette out in the ashtray before gathering up her keys and jacket.

"Abby, I have some running around to do this morning. If anyone is looking for me I'll be on the radio."

"You got it, Chief."

She had almost made it to the car when an elderly man, wearing a baseball hat with the words *World War II Veteran* emblazoned on it, approached her holding a black metal mailbox in his hands.

"Chief Taylor?" the man called out.

"Yes, sir," she replied.

"I wanted to talk to you about this," he said, raising the dented mailbox up for her to see.

"Let me guess, boxball?" she said.

"If I catch those silly *sonsofbitches* I'm going to box more than their balls," the old man replied.

Alex stifled a laugh.

"I'm sure you would, Mr.?"

"Foery," the man replied. "Martin Foery."

"Where did you serve, sir?" she asked.

"I was with the 165th Infantry, on Saipan."

"Thank you for your service, and I'm sorry for the damage to your mailbox. If you go inside and ask for Officer Hutchinson, he'll take a report from you on the damage. I'll make sure the officers keep an eye out in the area."

"I appreciate that," the man replied. "Thank you, Chief."

She watched as he turned to head toward the steps of city hall.

It still amazed her, the differences in people. Why was it that some young men went off to war and sacrificed themselves, while others remained safely at home, engaging in boorish behavior for their own amusement?

Alex had studied the battle of Saipan for a college history course she had taken. It had been a brutal proving ground for many a young soldier during World War II. In three weeks of fighting on the island nearly one out of every five American soldiers was wounded or killed. Some of the nicknames given by the soldiers, to the topography of the island, speak volumes as to the severity of the fighting: *Hell's Pocket*, *Purple Heart Ridge* and *Death Valley*. In the end, it would be one of the most decisive victories in the Pacific and would see the awarding of five Congressional Medals of Honor and one Navy Cross.

Alex only wished she could catch those little bastards and make them have to come face to face with that veteran. Then they would see just how *tough* they really were.

She'd make a point to see what she could do to arrange that meeting, but for now it would have to wait. Alex got in the car and headed off to the first of the three lakeside motels.

The Wallingford Inn must have been something special back in its heyday, Alex thought, as she pulled the unmarked car up to the covered portico front entrance.

The six story hotel sat on the southern bank of Lake Moriah. As Alex got out of the car she heard howls and laughs coming from the nearby pool. The summer crowds had already descended. She walked toward the entrance and opened the glass door, feeling a blast of cold air hit her.

She walked over to the front desk and introduced herself to the young woman standing there.

"I'm Chief Taylor from the Penobscot Police Department," she said. "I need to speak with the manager on duty."

"Any problems, Chief?" the woman asked.

"No, just going around and introducing myself. I'm trying to speak first hand to the people who deal with the summer crowds and address any needs before it gets too busy."

"Well, please have a seat, and I'll call him."

"Thank you."

Alex walked into the reception area which afforded a panoramic view of the lake. She could see why it was still a popular destination despite the dated look.

A few moments later the day shift manager walked in and greeted her. He was a middle aged man with a pencil thin mustache and dark hair parted over to the side. But what got Alex's immediate attention was his attire. It struck her as off that the blue and white checkered pants, partnered with a powder blue dress shirt, actually seemed quite at home inside the hotel. It was as if the Wallingford was caught in a 1970's time warp.

"Chief Taylor, so glad to meet you, the man said, extending his hand to shake hers. "I'm Dan Johnson, the manager. Everyone just calls me Danny."

"It's nice to meet you, Danny. I'm Alex Taylor."

"To what do we owe this visit?"

"Since I'm new to Penobscot I just thought I would reach out to the folks that handle the accommodations for the summer crowd and see if they have any needs or to address any problems."

"Well that is quite a departure from what we grew accustomed to. Chief Parker always made us feel bad if we asked for help. He treated us as if the occasional unruly guest was our fault."

"Well, I'd like to change that relationship," Alex replied.

They spent a few minutes discussing the prior issues the hotel had, and Alex promised that the Department would do anything it could to mitigate any problems they might have.

"I was wondering if you might be able to show me one of your rooms, Danny," she asked. "I have family that might come up for a visit after Labor Day, and my mother can be so picky."

"Aren't they all," he said with a laugh.

He led her down the hallway to one of the vacant rooms and opened the door, stepping aside to allow her to go in.

"Thank you," she replied, and stepped inside.

It wasn't the worst place she had ever seen, but it was certainly in dire need of some updating. What was most important to her was the fact that the rooms were bright. Even if the furniture hadn't been replaced in a while, the rooms appeared to have benefited from a fresh coat of paint.

"After each season we repaint and have the carpets professionally cleaned," the man said.

"That's a very nice touch, Danny," Alex replied. "Thank you for taking the time to show me the room. I'm sure it would meet my mother's expectations."

"We'd be very happy to arrange accommodations whenever you need it, Chief."

As she was leaving, the man handed her his business card.

"If you need anything, at any time, you let me know personally."

"Thank you, Danny."

The next stop on her journey was the Lake View Cottages, which had the distinction of merging a quaint exterior charm with an updated interior. There were a total of a dozen and a half individual white clapboard cottages which had either a queen or two full beds inside along with a small seating area, complete with wall mounted flat screen TV's, *Wi-Fi* and a half kitchen.

The manager, Jenny O'Day, explained to Alex that a few years back they had signed a long term lucrative contract to host the organizers of both the fishing tournament and the annual regatta, along with the top seeded contestants and select media. As a result, they had invested in numerous interior upgrades, which effectively bumped them off of the suspect list.

The manager was grateful for Alex's concern, but, as she explained, they really had no problems at their location because of who they hosted.

When she was done, Alex got back in her car and made her way north along Route 1.

After being shutout at all of the other locations, she was beginning to think that she would have to head back to the office and expand her search parameters. She wondered how many other places there were surrounding Penobscot.

She pushed the thought away as she saw the sign for the Cedar Edge Cabins appear, just ahead of her on the right.

She had just been about to pull off into the parking area when she caught a glimpse of a vehicle parked adjacent to the main house.

It was a late model gray Jeep.

Alex straightened out the unmarked car and pulled back onto the main road, continuing north. About a mile ahead she pulled over onto the shoulder.

She felt that nagging cop intuition that told her something wasn't right. She had seen the same type of vehicle parked near the back of Rebecca Waltham's a few days earlier.

Yes, she knew that Jeeps were popular vehicles, especially up here, and to most folks it could simply be a coincidence.

But Alex was a cop, and she did not believe in those things.

Alex reached down and grabbed the radio mic from its holder on the dashboard.

"M-11-1 to M-11-3 are you on the air?"

"M-11-3, that's affirmative. Go with message."

"M-11-3, 10-3 me," she replied, using the radio code for Hutch to call her by phone.

A moment later the cell phone rang.

"Hutch?"

"Hey, Chief, what do you need?"

"Are you doing anything right now?"

"I'm just running radar up on Highway 29, but it's really slow."

"I need you to meet me up by Cedar Edge Cabins."

"When?" he asked.

"Now, but we have to time it right. I'm a mile north of the location. Come in from the south. Call me back when you are about a mile south of the place."

"Okay, I'm on my way," Hutch replied.

Alex reached up and loosened the mounting screw for the in-car camera system. She removed the camera from the cradle and set it sideways on the dashboard. She then powered up the video display on the car's computer and watched as the image, looking out the driver's side window, appeared.

A few minutes later her cell rang.

"Okay, I'm in position," Hutch said when Alex answered the phone.

"Start heading north," she replied. I'm going to pull off to the side of the road, and you pull up next to me like we are just talking."

"10-4, Chief," Hutch replied.

Alex pulled the car onto the shoulder just as Hutch's marked patrol car came around the bend. To anyone watching it would have appeared completely normal to see the two police cars stopping to chat.

Alex rolled down the window and adjusted the camera on the dash.

"What happened to the camera?" Hutch asked.

"I'm making lemonade out of a lemon," she replied.

"I assume you're going to explain that to me, aren't you?"

Alex watched the computer display as the camera brought the Jeep into view.

"Uh huh," she said as she began writing on a scratch pad.

"Thank you," Hutch said. "Sometimes I don't think my brain works as well *outside the box* as yours."

"You'll learn, Hutch," Alex replied and handed him the paper.

"What's this?"

"Don't look around. I believe that is the license plate of the same Jeep that was parked at Rebecca Waltham's the other day."

"It's parked across the street, isn't it?"

"Yes it is."

"And that's why you took the camera apart, so you could see it without someone thinking you were looking?"

"See, you're learning."

"What do you want me to do with this?"

"Run it, but quietly, not on the air. I don't want anyone with a scanner knowing what we are doing. Go back to the station and do it. After you have the information, then I want you to do a background check on the registered owner and see what you can dig up."

"You got it, Chief," Hutch said. "I'll call you as soon as I have the information."

"Thanks," Alex replied. "Hey, by the way, did you take that report this morning from the old man and the mailbox?"

"Mr. Foery? Yeah, I did. I left a note for the evening and late shift to keep an eye on that stretch of road. It's out in the rural area of town, and we've had problems out there before."

"Good work. Let me know what you find out on the Jeep."

As soon as Hutch had pulled away she rolled up the window and dropped the car into drive, heading south on Route 1 back to town.

Well, this could be a very interesting twist, she thought.

CHAPTER ELEVEN

"I have that information you wanted, Chief," Hutch said over the phone.

"Great," Alex replied. "Meet me over in the high school parking lot. You want coffee?"

"Sure," Hutch said. "Regular."

"Donut?"

"Again with the stereotype?" he asked.

"Suit yourself," she replied. "But you'll be a much happier individual when you learn to just embrace it."

Fifteen minutes later Alex watched as Hutch pulled into the parking lot and up to her car. She rolled down the window, handing him a coffee container and a bag.

"It's okay," she said. "You don't have to open the bag until after I leave."

"What is it?"

"A toasted coconut donut," Alex replied, "A culinary masterpiece. What do you have for me?"

"The registered owner of the Jeep is a Hazel Jenkins, year of birth 1967, who resides in New Hampton, just north of Concord."

The wave of excitement that Alex previously experienced, when she had first spotted the vehicle, began to dissipate.

Guess it's back to square one, she thought.

"However, that last name sounded very familiar to me. So, remembering what you told me before, I put on my 'investigative cap' and began to dig a little deeper," Hutch continued. "I did a check by address and found a record for a Louis Jenkins, year of birth 1990."

That got Alex's attention.

"Any local record for him?"

"He doesn't have a criminal background on file," he replied. "But then I remembered doing a background check about two years ago for the high school on a new part-time employee in the Maintenance Department, so I pulled the folder. *Lo and behold*, it was for a Lou Jenkins, same year of birth."

"*Outfriggenstanding!*" Alex replied. "You're going to make one helluva detective, Hutch."

"We don't have any detectives," He replied.

"Not yet," she said, sipping her coffee. "So is Jenkins still employed at the school?"

"I can only assume he is. I haven't heard of them replacing anyone."

"What else did the employment application say?"

"At the time he was going to school at NNHU. Not sure if he still is. The application listed an address for an apartment over on Atlantic Avenue, in the northern part of town. That area is known for renting out to college kids."

Alex began to process everything. She needed to take a look inside the motel, but she wanted to do it when Jenkins wasn't around. She couldn't take the chance of tipping him off. At this point his connection was tenuous at best and she would need something more substantive before she would even contemplate questioning him.

Alex checked her watch. It was nearly three thirty, and the evening shift would be coming on soon.

"Do you have any plans tonight, Hutch?"

"Ripping out some old kitchen cabinets, why?"

"How'd you like to earn a little extra money for some new ones?"

"That'll work for me," he replied. "What do you want me to do?"

"Take a ride by the motel and see if the Jeep is still there. If it is, sit up the road and watch the location. When it leaves, call me and follow it to wherever it goes."

"Where do you think he will go?"

"Hard to say," she replied. "But my guess is, if it is the same Jeep, the first stop will be to Rebecca Waltham's. I wouldn't think they would want to go and waste any of her husband's precious business trip time."

"What are you going to do?"

"I'm going to snoop around inside the motel, make sure I'm on the right path, before I go and drop the hammer on some college kid's extra-curricular activities."

"Okay, Chief," Hutch replied. "I'll head up there now and keep you posted."

"Enjoy the cop food," she said with a laugh, before pulling away.

It was after four o'clock when she pulled up in front of city hall. She grabbed the bag of Chinese food she had picked up and headed inside. The night shift had already come on duty.

"Evening, Chief," Bobby Willis said as she walked in.

"Good evening, Bobby."

"Abby said to tell you that she left the paperwork you asked for in your in-basket."

"Okay, thanks," she replied and went into her office, setting the bag of food on the desk.

It was a strange feeling to be eating dinner without having something, other than the can of coke, to wash it back with.

Maybe this is the start of a new me, she thought.

She reached over and removed the stack of papers, including the ones that Abby had left her, from the in-basket. There was a sticky note attached to the purchase order she had prepared.

Chief – Attached is the P/O for the ammo. I couldn't find any listings for Mountain View Sporting Goods in Belkin. I checked with the Chamber of Commerce there, but they had no information. Abby

Alex took a sip of soda.

She'd like to say that she was surprised by the revelation, but she wasn't. In fact, in light of everything else that she had seen in recent days, it made perfect sense.

Alex opened the food container and began to eat.

She signed off on the purchase order and continued reading the remainder of the reports, initialing each of them.

When she was done, she walked outside, putting the reports into the basket to be forwarded and filed. Then she walked the P/O up to Sheldon Abbott's office. He was already gone for the day, so she slid it through the mail slot on the exterior wall.

As she made her way back down the stairs her cell phone began to ring.

"Hello?"

"Chief, it's Hutch. He's moving."

"Which way are you headed?"

"South on Route 1," he replied. "I'll let you know in a few minutes if he heads toward the apartment or somewhere else."

"Great," she said and ended the call.

Alex started taking the steps two at a time. She didn't want to waste any time.

As she headed toward the front door she peered back into the office.

"Going out, Bobby," she said. "I'll be on the radio if you need me."

"Okay, Chief," Willis replied, looking up to a now empty doorway. "Have a great weekend."

Alex raced north, hoping that Jenkins was done for the day and not just going out for dinner. Half way to the motel her phone rang again.

"What do you have for me, Hutch?"

"You were right," he said. "Lou Jenkins is banging Rebecca Waltham."

"Damn," she said. "I love it when a plan comes together."

"Huh?"

"Forget it," Alex replied. "I'm dating myself. Where are you now?"

"I'm about a quarter mile past the driveway. I have a perfect view if anyone comes or goes."

"Okay, just sit on the location and let me know if he moves. I'll call you back as soon as I'm done."

Five minutes later Alex pulled up next to the large main house of the Cedar Edge Cabin and walked inside.

A young woman sat at the front desk, her attention focused on the social media site on the computer in front of her.

"Good evening," Alex said.

The woman glanced up from the screen.

"Can I help you?" she asked, sounding rather bored.

"I'm Chief Taylor, the new police chief in Penobscot. I've been going around to some of the motels to get familiar with the locations before things get too busy."

"The manager is probably the best person to talk to," she replied.

"And who would that be?"

"Lou Jenkins, but he's not here right now."

"When will he be around?"

"Monday," she replied. "Around noon."

"Okay, I'll come back then," Alex said, and headed toward the door.

"Oh, you know what. My mom's thinking about coming up for a visit. You mind if I take a look at one of the cabins?"

The woman, who had already returned her attention to the computer screen, reached behind her without looking and grabbed one of the gold, shield shaped, plastic key chains. She tossed it to Alex, who caught it in midair.

"Cabin fourteen is free," she said. "Go out the door and walk along the driveway. It's the second to the last on the end."

"Thanks," Alex replied.

The cabins were all cookie cutter designs, with faded yellow clapboard and green shingled roofs. Each overlooked the lake and a small rocky area that served as the locations version of a beach.

It was obvious that they had seen their *best days,* decades earlier.

Alex walked up the wooden stairs, which creaked with each step she took, and entered a small screened-in front porch. On the far side was a small refrigerator next to a base cabinet that had a hot plate sitting on top of it. A small table and two chairs provided the occupants with an obstructed scenic view of Lake Moriah.

She slipped the key into the front door lock and opened it.

The large one room cabin featured a queen size bed in the center, which was flanked by a pair of vintage night tables that each held lamps. On the opposite wall was a squat dresser, on top of which sat a bulky color television. The interior walls were outfitted in cedar wood paneling that had darkened considerably over time. It gave the occupant the feeling that they had been teleported back in time to the 60's.

It was a dead match for the room she had seen in the photos.

Alex wanted to spend more time looking around, but she wasn't sure whether there were any hidden recording devices. She began focusing on the little things: an old clock radio on the night table, a blue Naugahyde chair in the corner, the curved chrome drawer pulls.

Any detail that she could potentially use to link the room to the ones in the photos.

She walked to the back of the cabin where the bathroom was and peeked inside. When she was done she headed out the front door and relocked it.

Had anyone been watching it would have appeared that she was doing exactly what she had told the woman at the front desk.

She walked back up to the main house and dropped off the key.

"How much are the cabins?"

"Forty-nine dollars Monday through Thursday," the woman said. "Sixty-nine on the weekend."

"Thank you so much," Alex replied and walked outside.

Hope that girl has some outstanding attributes other than her stellar personality, she thought.

When she had driven out of sight she pulled out her cell phone and called Hutch.

"Any change?" she asked.

"Nope," he replied. "He's still inside. How did you make out?"

"I think we need to sit down with Mr. Jenkins and ask him a few questions."

"Tonight?" Hutch asked.

"No, just sit tight and see where he goes when he leaves Rebecca Waltham's," Alex said. "But don't let him pick-up the tail. I don't want lover boy getting spooked before we are ready to talk to him."

"Gotcha."

"I'm going to compare what I saw to the photos and make sure there is a match. You need me to bring you out anything?"

"No thanks," Hutch replied. "I have some *cop food* if I get hungry."

"Good man, call me if he moves."

Alex hung up and headed back to her place.

She flipped on the lights in the apartment and tossed her jacket onto the couch as she headed toward the kitchen. She grabbed a glass, filling it with ice and pouring herself a drink. It was a nice try earlier, but the Coke just hadn't done anything for her.

When Alex was done, she grabbed the photocopies of the books from the end table drawer and pulled the foam boards with the pictures out from behind the couch. She sat down on the couch, laying the boards out on the table in front of her.

Alex took a sip of the whiskey and lit a cigarette, taking a drag, as she began to look through the photos. Despite the graininess of the images it took less than a dozen before she had a confirmed match. The photo with Charlie Parker showed the exact same night table, with the chrome drawer knob, that she had seen in the cabin earlier that evening.

She felt a wave of exhilaration come over her. It was a feeling she hadn't felt in a very long time, that sense of knowing you had caught someone before *they* knew it. There was still a lot of work to be done, but she had the working foundation.

CHAPTER TWELVE

It had been a very long weekend.

Alex had systematically gone through every photo, matching them up by the small characteristics that she could identify. When she was done she had come up with four, possibly five, separate rooms and still had a pile of photos that were too obscured by bodies to positively say.

Hutch had called after midnight on Friday to let her know that he had followed Jenkins from Waltham's house back to his apartment on Atlantic Avenue.

She had thought about keeping the tail on him but decided to pull back. There was just no reason to spook him at this point.

Alex had spent the weekend taking the two diaries, and rewriting them into one cohesive chronology of events. It painted a stark portrait of the girl and the last few months before she had disappeared.

She had also made a conscientious effort to limit her drinking. As a result, she was relatively clear headed when the alarm clock rudely interrupted the pleasant dream she had been having.

It was just before seven when she walked into her office.

Well, it's the start of week two, she thought. *I can't wait to see what surprise this little town has in store for me now.*

It took less than twenty minutes for her to get her answer.

Alex looked up from her desk as Sheldon Abbott walked into the office, closing the door behind him.

"Alex, just the person I was looking for," he said.

"What can I do for you, Sheldon?"

"I wanted to let you know that someone in the Department is playing a joke on you," he said conspiratorially. "I just got a purchase order for almost sixteen hundred dollars for ammunition, and they signed your name to it."

He handed her the purchase order.

Alex took the proffered paper and examined it, before handing it back to him.

"No joke, I authorized it."

"You did?" he said, the words coming out with a slight stutter. "Are you serious?"

"That's generally not something I would kid around about," she replied.

"Who uses that much ammunition?"

"I do," Alex said

"Haven't they already shot this year?"

"Allegedly," she said.

"I don't understand."

Alex got up and walked over to the filing cabinet where she removed the folder with the invoices. She dropped them on the desk in front of Abbott.

"Did you authorize those, Sheldon?"

Abbott picked it up and began sorting through them.

"I've never seen these before," he said, handing the papers back to her.

"Well, if you didn't authorize those orders, then I would say it is probably safe to assume that Charlie Parker was skimming money from the police budget," Alex said. "Bottom line is that no one here has qualified in years."

Abbott looked up at her.

"But, Alex, this is a lot of money."

"No it's not, Sheldon. You know what's a lot of money? Funerals and lawsuits, those cost a lot of money."

"Is this going to be every year?" the man asked.

"No," Alex said.

"Oh, thank God."

"It's going to be twice a year," she replied.

"Are you serious," Abbot replied, his eyes going wide.

"Maybe three times, but I won't know that till I get them out on the range."

"Alex, I don't think you understand the delicate financial situation we are in here. I mean, running a city takes money, and that means sometimes we have to do more with less."

"Actually, I do understand. I just don't particularly care about such things when it comes to my people's wellbeing. You see when you under fund the Highway Department they can't patch all the potholes. If you under fund the Sewer Department sometimes you get a backup or a bad smell. But when you under fund training for the police you get a tragedy. You don't want a tragedy do you Sheldon? They cost a lot of money and involve a lot of bad publicity."

Abbott stared at Alex for a moment longer. Mentally, he conceded that he had lost this one before it had even started.

"Alright, Alex," the man said. "Just please try to keep me in the loop before you plan on spending anything extra."

Alex knew she had won this battle. But she was also aware that discretion was the better part of valor and extended an olive branch to the man.

"I give you my word that I will *never* ask you for anything that I truly do not need and that I will treat the budget as seriously as my own personal finances. However, when I do ask for funding, I will tell you exactly why I need it, and I expect that you will support me."

"Agreed," Sheldon said.

He removed a pen from his jacket pocket and signed off on the purchase order, handing Alex one of the copies.

"I'll drop this off at the clerk's office and have them cut the check."

"Thank you, Sheldon."

"I'll let you get back to work," he said and stood up. "By the way, any progress on that girl in the lake?"

"Nothing yet, still waiting for the lab reports to come back from the state police," Alex replied. "As soon as I hear something, I will let you know."

"Thank you," he replied.

Alex watched as the man waddled out the door and just shook her head.

"I hate politicians."

She reached over and picked up the phone then dialed a number, listening as it rang.

"Major Crimes, Blackshear."

"Tom, its Alex Taylor."

"Hey, Alex, how was your weekend?"

"Good, I just wanted to call and make sure you got that brush I sent up on Friday."

"I did, I walked it over to the lab myself. Is it from your local missing?"

"Yeah, she fits the vic. Seventeen year old runaway back in May. Typical teenage angst," she said. "Knew everything and thought there was a better world outside the parent's home."

"If I had a dime for every kid I knew like that," he said, his voice trailing off at the end.

"I guess we all go through it, just depends on what side we come out on."

"I was going to call you today anyway. The toxicology report came back negative, no drugs or alcohol."

"Well, I guess she went in alive, sober and pregnant."

"It's one fucked up world we live in, huh?"

"Eh, I look at it as job security, Tom. It keeps me from going insane."

"True enough," Blackshear replied. "Anyway, I'll keep on the lab weenies and see what I can get you back."

"I appreciate it, Tom. I'll talk to you later."

Alex hung up the phone and reached into her pocket, pulling out the pack of cigarettes. She heard a knock on the door and looked up to see Abby standing there.

"Mind if I join you?" she asked.

"No, not at all," Alex replied.

Abby sat in the chair across from Alex, lighting up a Virginia Slims.

"I saw Sheldon Abbott walk out of your office before," Abby said. "Let me guess. He wasn't happy with the purchase order."

"Not even remotely happy."

"It was a good try, boss."

"Oh, I didn't say he said no," Alex said as she lit her own cigarette. "I just said he wasn't happy about it."

She handed Abby the piece of paper. "Call up the vendor when you get a free moment and tell them that the purchase order has been approved, and I need the ammo shipped ASAP."

"I'm impressed," Abby said, as she took a drag on her cigarette. "Chief Parker was never able to get us ammo to train with."

"I learned a long time ago that it is sometimes easier to ask for forgiveness than it is to seek permission," Alex replied. "Just remember it helps to be on the right side of the issue at hand."

"Sounds like good advice."

"By the way, I've been meaning to ask you where you work out."

"I just go out to the school. I figure my tax dollars paid for that gym. They have a really nice weight room. Just don't go on Monday, Wednesday or Friday afternoons, because then you have to contend with all the high school kiddies. There's just way too much testosterone for me."

"They give you a hard time?"

Abby lifted her right arm up and flexed, the material of her uniform shirt stretching tautly over a very large bicep.

"Holy shit," Alex exclaimed.

"They only did it once," she said with a laugh.

"I was beginning to wonder why you always wore long sleeve shirts."

"Self-conscious," Abby replied. "Which is kind of ironic considering that I do all this just to compete on stage. I just don't think it looks professional in uniform."

"Probably makes the boys feel a bit *lacking* as well."

"After they opened the gym at the school, a few of us would go over, but that didn't last too long. It requires a big commitment, and most of the guys here would rather fish or drink."

"After things settle down here I might join you."

"I wouldn't mind the company," Abby said. "But once we leave the office, you're in *my* world."

"Fair enough," Alex replied. "I know my way around the gym, and I don't ask for any special treatment."

"Just let me know when you're ready."

"I will. By the way, I wanted to ask you a question. What did you think of Charlie Parker?"

"Nice enough when he wanted to be. But he could be prickly at times. Still, I don't like to talk about the dead."

"No, I don't want you to either," Alex said. "I'm just trying to figure out how he fit with Sheldon Abbott."

"Oh they'd known each other for a very long time. Abbott was the one who promoted him to Chief."

"Were they friends?"

"Yeah, I think they knew each other from grade school. From what I heard Abbott went away to college, and Parker joined the department. When Abbott came back he got married and went to work for his father-in-law. Then he got into local politics, and as his power grew so did Parker's promotions. It supposedly rankled some of the more senior officers at the time, but what can you do? Small town politics."

"So I've heard," Alex said. "It seems as if everything here is driven by it."

"Someone here once said that we swim in a very cloudy gene pool and I think that was a pretty accurate analogy."

"Were there ever any *waves* in that pool from time to time?" Alex asked.

"Oh God, yes," Abby said. "Actually, just prior to your arrival things had reached a very tense period here. In the past, knowing or being related to the right people was always much more useful in terms of getting ahead than ability ever was. That being said, it appeared that even friendships could hit a rocky stretch."

"Abbott and Parker?"

"Nothing publicly," Abby replied, taking a drag on her cigarette. "But internally we knew their *ships* were in rocky waters. To make matters worse, something had happened between Mike Williams and Abbott almost a year ago. He was a sergeant here. That's when the big chill really set in between Parker and Abbott."

"I heard about him. He moved out west, right?"

"Yeah," Abby replied. "He came into work one day and flipped his badge onto Parker's desk. Said he was done with the cold weather and left that same day. He gave us a forwarding address for a place called Aptos in California."

"That's a drastic change."

"You're telling me. During the winter we'd get a postcard every other week that depicted beach scenes or Palm trees. Heck, one even showed an old *cement* ship folks used to fish off of."

Abby reached up to the cork board above her desk and pulled off the card, handing it to Alex. She looked at the card which showed the old, half submerged, S.S. Palo Alto. The ship had been built too late for war service and was eventually sold to a private entity that turned it into an amusement ship with dance floor, casino and night club. A pier, nearly twice as long as the ship, extended as far out as the ship's bow, while the cold blue water of the pacific broke in waves against a beautiful sandy beach.

"Then they just stopped," Abby said. "I guess after a while he just moved on with his life."

"Was Williams friends with Parker?"

"Yeah, back in the day they were inseparable. Chief Parker was the one who promoted him to sergeant. But after his run-in with Abbott the two hardly ever spoke. That went on for about a month, and then he left."

"Reminds me of New York City," said Alex. "Just on a slightly smaller scale, of course."

Abby was about to reply when Hutch stepped into the office.

"Good morning," he said.

"Good morning, Hutch," Abby said.

"Hey, Hutch, grab a chair," Alex replied.

"Well, if you'll excuse me," Abby said, getting up from her seat. "I'm going to go and get that order in."

"Thanks, Abby."

Hutch took the empty seat across from the desk.

"How are you feeling?"

"Tired," he replied. "They never really tell you how much work is entailed in home renovation."

"Are you ready to ruin someone else's day?"

"Sure, who?" Hutch asked.

"Lou Jenkins," Alex replied.

"You think we have enough to bring him in for questioning?"

"Absolutely," Alex said. "But I'd rather he come in thinking we need his help, than for it to be adversarial from the start."

"What do you need me to do?"

"Go find him and say we need to ask him some questions regarding a problem over at the school. That should put him at ease."

"You want me to go get him now?"

"Yeah, there's no time like the present."

"You got it, Chief," Hutch replied.

CHAPTER THIRTEEN

Lou Jenkins sat in the small interview room in the Penobscot Police Department, his reflection staring back at him in the one way mirror. On the other side, Alex stared at Jenkins, gauging the man's response to being kept waiting.

He was in his early twenties, with long brown hair, that was slicked back over his ears, and a bit overweight. He wore a faded concert t-shirt, from a popular metal band, along with khaki shorts and a pair of flip-flops.

Ah, America's youth, she thought. *They're always dressing for success.*

Jenkins reached down, picking up the coffee cup that sat in front of him on the table, and took a sip. It had long ago grown cold as he waited, with each passing minute, for someone to come in and talk to him.

He was beginning to think that they had forgotten about him, when he heard the door open.

"I'm so sorry, Mr. Jenkins," Alex said, as she entered the interview room.

"Oh, no problem," the man replied.

He was pleasantly surprised when she walked in. He'd heard that the city had hired a new female chief of police. Jenkins had just assumed that it would be some old hag and not the hot blonde that had taken the seat across from him.

"The mayor seems to think everyone else's time is unimportant."

"Politicians!"

"My sentiments exactly," she said.

Jenkins watched as she put a large coffee container down on the table, along with a large manila folder.

"I'm Chief Taylor," she said. "I'm sorry to drag you down here on such short notice, but they pretty much have me going in fifty different directions lately. I figured it would be easier this way. Can I get you more coffee?"

"No, I'm good," Jenkins said. "Do you mind if I ask what this is all about?"

"We are conducting an investigation into a missing high school student, Susan Waltham."

"Well, I'm only the part-time janitor there. Not sure what I can tell you."

"The missing girl's parents said she had recently broken up with her boyfriend. I'm just trying to speak to everyone over at the school to see if they might remember anything unusual, something that might help us figure out what happened."

Alex noticed the physical change in the man as he visibly relaxed. That was the reaction she had been hoping for, and she was betting that it would lull him into a false sense of security.

"Oh, you mean Paul Bollinger."

"You know him?"

"Oh yeah, he's on the football team. Bollinger is your typical jock, long on brawn and short on brains."

"See, that's the kind of information I'm looking for, Lou," Alex said. "Parents rarely know anything more then what their children *tell* them and that information is normally useless."

"I'll try to help in any way I can."

"What can you tell me about Susan?"

"Susan was a really sweet girl and very smart," Jenkins said. "She was also one of the more attractive girls, as I recall."

"Had you ever seen any problems between Susan and Bollinger?"

"Well, I don't want to sound like a gossipmonger, but Susan was only one of the many girls in his *stable*."

"Really?" Alex said.

"Oh yeah, he had a reputation as a big time player. He tells them what they want to hear until they drop their pants for him. When he'd had enough he kicked them to the curb and moved onto the next one. It's pretty sad actually."

"They had broken up before she went missing," she said. "Did you happen to notice anything unusual?"

"Yeah, I saw him hanging around with one of those girls who had a reputation for being a big *team* supporter. If you know what I mean."

Jenkins leaned forward, and when he spoke, he did so in a hushed tone, as if Alex had suddenly become his confidant.

"You'd be surprised at what goes on in that place," he said, with a wink. "Not just between the kids, but the faculty as well."

Alex leaned back against the chair and let out a soft whistle.

"That's why I wanted to talk with you first, Mr. Jenkins," Alex said. "Those snotty brats and high-brow teachers probably never even notice the blue collar folks who make their daily lives easier. But it's folks like you who know what is really going on."

"Please call me Lou," He said. "And you're right; they take everything for granted and look down on us. That is until they need something."

Alex took a drink from the coffee cup and pulled out the pack of cigarettes.

"You smoke, Lou?"

"No," the man replied. "But please go ahead. It doesn't bother me at all."

"Thanks," she said. "I've been trying to kick the habit, but you know how that goes."

Alex lit one and inhaled deeply.

She could feel his eyes on her, knew instinctively what he was thinking. It had all been part of her plan, even to the point of opening one extra button on her blouse.

Like they say, all's fair in love and war, she thought.

"I can only imagine what you have seen there."

Jenkins let out a laugh and leaned back in his chair.

"You'd be amazed. Spend one week cleaning out the faculty lounge garbage cans and you'd never send your kids to school again."

"Good thing I don't have any," she said.

"If you think that place is bad, you should spend some time at my other job."

"Where is that, Lou?" Alex asked with a quizzical look on her face.

"I'm the manager over at the Cedar Edge Cabins, just north of town," he said. "People think that just because it isn't *inside* the town, that no one sees what they are doing."

Alex smiled and took a drag on her cigarette.

"You know I'm new here, Lou. I can only imagine what goes on in a small town."

"Well, Alex," he said. "Do you mind if I call you Alex?"

"Not at all," Alex replied, leaning back in her seat.

"I was just going to say that if the folks upstairs were to ever give you problems, I could always give you a call and invite you down to the motel for some coffee. You might even be surprised as to who you might run into there."

"Really?" she asked. "You'd do that for me?"

Jenkins leaned forward on the table, his voice dropping law again.

"You and I are *out-of-towners,* Alex. We'll never fit in here," he said. "These folks here know that. All they will do is use you up and spit you out. I figure we outsiders have to look out for one another."

"Sort of like you scratch my back and I scratch yours?" she asked.

"I don't know, do you like having your back scratched?"

Alex squirmed in her chair, biting her lower lip playfully.

"Has anyone ever told you that you are incredibly beautiful, Alex?"

"You know I'm almost old enough to be your mother, Lou."

"You might be old enough, Alex, but I can guarantee you, that is the only resemblance you have to *my* mother."

"What is it that you are suggesting?"

"Everyone else seems to like the accommodations over at the motel, why don't you stop by and I'll show you around. See how it works out for you?"

"I don't know, Lou," she replied. "Like you said, I'm an outsider. I have no way of protecting myself. I've already had one run in with the mayor that left me feeling uneasy."

Jenkins smiled and leaned back in the seat.

"What if I could give you all the protection you would ever need, Alex? What would that be worth to you?"

Alex looked at him, contemplating what he was saying.

"I sure wouldn't mind having some *insurance* to keep that from happening again."

"How'd you like to wake up one morning and find an envelope, with an insurance policy in it, slid under your door?"

"Most insurance policies I know have a lot of words that are open to *interpretation*," Alex replied.

"Let's just say that my idea of an insurance policy is that a picture is worth a thousand words," Jenkins said with a smile.

"Sort of like this?" Alex asked, opening the folder and sliding a copy of one of the photos across the desk.

The smile quickly dissipated from the man's face, as his eyes grew wide in horror.

"I..... I.... don't..... understand," Jenkins stammered as he picked up the photo. "Where did you get this?"

His eyes were darting frantically back and forth between the photo and Alex.

"Oh, I think we both know the answer to that, Lou. The question is what more can you tell me about them?"

The man was in a state of panic, trying to resolve what had just happened and failing miserably.

"I don't know........," he muttered. "I think I need to speak with someone."

"Suit yourself, Lou," Alex said.

She stood up; pulling the photocopy from the man's hands and placing it back in the folder. "But just for the record, right now you're the prime suspect in Susan Waltham's disappearance and it's not looking good for you."

"No, wait, you have it all wrong," Jenkins blurted out. "I wouldn't do anything to Susan, I loved her."

"Really? And you showed her this love by putting x-rated photos in her locker?"

"No, it's not like that, not like that at all," he said, his voice cracking under the strain. "I was only trying to protect her."

"I don't know, *Louie*," Alex said sarcastically. "It sounds to me like you were getting off, on rocking little Susie's world."

"No, I was just trying to warn her about her father."

"Wow, that's kinky, Lou..........." she said, her voice trailing off seductively. "I kind of like it."

"No, you don't understand. I saw him check in and recognized the girl he was with from the school. I thought Susan had a right to know, but I just wasn't sure how to go about it. I decided that the best way was to make it part of a bunch of photos. This way it wouldn't appear suspicious to her. Let her figure it out on her own."

"And what, Lou? You just thought that would be the end of it?"

"I don't know what I thought," the man replied. "But it didn't matter. She ultimately figured it out."

"How?"

"I don't know. I didn't think she would, but somehow she figured out that the photos were from the same place. One day she showed up at the motel when I was working. She recognized me from the school and realized that I was the one putting them in her locker."

"What did she do?"

"She was really pissed, threatened me, said she'd have me locked up," Jenkins said. "I told her I was sorry, that I loved her and felt she needed to know what was going. I didn't know what else to do. She just stormed off. Then a few days later she showed up at the motel saying she had no place to go. So I gave her a place to stay. I figured it was the least I could do under the circumstances."

"Well wasn't that magnanimous of you," Alex said sarcastically. "I bet you even enjoyed the view as well."

Jenkins got quiet.

"So, let me see if I have got this right, Lou," Alex said. "First you go and shatter her world by showing her photos of dear old dad, getting *biblical* with one of her friends, along with a bunch of other select viewing material. Then, when she confronts you about it, you want me to believe that you just offered her a place to call home for a bit."

"I know it doesn't sound great."

"You're right, Lou, it doesn't. Actually it sounds like a crock of shit to be honest."

"But it's the truth!"

"Ok, so where is she now?"

Jenkins hung his head down in his hands.

Alex slammed the folder down hard onto the metal table, eliciting a sharp *crack* sound, which filled the small room and made the man jump.

"This isn't really a good fucking time to get all *introverted* on me, Lou."

"I don't know where she is. We got into an argument and she split."

"Wow," Alex muttered. "If I were you, I'd go straight home, lock your doors, close your blinds and never leave again, because you are the world's most unluckiest motherfucker that I have ever met."

"I don't think I want to say anything more," Jenkins replied.

"Suit yourself, Lou," she replied.

Alex gathered up the folder and headed toward the door.

"Oh, I did have one more question," she said. "I'm wondering did Susan split before or after she found out you had been interviewing for the role of *future* step-daddy with her mother?"

"Hey, Rebecca came on to me!"

"Sure she did, Lou," Alex replied. "I hate to break the news to you, but you really aren't *all that*."

"Can I leave now?" the man asked.

Alex stopped and turned to look back at him.

"Leave? Are you for real? The only place you're going is to the county jail, where you can make some new *friends*."

"What?!?! I came here willingly. I have things to do. I have to go to work!"

"That would probably be a good thing to consider, the next time you think of a career in the film industry."

Alex walked out of the room.

Hutch stood outside, staring at the man through the one-way mirror, and took a sip of coffee.

"Wow, you were good," he said.

"Book 'em, Danno!"

"What charge?"

"Slap him with violation of privacy for now. I'm gonna chat up my new friend, the county attorney, and see about getting a search warrant for the motel."

"You got it, Chief," Hutch replied. "By the way, who's *Danno*?"

"Ask me again after the dust settles," Alex said with a laugh.

She walked into her office, closing the door behind her, and lit up a cigarette. She sat down and rummaged through her desk drawer for the business card, then dialed the number.

"Nichols."

"Scott, Alex Taylor."

"Hey, Alex, what do I owe the pleasure?"

"I need a search warrant."

"Damn, girl, you sure do move quickly."

"Sorry, I just had my foreplay with the dickhead in my interview room."

"I assume you have a good reason."

"I'm booking a guy on a violation of privacy charge. He's the manager over at a local motel, and I think he might have a room or two wired for video."

Alex spent a few minutes *selectively* explaining what had transpired.

She didn't want to play her entire hand, as it pertained to *all* the photos. She still wasn't sure what side anyone was on, and before she gave up everything, she wanted to see what other images might be running around out there.

"Sounds like you have sufficient grounds," Nichols replied. "I'll need you to come over to court and make the application in front of Judge Garrett. He's the presiding judge, and he refuses to do anything by phone."

"Can we do it now?"

"No, it's gonna have to wait till one o'clock. He's hearing motions on a case this morning."

She looked at her watch, it was just after nine.

"Okay," she replied. "I'll meet you at court at one o'clock."

"Great, see you then."

CHAPTER FOURTEEN

Alex sat behind a small wooden table, in the third floor courtroom, and listened as Scott Nichols explained the grounds for the search warrant application.

"We're asking for two search warrants, your Honor. One for the place of employment, where we believe the images were initial obtained, and the other for the residence of the defendant, where we believe additional evidence may be stored."

Judge Preston Garrett III sat on the bench going over the array of photos before him.

He was an older man, having just turned sixty-nine the previous May, and he was in his final year of office, under New Hampshire's age limits. He had served this area for nearly four decades, and it was clear to Alex that his time on the bench had taken its toll.

"Chief Taylor, where did you say you found these photos?"

"In the locker of a missing person, your Honor."

"And how exactly do you know that these photos were taken at the motel in question?"

"I determined, based on an analysis of the details in the photos, that they were all taken at a similar location. I concluded that this most likely indicated a motel. I conducted in person examinations of each of the establishments, which fit these criteria, in Penobscot and found a positive match to one of the rooms at the Cedars Edge Cabins."

"And how did you link this to Mr. Jenkins?"

"Mr. Jenkins is both the manager of the motel, as well as an employee of the high school. His employment provided him with both the means to obtain the images as well as the ability to disseminate them to our missing person, via her school locker."

"It's a disgusting world we live in, isn't it, Chief?"

"That it is, sir," she replied.

"I guess I shouldn't complain too much though, it has kept me employed all these years."

"Our line of work does enjoy a sense of job security."

"What are you going to be looking for here, Chief?"

"Anything that could facilitate the crime, sir," Alex replied. "Audio / video equipment, computers, storage devices."

"How small can these things be?" Garrett asked.

Alex reached into her pocket. She removed a flash drive and held it up.

Garrett frowned noticeably as he stared at the diminutive size of the device she held.

"I guess they can be hidden just about anywhere."

"Yes, sir," Alex replied.

"Mr. Nichols, have I told you how much I loathe search warrants pertaining to electronic devices like computers?"

Scott Nichols looked up from the paperwork in front of him.

"No, sir, I don't believe we have had that discussion as of yet."

"My concern is that we must balance the *pursuit of justice* while doing our best to protect a person's privacy," Garrett replied. "Yet in terms of the diversity of data that a computer can hold, can anything be considered private?"

"Well, your Honor, if it helps at all the Fifth Circuit Court determined that a computer disk containing multiple files is a single container for Fourth Amendment purposes."

"Yes, but the Tenth Circuit held that a warrant authorizing seizure of all storage media and not limited to any *particular* files violated the Fourth Amendment."

"If you look on page two, your Honor, you will see that, in terms of the computers and storage devices, we are only specifying image files at this time, your Honor."

Garrett picked up his pen and signed the documents.

"Okay, Chief, you've got your warrants. However, since we have not had the pleasure of working together before, let me make myself abundantly clear. I won't stand for any nonsense. You can search the computer for forensic evidence related to the recording of guests at the hotel. However, should that investigation identify any other criminal activity, not directly related to the issue at hand, I will expect you and Mr. Nichols to come before the bench and request an additional warrant. Is that understood?"

"Yes, your Honor," Alex and Nichols said in unison.

"Your warrant is good for thirty days."

As they walked out of the courtroom, Nichols reached out and took Alex's arm.

"Just for the record, Alex, Garrett's time on the bench might be short, but he's mentored just about every judge there is around here. If you cross him, it'll bite you, big time."

"I understand," she replied. "Trust me, if I see anything else during the search you'll be the first to know. I don't want this little douche bag walking away on a technicality."

"Alright, Alex," Nichols replied. "Happy hunting."

Alex made her way out of the courtroom and headed to her car. Along the way she lit up a cigarette and pulled out her cell phone.

The phone rang on the other end a few times before it connected.

"Hey, Chief," Hutch said when he answered the phone.

"We've got the warrant. Where are you?"

"I'm just pulling back into town."

"Head straight over to the motel and wait for me."

"Will do," Hutch replied.

Alex ended the call and then dialed the main number for the Department.

"Penobscot Police Department, Officer Simpson, how may I help you?"

"Abby, I need you to do me a favor. Call all the night shift people and tell them I want them to come on duty now. Send Bobby Willis over to the Cedar Edge Cabins. Then tell Steve Marshall go to 116 Atlantic Avenue and secure apartment #102. No one goes in or out until I get there."

"Yes, Chief," Abby replied. "I'll get them out there immediately.

"Can you stay late tonight?"

"Yes, I can."

"Great, you man the office and call me if you need anything."

Forty-five minutes later Alex pulled up to the motel and found Bobby Willis standing outside.

"Where's Hutch?" Alex asked, as she got out of the car.

"Inside, he wanted to make sure someone was watching the desk clerk."

"Good thinking," Alex replied and headed toward the main office.

She found Hutch sitting at the desk, next to the same young woman she had spoken to the previous night.

"This is bullshit," the woman yelled as Alex walked up. "I demand to see a warrant!"

She held the paper up to the woman's face.

"If you want I can help you with all the big words," Alex said. "But basically it says I can search the premises, and if you try to interfere with me, you can have adjoining cells with your buddy, Lou."

"Lou's in jail?" the woman said.

"Probably learning why they call it the *pokey,* as we speak."

"Hey, I don't know anything about him," she said. "I don't even like the jerk."

"What's your name sweetheart?" Alex asked.

"Lori, Lori Meadows."

"Okay Lori, let me make this easy on you. I just want to know where Lou hung his hat around here."

"He has an office in the back," the woman said.

"See, that wasn't so hard now, was it?" Alex said. "Hutch, take Ms. Meadows outside and have Bobby keep an eye on her while we see what trouble we can find in little Louie's office."

"Yes, Chief," Hutch said and escorted the woman outside.

Alex walked to the back of the location until she found a door marked *Manager*. She tried the doorknob, but it was locked.

Hutch was just coming down the hallway, when he saw Alex emerge from a side room, carrying a large, red fire extinguisher.

"What's that for?"

"Master key," she said.

"Master key?" Hutch replied.

Alex gripped the handle in her right hand and brought the fire extinguisher up, cradling the metal cylinder in her left palm. With her right hand, she drew the device backward, and then swung it forward forcefully, the bottom of it crashing into the door directly into the lock.

The hollow wooden door splintered under the force of the projectile and flew inward, the shattered lock tumbling to the floor.

Alex set the fire extinguisher down in the hallway and turned to look at Hutch, who stared back at her in amazement.

"*Master key*," she replied, and stepped inside the office.

The room itself was fairly small and matched the décor of the rest of the establishment. The walls were clad in the same wood paneling and were offset by a lime green shag carpet that had seen much better days. In the center of the room sat an old wooden desk with an ancient looking computer on it. The only other furniture in the room consisted of a couple of chairs and a metal filing cabinet.

"Check the filing cabinet for anything *suspicious* looking, Hutch."

"As in naked photos suspicious?"

"Exactly," Alex replied. "But also look for anything strange that might link Jenkins to something bigger."

Alex sat down behind the desk and turned on the computer, waiting for it to power up. While the machine *whirred* to life, she began to rummage through the desk.

Almost two hours later, Alex began to lose hope of finding any evidence linking Jenkins to the photos.

They had combed every inch of the room, from top to bottom and then when they were done, from bottom to top.

"Find anything, Hutch?"

"Nothing at all, Chief," the man replied as he closed the last of the drawers. "You think we missed something?"

"I *know* we missed something. The problem now is how do we find it before it's too late?"

Alex slid the center desk drawer open and removed a pen to copy down the serial number for the office computer on the inventory list. Next she pulled out a scrap piece of paper and copied the number for the office phone. Maybe she could convince Nichols to get a subpoena for the phone records.

She was about to put the pen back in the drawer when she noticed the plastic keychain. She reached down, picking it up and looked at the key dangling from it. It was the same style room key that Lori Meadows had given her the previous night.

"What's that, Chief?"

"Good question," Alex said. "I'll let you know in a few minutes. Grab the computer."

Alex headed outside, walking over to the car where Meadows sat and opened the back door.

"Okay, Lori, we're all done in there. One quick question though. Would you have any idea why Jenkins would have a cabin key in his desk?"

The woman looked at the key and rolled her eyes.

"Lou always kept one of the rooms vacant in case he, or any of his friends, needed it. Manager's *prerogative,* he used to say."

"And where would this cabin be?"

"Cabin three," the woman replied. "Head down toward the water's edge and hang a left."

"Thanks."

Alex and Hutch made their way down a grassy hill and headed toward the lake. They turned left and then followed a small stone walkway toward the last cabin at the edge of the property.

"Guess it's time to see what's behind door number three."

Alex slid the key inside the lock and opened the door.

The cabin was a duplicate of the one she had seen last night. The only difference was that someone else had been here first.

The interior of the cabin had been trashed. The mattress laid askew, half on the box spring and half off. The coverings had been cut open with a knife.

In the corner Alex spotted a desk. A computer case was lying on top of it with its side open. She walked over and peered inside the metal box. Someone had already removed the hard drive.

The desk drawers had been pulled free and tossed to the side. Judging from the amount of papers that lay strewn across the floor it had been thoroughly searched.

Apparently they weren't the only ones looking into Mr. Jenkins' activities.

"Holy crap," Hutch said. "I guess we're too late."

Alex scrunched her lips up.

"Maybe," she replied. "Maybe not."

"I don't understand."

"Don't assume that they found what they were looking for. First go back to the car, and grab your print kit and the camera. Work the room as a crime scene. Take photos of everything you see and then dust everything that you think might yield a print. Start from the door and work your way forward. Then we are going to do the same methodical search."

"Yes, ma'am."

"In the meantime I'm going to go and have a chat with Ms. Meadows. Let me know when you're done and I will help with the search."

Alex went back into the main house and located the woman.

"You mind if I ask you a few questions?"

"Do I need an attorney?"

"Don't worry, Lori; you're not the one I'm interested in."

"Okay," the woman replied.

The two women sat down on the couch.

"How long has Lou Jenkins been the manager?"

"Well, he started here when he was in school so that would have been about two and a half years ago."

"Were you here then?"

"No, I only started here a year ago. But he likes to brag about how important he is."

"That must wear thin after a while."

"Only after about the one hundredth time."

"So I take it you didn't like him?"

"He was an asshole. After he hired me he spent the first few months trying to get in my pants. As if he ever had a snowball's chance in hell. Since then he has spent the remaining time breaking my shoes about every little thing and scheduling me to work the worst possible shifts."

"I've worked for a few people like that in my day," Alex replied.

"Really?" Lori asked.

"Oh, sweetie, just because they pin a badge to your chest doesn't mean they're not checking out your ass when you walk out the door."

"Great," the woman replied. "Nice to know things don't improve."

"Eh," Alex said. "Someday *you* might get a chance to be the boss."

"I'll try and remember that."

"You said he changed your shifts, any reason why?"

"Yeah, I used to work the day shift and then out of the blue he changed me to nights. Said it wasn't busy enough for both of us and it was more important for him to be here during the day."

"You remember when that was?"

"Late September?" she said. "Maybe the early part of October."

"What about Jenkins," Alex said. "You said he hit on you. Was he a player?"

"Lou?" Meadows said with a laugh. "Yeah, but only in his mind."

"So you never saw anyone around here with him?"

"Not really," she replied. "I mean there were a couple of young girls that came here from time to time. I'd see him leave with them when I came in for work. But no one ever hung around for very long."

"So he reserved cabin three for him and his friends?"

"Yeah, but even that stopped. When I first started, there was almost a constant stream of people shacking up here. I hated it because housekeeping would yell at me when the room was trashed. I guess after a while that novelty faded away. Now just Lou uses it."

"You go to school up here?"

"Yeah, I'm in my senior year at NNHU."

"What's your major?"

"Business Administration," she said. "Any advice?"

"Yeah, do your job well and be a bitch."

"Really?"

"They're going to call you it behind your back anyway. You might as well get some satisfaction out of it."

"Thanks."

"Hey, Chief?"

Alex looked up and saw Hutch standing in the doorway.

"I'm done with what you asked me to do," he said. "You want to come down and have a look?"

"Sure, be right with you."

Alex stood up.

"Thanks for your time, Ms. Meadows. If you think of anything else, please give me a call at the police department. "

Alex returned to the cabin and found Hutch waiting for her.

"Were you able to get anything?"

"Nothing really," he replied. "The surfaces are all porous or rough. I wasn't able to get a decent print from any of them. I did manage to pull a partial off the bathroom mirror, but that's it."

"Oh well, it was worth a try. Let's divide the place up. You do the bedroom. I'll do the desk area and kitchenette. When we are done we will switch and double check each other's work."

"Sounds like a plan," he said.

The search of the cabin took less time than the office, simply because there were fewer places to hide anything. Hutch was just finishing up the secondary search as Alex sat down on the bed and began going through the discarded papers.

"You find anything?"

"No," Alex replied. "There *was* something here, but it's long gone."

She found an open notepad halfway through. She flipped through the pages, but it was empty and still had the majority of its pages left. She slid it into her inner pocket.

"Did you give up on stealing books?" Hutch asked.

"Yeah, at my meetings they told me to take baby steps," Alex replied. "Besides, these notepads come in handy."

Alex stood up and handed the papers to Hutch.

"Bathroom break," she said. "Keep looking and see if we missed anything.

Alex walked down the short hallway and stepped into the bathroom. She unhooked the holster from her belt and balanced it precariously on the edge of the porcelain sink.

Alex turned around and looked down at the toilet.

You've used worse, she thought.

She reached down and began to undo the top button on her pants, then stopped. Her eyes moved slowly upward from the seat to the tank behind it.

She reached out and lifted the cover off the back of the tank, resting it on the seat and put her hand into the cold water. She felt along the bottom and then moved her hand up along the overflow tube until she felt a bulge.

"*Sonofabitch!*"

Alex leaned down, turning off the water supply valve and flushed the toilet, watching as the water drained out of the tank.

"Hutch, get in here!"

"Do I have to come in?" he called from behind the door.

"Yes!"

The door opened slowly and he saw her bent over the toilet.

"Come over here," she said.

He walked over to where she was standing.

"You have a knife?" Alex asked.

"Yeah," Hutch said and removed a tactical knife from his pant pocket.

"Reach down and cut the bag on your side of the overfill tube," she said.

Hutch leaned down and ran the tip of the knife down along the slender tube, until he had cut through the two miniature zip ties, which held the plastic bag in place around the tube."

Alex withdrew the bag from toilet and patted it dry with the towel hanging on the wall.

"What is that?" Hutch asked.

Alex slowly opened the plastic bag and removed a small hard plastic storage container. She opened it slowly to reveal a USB flash drive.

"That, my dear Hutch, is *Jenga*."

Alex put the device into her pocket and clipped her holster onto her belt before walking back out into the main room.

"Did you find anything in the papers?"

"Nothing to do with the photos or who might have been in the rooms."

"That's okay," she said. "I think we found what we needed."

"What about the computer?"

"Forget it, without the hard drive it's nothing but a paperweight," Alex said.

"What do we do now?"

"You and Bobby go through each cabin. Look around for signs of wires or recording devices. Focus on the areas in front of or on top of the beds. If you can't find anything call me and I will have the state guys come up and do a sweep."

"Okay, Chief," Hutch replied.

"In the meantime I'm going to head over to his apartment and see what I can find there."

CHAPTER FIFTEEN

Alex walked through the door of the Penobscot Police Department, just before ten o'clock in the morning.

It had been after two in the morning when they had finally left Lou Jenkins apartment. Despite the intensive search, they had not uncovered anything substantive that would aid in the investigation. It seemed that whatever Lou Jenkins did, he hadn't brought it home with him.

Hutch and Bobby had better results. They had located a series of cables that originated at Jenkins' cabin and ran underground to three other cabins that were closest to his.

Each cable came up out of the ground and ran up into an exterior wall. Inside the cabin they conducted an examination of the walls where the cables came into. They found that there were no electrical outlets or television cable connectors that would account for them. It was Hutch who had decided to get a better look and removed a sheet of paneling from the wall, revealing a small fiber optic camera mounted behind it. Upon closer examination of the paneling itself, Hutch found that that one of the original nails was missing, leaving a small pinhole for the camera to see through.

The fiber optic cameras were all connected to a USB portal, which allowed Jenkins to record or view any of the rooms, from the computer in his cabin.

Despite the physical evidence of the hidden cameras, it seemed as if the only hope of finding further incriminating photos or files rested with the small USB drive that Alex had in her pocket.

She'd gone to great lengths, to instill in everyone involved, the need for absolute security as it related to the purpose of the search warrants that they were conducting. Alex wanted to believe they would all keep their mouths shut, but realistically she knew the clock was already ticking on when the news would leak out.

"Good morning, Chief."

"If you say so, Abby," Alex replied, her raspy voice belying the exhaustion she felt inside. "Has Hutch come on duty yet?"

"Yeah he called on about a half hour ago. I let the late tour guys go home."

"Good job," Alex said.

"So how did the warrants go?"

"I've been on worse," she replied. "Then again, I've been on a whole lot better too."

"Sorry to hear that. Anything I can do to help?"

"Not unless you happen to have a spare *TARDIS* lying around here and can transport me back in time."

"I doubt I could help, even if I knew what *that* was."

"How about a cup of hot coffee?"

"That I can do," she said.

Alex walked into her office and sat down at the desk. She took the USB drive from her pocket, along with a brand new drive she had purchased on her way into work, and put them on the desk.

Abby walked in and handed her the coffee cup.

"Thank you so much," Alex said.

"Enjoy."

Alex fired up her laptop and lit a cigarette as she watched the machine load up. Once she had logged in, she started a specialized program which allowed her to clone the contents of the evidence USB drive onto the one she had purchased. When she was done, she secured the original in a sealed evidence envelope placing it in the file cabinet, along with the original photos and books. She then went back to her desk and began opening the files.

It was a treasure trove.

The photos Lou Jenkins had sent Susan Waltham were actually screen grabs of videos he had recorded. Each was kept in its own file along with a scanned image of the motel registry card. The cards contained the name the person signed-in with when they registered. It was evident that, in most cases, they were using fictitious names, but Jenkins had also written their real names, along with the names of the women they were with, if he knew them.

So, in the case of Sheldon Abbott, the registry card indicated that he had signed in as *John Williams* and then Jenkins had written Abbott's name next to it, along with the name Heather Mills.

The USB was a veritable *who's who* and there were hundreds of files to go through. It dawned on Alex that this investigation had gotten to the point where she needed to bring someone in to help her.

"Morning, Chief," Hutch said from the doorway.

Alex looked up from the laptop.

"Hey there," She replied. "Good work last night on finding those cameras."

"Thanks," he replied. "I almost missed it to be honest. I took a walk around Jenkins' cabin and was about to call it a day when I saw the cable TV line coming in, but then I saw a separate line, running down from the interior wall into the ground. I matched them up to similar cables in the other cabins, and then I began looking closer at everything. The lines all came up into the walls that were directly across from the beds."

"That was a good catch," Alex said. "Go grab some coffee and come back."

"Okay," Hutch replied.

She took a drag on the cigarette and slowly began to blow smoke rings, watching as they floated through the air before dissipating.

"Got my coffee," Hutch said as he walked back into the office.

"Close the door and grab a seat," she said.

"Am I in trouble?" he asked.

"Trouble? No," Alex replied. "Tell me, Hutch, do you like watching porn?"

The man stared at her across the desk, swallowing hard as he fumbled with the coffee cup in his lap.

"I don't know exactly how to answer that question, Chief," he said.

"I'll take that as a yes," she said. "Congratulations, you've just inherited a lot of overtime."

"Starting when?"

"Tonight, over at my place."

"You want me to come over to your place and watch porn with you on overtime?"

Alex looked at him with a smile and took a drag off the cigarette.

"Ain't this a fucking great country or what?"

"Yes, ma'am," he said.

"Meet me at my place around six," she said. "Do have a laptop? You like Chinese?"

"Yes and yes."

"Good, bring it with you and stop by *Bamboo Garden* to pick up dinner on your way over. I'll take a container of chicken lo mein."

"Anything else?"

"Nope that'll do for now," she replied. "I think I'm going to go pay a visit to our little friend over in county and see if he wants to talk now."

Alex ejected the thumb drive from the laptop and shut it down.

The ride to the county jail took about forty-five minutes. It gave Alex the opportunity to sit back and enjoy the countryside. It was a far cry from the urban jungle she had patrolled back in New York City for so many years. However, with each passing day, she found that she was becoming more accustomed to the pristine nature of her new environment.

Not that the people were any different. Human beings had an amazing capacity for self-deception. They thought that just because they lived in quaint little towns, with tree lined roads and white picket fences, that crime was something that happened only in the *big city*.

How naïve they were to believe that.

Granted, an organized sex ring; matching school girls with creepy old men, wasn't exactly a cutting edge crime spree, but she'd seen worse things grow out of such prosaic crimes. The case wasn't really about who was doing what to whom. No, at the core of it, was about who was controlling the strings. Sex sold and it was a very lucrative business.

In her career, Alex had come to realize that, to some people, those things were no different than drugs. Some people chased a high, others chased money and power. Both were an addiction and you could never have enough.

Alex pulled the unmarked car into the parking lot of the County Correctional Center. She parked the car in a vacant spot near the front door, then got out and walked inside.

"May I help you," asked the uniformed corrections officer, who sat at the reception desk, behind a partition made from bullet resistant glass.

"I'm Chief Taylor from the Penobscot Police Department," she replied, showing her badge to the officer. "I need to interview an inmate, Louis Jenkins."

"Step through the magnetometer, Chief, and secure your weapon inside the gun locker."

When Alex was done the officer buzzed her through the door.

"Go straight down the hallway to the steel security door and they will buzz you back."

"Thanks," Alex replied and headed back.

At the steel door she was buzzed through and entered a large in-take processing area.

Another corrections officer sat up behind a raised desk, looking down at her.

"Can I help you?" he asked.

"I'm Chief Taylor from Penobscot. I need to speak with Louis Jenkins."

The man looked down and she could hear him tapping the keys of the computer keyboard in front of him.

"Sorry, Chief, I can't help you," the man replied.

"Why not?"

"He's not here."

"He just came in yesterday?"

"Yeah, but he got arraigned this morning and posted bail."

"Are you friggen' kidding me," she said.

"Nope, he came up with the two thousand *cash only* bail."

"Did he post it from his own funds?"

"No, he had a bail call. It says here that he placed a call to a Becky Riggs."

"*Sonofabitch*," Alex muttered. "Does it say who posted the bail?"

"Yeah, same person."

Alex looked up at the man. Behind him an array of video screens showed every angle of the correctional complex.

"Who takes the bail?"

"The officer at the front desk," he replied.

"You have a video feed out there?"

"Yeah, you want to see who showed up?"

"Yeah, I do."

"Come on back," the man replied.

Alex walked behind the desk and pulled up a chair as the officer scrolled up the video camera for the front desk. He keyed in the time range search and the video began to play. As she watched, the computer screen showed a figure approach the front door and walk inside.

The woman wore a scarf and oversized dark sunglasses. If she was hoping to maintain her anonymity she had failed miserably. Alex immediately recognized the woman.

It was Rebecca Waltham.

As Alex watched the woman counted out bills and then slid them through the slot in the glass partition to the officer inside. When she was done she left and walked outside.

"Can you scan the parking lot?"

"Absolutely," the man said pulling up a different camera.

In the parking lot Alex could see a silver Mercedes Benz sitting in front of the location, with Waltham behind the wheel. Fifteen minutes later Jenkins walked out and got into the vehicle.

The conversation was animated and included Waltham hitting him several times before abruptly putting the car in drive and speeding out of the parking lot.

"Lover's quarrel?" the man asked.

"Oh you have no idea," Alex replied. "Can you do me a favor? Can you print out a shot of her paying and also one in the car with him?"

"Sure thing," he replied. "You want a copy of the bail sheet with her information?"

"That would be fantastic."

A few minutes later Alex walked out of the correctional center holding the two color pictures, along with the photocopy of bail sheet, and headed toward her car.

This was certainly an interesting twist to a story that was already chock full of them.

It wasn't the fact that Rebecca Waltham had posted bail for Lou Jenkins that seemed odd to her; it was that she did it while attempting to conceal her identity.

As she pulled back into town she passed the high school and saw a number of cars parked in the lot.

She remembered Abby saying that the members of the sport teams worked out there and it was Wednesday.

Wonder if Paul Bollinger is in there? she thought.

Alex had found out that he had graduated and was planning on attending NNHU. He'd played basketball for the high school team and had picked up a partial sports scholarship.

She figured it wouldn't hurt to take a look and pulled the car into the parking lot.

If she was lucky, he would be here trying to keep up his conditioning for the upcoming season.

As soon as she walked inside she could hear the sound of sneakers on the hardwood floor in the gym, along with shouts and the sound of a basketball being dribbled.

She walked down the darkened hallway until she came to the gymnasium. Inside there were a bunch of kids playing a game of three on three.

Alex stood in the doorway watching, seeing if she could pick him out based on the image in the photo. As they ran down the court in her direction she saw him.

The graininess of the photo had been kinder to him than real life. He was tall and lanky, with close cropped blonde hair.

As she watched, he passed the ball to his teammate at the three-point line and then ran up the middle. Just as he approached the net his teammate passed the ball back and he went in for a lay-up, which got blocked.

He'd have to add at least twenty pounds of muscle if he was going to make it in college, she thought.

"Paul Bollinger," she called out.

"Yeah," he said. "Who wants to know?"

"Police," Alex replied, holding up her badge.

"What do you want?"

"I'd like to talk to you."

"About what?" he asked.

Behind him the other kids began whispering. She knew what they were doing. Teenage boys seemed to have a tough time with female authority figures.

"I'm kind of busy here."

"That's fine, we can do this down at the station if you'd prefer."

Behind him one of the big mouths just couldn't resist the opening.

"She wants to do you down at the station, dude."

That started all of them laughing.

"Is that what you want, officer?" Bollinger asked with a smirk. "To do it down at the station with me?"

Alex walked out onto the court and approached the group, stopping right in front of Bollinger. Clearly it made him uncomfortable to have her so close to him.

"It's chief, not officer," she said. "And don't flatter yourself, junior. You wouldn't know what to do with a woman if you had a picture book and your fan club back there to cheer you on."

"You couldn't handle…"

Alex knocked the basketball that Bollinger was holding, out of the kid's hands and stepped in even closer.

"This seem like a joke to you, junior?" she asked, her voice low and measured.

The formerly vocal team members slowly began walking away.

"No," he replied.

"Then I suggest we have our little chat and then you can get back to playing games with the village idiots over there."

Alex turned and pointed toward the doorway she had come through.

"What's this about?" Bollinger asked, once they were in the hallway.

"Susan Waltham," she replied.

"Isn't she missing?"

"Yes, she is."

"I don't know what you want from me then."

"What happened between the two of you?"

"I got bored. It was time to move on."

"You mean you got what you wanted from her and went looking for a new conquest."

"Yeah, whatever," Bollinger said. "She couldn't accept that we had our thing and it was time to move on."

"You ever think that maybe she wanted more than a *thing*?"

"Look, I'm young and life's short. I just wanted to have fun. If she couldn't handle that, well that's her problem, not mine."

"When was the last time you saw her?"

"At school," he said. "It was just before graduation."

"And you haven't seen her since?"

"No, but like I said, I moved on. I really wasn't looking for her."

"So it really doesn't bother you that she is missing?"

"What do you want me to say?" he asked. "I miss her? I've been through two other girls since Susan. Things move quickly at my age."

"When you saw her last did she say anything to you?"

"She was always saying something. She just couldn't come to terms that it was over between us. Kept telling me we could still make it work. It was sad."

"Did you say anything to her?"

"Just that I was going to college and I didn't need an anchor."

"Wow, you certainly do have a way with words."

"Listen, who wants to get saddled down so early in life? I mean we just met and who knows what might happen next? You're pretty hot for a cop."

Bollinger reached his hand up toward Alex's cheek. It never made it.

Before he knew what happened she had grabbed his wrist, twisting it violently behind his back and planting him face first into a locker.

"This is my idea of foreplay, dickhead," she whispered into his ear, twisting his wrist as he grunted in pain. "Are you still interested in seeing what happens next?"

Alex let go of the kid and took a step back.

When he turned around his eyes were wide in fear and he cradled his wrist with his other hand.

"Are you fucking insane? You could have broken my hand!"

"Don't be such a pussy. If I wanted to hurt you, you'd be on the floor with your hand shoved up your ass, crying for your mommy."

"You are nuts."

"Here's a word of advice, Mr. Bollinger. When you're spewing out that whole 'life is short' bullshit, remember that Karma's a bitch. When she comes for you, and she will, you're going to wish life really was short."

"Are we done here?"

"Oh yes, we are most certainly done. You can run along, I think your *village* misses you."

Alex turned and walked away. She could feel his stare burning into her from behind.

She smiled as she opened the door and stepped outside.

CHAPTER SIXTEEN

Alex was just coming out of the shower, drying her hair, when she heard the knock on the door.

"Coming," she called out.

She opened the door partially and saw Hutch standing on the other side holding a bag of food.

"Room service," he said.

"You're early," she replied, opening the door fully and letting him step inside.

"I like being punctual," Hutch said as he watched Alex lay the .9mm on top of the coffee table and head toward the kitchen.

"Were you expecting trouble?" he asked.

"Hell no," she replied. "If I was expecting trouble I'd have had a rifle in my hands."

"You scare me sometimes, Chief."

"Funny, that's what all my boyfriends used to say. You want a drink?"

"Sure, I'll take a soda."

Alex grabbed a coke from the fridge and handed it to him, along with a glass. She then poured a whiskey for herself.

"Cheers," she said. "Let's eat and I'll fill you in on my excellent trip to county today."

"Unbelievable," Hutch said, after listening to Alex's story about Waltham paying Jenkins' bail.

"Makes you wonder what else might be going on," She said, digging out a piece of chicken from the container in front of her.

"So what do you need me to do tonight?

"At first I thought Jenkins was just a pervert," Alex said. "But the more I looked at the files on the drive the more I realized that there is something more going on here."

"What do you mean?"

"Jenkins isn't just getting lucky that every well connected man in Penobscot just happens to be tapping young girls in his motel. No, this has all the hallmarks of an organized operation. Either Lou is taking advantage of what's going on or he is directly involved in it. At the very least he knows more then he let on."

"So what are we going to do?"

"We need to go through every video and look for clues. We need to find out if there are any indications as to who is arranging these little get-togethers."

"And you think we'll find it on that drive?"

"The first thing you do when you're going to commit a crime is to have an accomplice."

"Why?"

"Because if the cops catch you red handed, you want to be able to give them someone else. It's the nature of the beast. Trust me; there is no honor among thieves."

"So you think there is something on the USB that implicates someone else."

"Yeah," Alex replied. "At least I hope so."

"So you don't believe the story Jenkins told you about wanting to warn Susan Waltham?"

"I don't know," she said. "Lou's a bit of an anomaly. On one hand he seemed genuinely stupid enough to do something like that. But the fact is he had the equipment set up *before* the father ever came into the proverbial picture. How else would he have been able to get the screen grabs of him to send to Susan?"

"Good point," Hutch replied.

"Which begs the question, why was he recording in the first place?"

"My guess is money."

"It's a perennial favorite," She replied. "But he needed someone to bail him out, so I'm not sure how much access he has to money right now. That makes me think he is just a cog in a bigger machine."

"So why do you think he would be taking videos?"

"If I had to guess I would say most likely *insurance* of some sort," Alex replied. "Now the real question is whether it was sanctioned by someone else or is Lou just freelancing."

"I guess that means we have to go looking for clues."

"Welcome to my world, Hutch."

Alex had already downloaded the files onto her computer and gave Hutch the USB drive to work off of. Alex had him work from the newest folders back, as she worked from the oldest ones forward.

Viewing the images proved difficult at first for Hutch. Occasionally Alex would look over and catch him staring at the videos with a mixture of disgust and interest.

She stifled a laugh the few times she caught him having to make some physical *adjustments*.

Guess there are times when being a woman comes in handy, she thought.

Alex knew from firsthand experience that it was a difficult thing to separate the personal from the professional at times.

They each took copious notes as they reviewed the videos. From time to time she would have to ask for his help in identifying the people involved when Jenkins didn't identify them on the registration card. They compiled lists of the dates, times and persons involved along with anything that might prove relevant down the road.

As time progressed a pattern began to emerge.

For the most part the men involved changed frequently while the same young women appeared on a fairly regularly basis. Clearly these were not simply mass cases of May-December romances.

While none of the videos showed an exchange of money, clearly there was a strong argument to be made for an organized sex ring. The only question that yet remained to be answered was: who was in charge?

"Holy Crap," Hutch replied.

Alex looked up from her laptop.

"Whatcha got?"

"You need to see this."

Alex got up from her chair, made her way over to the couch and sat down. Hutch reached down, hit the play button and Alex watched as the scene began to unfold.

A middle aged man sat in the chair next to the bed, his fingers scrolling through the smart phone he held in his hand. The camera picked up the change of light in the room as the door opened off-screen. The man looked up and smiled as someone walked into the room. He stood up and extended his hand in greeting. Alex could see it was a woman with dark hair, but her back was turned to the camera.

"You know this guy?" she asked.

"No," Hutch replied. "Never saw him before. I checked the registration card, but there are no names listed."

The two continued to talk and from off screen the lighting changed again, as someone else entered the room. The woman turned slightly to greet the new arrival, but as she did she stepped out of view. For a few moments the figures hovered on the edge, just out of view. The woman stepped back into view and, as Alex watched, motioned the man's attention to another woman who came into view. A huge smile appeared on the man's face and he turned to the first woman, nodding his head enthusiastically.

"Guess he likes the merchandise," Alex said sarcastically.

"Keep watching," Hutch replied. "It gets better."

The first woman walked off camera as the second woman, who had blonde hair, pushed the man playfully until he fell backward onto the bed. A few moments later she had him undressed and laying on the bed. Then it was her turn and she began to remove her clothes in a slow, teasing manner, much to the *growing* delight of the man. When she was undressed she climbed on top of him and began to ride him.

Suddenly the first woman came back into view, naked this time. As Alex watched, the woman walked over to the bed and climbed on top of the man, lowering herself down to his face. As the man began to pleasure her, she arched her back and tilted her head upward in pleasure, giving Alex a clear view of who she was. Staring up at Alex was the face of Rebecca Waltham.

"*Sonofabitch!*" she said.

"Yep, things just got a whole lot more interesting, don't you think?"

"We're gonna need a score card to keep track of all the players here," she replied.

Alex stood up and walked to the kitchen

"You want a refill?"

"Sure," he said.

Alex refilled his glass and poured herself another whiskey.

"To strange bedfellows," she said, toasting him.

"Cheers," Hutch replied, tapping his glass against hers.

Alex took a drink and lit a cigarette.

"So what do you make of that video?" he asked.

"I'm not sure what to think," she replied, taking a drag.

Alex pressed her lips into a frown, as she absentmindedly swirled the drink in her hand. Her mind was moving rapidly from thought to thought as she tried to process everything.

"Lou Jenkins had to call Rebecca Waltham to bail him out," she said. "That means junior doesn't have enough cash which tends to rule him out as the head of this little ring."

"So if he doesn't have the money, then did he use the video as leverage against Waltham to get him out?"

"That doesn't seem to fit though. He's already *hitting* her; I wouldn't think that he would need to play that card. Then again that's not to say that he didn't use the video to get her into bed in the first place. It seems like right now, we have more questions and conjecture then we do actual facts."

"Do you think Waltham is involved?"

"Oh I know she is involved," Alex said. "The question is just how deep."

"So if the videos were meant to be insurance in the event that anyone grumbled, why would Lou advertise it?"

Alex pondered that for a moment

"What was the date on that file?" she asked.

Hutch got up, walking over to the laptop and scrolled through the files.

"It says here April 10th."

"That's almost two weeks before Susan got the photos of her father" she said. "Clearly he had videos of both Kevin and Rebecca. So why did our budding little filmmaker rat out dear old dad while giving momma a pass?"

"Maybe he was just trying to get rid of the competition."

"Could be," she said. "What if Lou just went off the reservation?"

"What do you mean?"

"Maybe it was for insurance, but maybe it's not. Say he did figure out what was going on and decided to get in on a little side action. So he demotes the daytime clerk to the evening shift and gets rid of her. Then he sets up the rooms and begins steering clients to them, where he videos everything."

"Sounds reasonable," Hutch said. "So why run the chance of screwing things up by giving Susan Waltham the pics?"

"Maybe he really did like her? So he figured he could parlay it into a 'come cry on my shoulder' moment."

"Helluva risk. What happened if it went south?"

"Guys rarely think with the head on their shoulders, Hutch. Maybe he thought the videos would protect him."

"So how did he go from shacking up with Susan Waltham to making house calls with her mother?"

"That, my dear Hutch, is a question that we are going to have to pose to Mr. Jenkins. For now, I guess we just go back to watching the videos and hope for a break."

"At this rate I am going to need a very cold shower in the morning."

"It's not just a job, it's an adventure," Alex said with a laugh.

"I never thought I would be working the Vice Squad in Penobscot," Hutch said as he headed back to the couch.

"Think of the stories you'll be able to tell your grandkids."

"I doubt this case makes the highlight reel."

Alex laughed and went back to her seat. She crushed out the cigarette in the ash tray and brought up the next video file. It was nearly 11pm when the break they had talked about came. As Alex watched the latest video begin to play she observed Rebecca Waltham once again enter the room and greet the man sitting in the room.

"Got it, Hutch," she said.

Hutch got up and joined her at the counter.

"Hot damn," he said.

"You know him?"

"I do," he said. "Give me a moment to remember where."

Alex let the video continue to play. Again another young woman entered the room and Waltham introduced the two.

"What about her?"

"She's new, never saw her before. If memory serves me correct I think he has something to do with the regatta."

"Really?" she said, turning her head back toward the screen.

A few moments later, the young woman and man were in bed. The camera captured the motion of the door opening and closing. They continued to watch the entirety of the video, but Rebecca Waltham never appeared back in the room.

"Well that was interesting," Alex commented, as the video ended.

"How so?"

"Two things," she said. "Rebecca is making introductions for an otherwise unknown female. It's the second time we have seen her do this so far. If she is making introductions, it makes me believe that she has a much larger part to play in all this. If you are right about that guy being involved in the regatta, then maybe she figured out a way to mix business with pleasure. Maybe we are actually looking at the ring leader."

"Why was she having sex the first time we saw her?"

"Maybe she likes it, Hutch. Or maybe she was fulfilling a special request. All I know is she is a smart woman with money and she was the first one Lou Jenkins called to bail him out. Right now she's the odds on favorite."

"So we should talk to her next?"

"No," Alex replied. "We're not ready for that yet. Rebecca Waltham is wealthy and wields a lot of clout. Besides that, she is smart and our first question about *sexscapades* at the Cedars Edge Cabins would be answered with her asking for her attorney."

"So what do we do now?"

"We go back to the weakest link in the chain."

"Lou Jenkins," he said.

Alex looked over at Hutch and smiled.

"I'll make a detective out of you yet, junior," she replied.

CHAPTER SEVENTEEN

The alarm on the cell phone on the night table chimed noisily, as it rudely interrupted the dream Alex had been thoroughly enjoying. She groaned audibly as she surrendered her hold on the land of enchantment and succumbed to the interruptions of the real world.

Alex swung her legs over the side of the pullout mattress and sat up, reaching for the pack of cigarettes on the end table. She closed her eyes and inhaled deeply as she tried to chase away the cobwebs.

Something wasn't right, and it took her a few minutes to realize that the air conditioning unit wasn't running.

"Isn't that just lovely," she said sarcastically as she stared at the silent machine.

She turned on the TV and got up, heading into the kitchen to pour herself a cup of coffee. She sipped her coffee and watched the local news anchor prattle on about the latest bullshit going on down in the nation's Capitol.

Nothing ever really changed down there. In fact, she had come to the conclusion, long ago, that the only thing that ever *really changed* was just which party was in charge of doing the screwing over of the American people, at the time.

The room was already beginning to get hot and Alex made a mental note to call the apartment manager when she got into work. She crushed the cigarette out and headed off to the shower.

Twenty minutes later she was in the car heading toward the station.

"M-11-1, are you on the air?"

Alex reached over and picked up the mic.

"M-11-1, that's affirmative. Go with your message."

"Chief, we have a report of a 10-55, vehicle accident with injury. Highway 23, about a quarter mile north of Birney Road. M-11-3 and EMS are in route, can you provide assistance with traffic?"

"10-4, show me responding."

Alex reached over and activated the vehicles emergency lights as she executed a u-turn and headed north. Five minutes later she slowed down as she approached the scene.

Hutch's patrol car was parked on the opposite side of the road. There was barely any traffic so she pulled off onto the shoulder on the northbound side.

Alex exited the car and walked across the road.

"Hutch?" she called out.

"Down here, Chief."

She walked over near the edge and looked down the embankment.

"Fuck me," she said. "Is that who I think it is?"

"Yes, ma'am," Hutch replied.

Alex navigated the steep slope carefully as she made her way toward the vehicle.

It had been traveling southbound when it veered off the road, barreling through the overgrowth and young trees. The vehicle sheered them off at their base, before it slammed head-on into a mature oak. Unlike the smaller trees, this one hadn't budged.

The front end of the vehicle had caved in and partially wrapped around the tree. Despite the violence of the initial impact the passenger compartment remained intact. This did little for the driver whose body was presently lodged halfway through the windshield.

"I don't friggen' believe this," Alex exclaimed. "Who called it in?"

"Some old timer on his way to work," Hutch replied. "He said it was still dark when he was driving down the road. He saw lights off to the side and stopped. Called us when he realized it was an accident."

In the distance she heard the wail of a siren.

"You got gloves?"

"I do," Hutch replied.

He opened a small black leather pouch on his gun belt and removed a pair of blue nitrile gloves which he handed to her.

Alex slid the gloves on and began to examine the driver. His face was torn up from going through the windshield. Blood covered the hood directly underneath him and ran off the side.

"What do you think?"

"I think it sucks to be us, but it sucks even worse to be Lou Jenkins."

Alex leaned down lower, staring up into the man's face. His eyes were wide open, and his mouth partially ajar, in a surreal image that made you believe that he had seen his demise unfold before him.

"I guess he should have worn his seatbelt," Hutch replied.

"Wouldn't have mattered," Alex replied.

"Why not?"

"He was already dead."

"Are you serious?"

"Yeah, come over here," she said.

Hutch approached Alex and knelt down beside her.

"Here," she said, pointing with her pen. "See how this skin is pulled backward? That shows where the glass broke and dug into the skin. It's a vertical tear, same with these areas here."

Alex pointed out different places on the man's skull.

"Now look over here, Hutch," she said, pointing to the horizontal gash along the side of the man's throat. "That's what killed him. When we look inside the car, I bet there is a lot more blood than there should be."

"So you're saying we have *another* murder," Hutch said.

Alex stood up and removed her gloves just as the EMT's were descending down the embankment.

"Either that or you find me a straight razor and shaving kit in the car along with a massive pothole back up there on the road."

"What have we got, Chief?" one of the EMT's asked Alex.

"The drivers in desperate need of a time of death," she explained as she reached into her shirt pocket and removed the pack of cigarettes.

The man looked over at the body protruding through the windshield.

"Damn," he said, as he donned a pair of gloves. "That had to hurt."

"I'm thinking that by the time he went hood surfing he wasn't feeling any pain."

He opened the car door and grabbed the man's wrist, feeling for the non-existent pulse.

"Call the time of death 0643 hours."

"Thank you," Alex said to the man. "Hutch call it in and have the medical examiner respond."

The EMT's began to climb back up to the roadway as Hutch removed the portable radio from the holder on his belt.

Alex took a drag on the cigarette as she stared down the embankment. Had he not hit the tree he would have traveled about another forty feet.

I wonder if the passing motorist would have seen your lights then, she thought.

"They're notifying the doc to respond now," he said. "So who do you think did this?"

"That is a very good question, Hutch," Alex replied. "I'm sure that the list could potentially contain any number of people, including someone who might have learned about Lou's extra-curricular film activities."

"Should we check the car?"

"Yeah, we will, but after the doctor does his medical examiner thing. This is a crime scene now. That means you document everyone that comes and goes, along with the times they were here."

"Gotcha, Chief," Hutch replied.

He took out his memo book and began making notes.

"Do we have any place we can have the car towed to? A secure location?"

"We have a garage back at city hall," he said. "In the winter Chief Parker used to park his car inside it. He hated shoveling it out when the plows came down the road."

"Okay, after they haul the body away I want you to have it towed back to the garage and lock it up. The killer was in the car with him. It's evidence now so we have to make sure we don't let anyone contaminate it."

"You think we'll get prints?"

"No," she replied, taking a drag on her cigarette. "But we have to play the game. Occasionally we get lucky. Remember, you only get one chance to be right so you make it count."

"Now what do we do? It's not like we can ask him any questions."

"That's true, but I also know that dead men don't tell lies. Now that this is a homicide investigation we need to start looking at everything."

"I hate to ask this, but what do you want me to do?" Hutch asked. "I've never handled an actual homicide."

"You can't stay a virgin forever, Hutch," Alex replied. "The first thing you're going to do is go up and grab your camera. I want you to take photos of everything, the deceased, the vehicle and the ground around it. Take them from every very angle, look for prints as well. I don't think they took the ride down here with him, but you never know. Also get some shots from the main roadway, as well as looking down the embankment."

"Yes, ma'am," Hutch replied.

Alex oversaw the photographic aspect of the investigation. Giving him advice on the proper angles as well as pointing out shots he felt he had missed.

"The purpose is to record everything because, at the end of the day, this will all be gone and you can't put it together again," Alex explained. "Cases can be made or lost depending on photos. Something that doesn't seem all that significant now might pop up in a photo and prove to be the key to solving a crime. Never skimp on photos."

"Gotcha," he replied.

As Alex had surmised, the examination of the immediate area around the vehicle failed to identify any footprints leaving the scene. Most likely whoever had done this had left the vehicle up on the main road.

When he was finished with the camera work on the roadway Hutch returned back to the vehicle.

"Got everything up top," he replied. "I took shots from both directions."

"Good. We'll let the state guys go over the interior of the car and see if our killer left a calling card. For now we secure the scene till the doc gets here."

"What do we do after that?"

"We figure out who might have had an ax to grind against Lou Jenkins. I'll get in touch with Nichols to get subpoenas for his phones and financial records. One door closes and another one opens."

"What do you mean?"

"Lou went from suspect to victim," she said. "Now we are tasked with finding his killer. It becomes a lot easier for us to get access to his personal records under the auspices of trying to catch whoever did this."

"Clever," Hutch replied.

"Start with his financials and work your way down. I want to know what his bank records look like. Was he getting funded by anyone or was money going out. I also want to know what his phone records say, both his personal phone as well as the work number. See if there is a pattern to the calls. Pay careful attention to whether or not Rebecca Waltham's phone number comes up and when. If she is involved, we may see a connection between the dates and times of those calls and when the videos were recorded. If you shake the tree hard enough something's bound to come loose."

"Okay, I'll get on that as soon as I get back to the office."

"Chief Taylor!"

Alex looked up to see Peter Bates carefully navigating his way down the embankment toward her.

"Good morning, Doctor," she replied. "Sorry to start your day out this way."

"Not a problem," he said. "I look at it as having job security."

"You and me both," Alex said. "Except that I could have used Mr. Jenkins here alive for one more day?"

"You know the deceased?"

"I guess you could say that. I arrested him the other day."

"So I take it that you don't think his departure from this life was of an accidental nature?" Bates said, looking at the mangled Jeep. "No pun intended."

"You're the expert, Doc," Alex replied. "You tell me whether my doubts are unfounded or not."

Bates began making his way around the vehicle, examining Jenkins' body from various angles.

For a small town doctor it appeared to Alex that he was quite meticulous. He recorded his observations in a small reporter's notebook, stopping at various times to sketch out the scene, from the angle that he had been viewing it at. When he was done, he put the notebook in his back pocket and donned a pair of gloves.

He began to examine the portion of the body protruding from the vehicle. When he was done, he opened the door and carefully looked around the interior. The driver's side was covered in blood, but nothing looked out of place. He then walked around to the passenger side of the vehicle and began to rummage through it.

"Well, should I chalk up Mr. Jenkins untimely demise to natural causes?" Alex asked.

"Oh I think we both know better than that," Bates said as he stood up. "Jenkins was most surely helped along in his journey into the afterlife."

"Yeah, that was my layman's guess as well," she said. "Anything else that you think might help me?"

"I would probably start out by speaking to the person who owns this."

Bates held up a small gold earring that contained a large pearl suspended inside ornate filigree.

"Where did you find that?" she asked.

"On the floor," he said. "It was between the center console and the passenger seat."

"Hutch, get me a photo of the Doc holding the earring in relation to where he found it."

Hutch walked around and snapped several photos of the earring as Bates held it in proximity to where he had originally found it."

When he was done, Alex removed a plastic security envelope from her jacket pocket and held it open. Bates deposited the earring inside and she sealed the bag up.

"Well, his death wasn't the result of an accident," Bates said. "But like you said, you had already figured that out. I can't be certain till I get him back and do the autopsy. However, judging from the laceration across the neck, and the blood inside the interior of the vehicle, I am fairly certain that someone in the vehicle slashed his throat, before the vehicle ran off the road."

"Yeah, that was my guess," she replied.

"You think this has anything to do with what you arrested him for?"

"I'm not a big believer in coincidences," Alex replied. "Especially under circumstances like this."

"I'll get you my report as quickly as possible," Bates said. "If there is anything else you need, just let me know."

"You know, there is something. Can you swab him and see if there is evidence that he had sex recently?"

Bates glanced over at Alex, a quizzical look on his face.

"Sex? Yeah I can, but you'd have to get something to match it to."

"I'll work on that," she said.

"Okay," Bates replied. "My work is through here. I'll send the fire rescue guys down to extricate the body for EMS. I'll get back to you as soon as possible."

"Thanks, Doc. I really appreciate it."

Bates began making his way back up the hill just as Hutch returned back to the scene.

"What do you need me to do now, boss?"

"Just baby-sit the car till they tow it out of here. Once you get it back to the garage I want you to take some interior photos. Don't go into the car, just from the outside."

"Okay," he said. "I called Abby and told her to send a flatbed tow. It should be here soon. I'll have them take it over to the garage."

"Alright," Alex replied. "I'm going to head back into town and get Nichols to work on those subpoenas. Call me if you need anything."

CHAPTER EIGHTEEN

Alex made her way back to town, the events of the last few days playing out in her mind. She stopped off at Dunkin' Donuts and grabbed an extra-large coffee, along with a toasted coconut donut, before she headed into the office.

"Good morning, Abby."

"Hey, Chief," she replied. "It's been a helluva morning, hasn't it?"

"That's an understatement," Alex replied. "But it pays the bills."

Alex walked into the office and opened the window, removing the pack of cigarettes from her pocket. She sat down at the desk, lighting one up and removed the cover from the coffee container.

Things have certainly taken an interesting twist, she thought.

She reached in and removed her cell phone from her pocket. She scrolled through the contact numbers and selected one, hitting the call button. It rang a few times before the call went through.

"Hey, kiddo, what's going on?" Maguire said.

For a moment she was silent, just listening to his voice on the other end.

"Alex?"

"Yeah," she said, snapping out of her revelry. "Hey, James, how are you?"

"Fine," he replied. "Are you okay?"

"Yeah, I guess I just zoned out for a moment. It's been a rough morning. I just called to see how you were doing and to pick your brain."

"Sure, just use me and abuse me."

"Ha," she replied. "Wouldn't you just love that?"

He laughed on the other end and she could almost see that roguish smile in her mind.

"What can I do for Penobscot's finest?"

"I've got another homicide."

"Are you friggen' kidding me?" he said, his tone becoming more serious.

"Yep, and I think they are related."

"What makes you think that?"

"Long story short, I tracked down that guy that was taking the photos. Turns out he was the manager at a local motel and had an extensive video recording system set up. Anyway, I busted him the other day and he made bail. This morning he turned up, sticking head first out of his car's windshield. That was apparently *after* someone slashed his throat."

"Ouch. Sounds like your shit list wasn't the only one he was on."

"Indeed," she replied. "Although killing the little prick had crossed my mind as well, I just hadn't acted on it."

"Any suspects?"

"One, but it's sort of a convoluted path to them."

"Investigations are rarely cut and dry," James replied. "Tell me your story"

"Remember the missing I talked to you about?"

"Yeah, your floater, right?"

"Yep, that's the one," she said. "Anyway, I tracked down the motel where the photos were taken and that is how I identified my newly deceased, as the manager. I got a search warrant and came up with the video system. In addition his car matches one I saw at the missing girl's house when her mom was home alone and daddy was away on business. I figure he was doing her on the side."

"Geez, Alex, what the hell have you done to that little town?"

"For the record, you got me the job and they were fucked up before I got here," she said. "But wait, it gets better. The next day they set bail for my little cameraman and guess who he calls to get his ass out of jail?"

"Your missing girl's mother."

"Give that man a kewpie doll."

"She's going to say they were just friends," Maguire replied.

"Yep, except I have video of her participating in at least two of the sex tapes he recorded."

"Having sex?"

"In one, but she was clearly doing introductions between the man and girl on both."

"That's really interesting."

"But is it enough?"

"Well, that depends," he replied.

"On what?"

"On whether or not you've lost any of your interrogation skills."

"Don't you worry about me, rookie. I can still make them squirm in their seats."

"I don't know, that country living might have started to make you a little lazy."

"You want to compare arrest records?"

"You know I love it when you get feisty."

"I know what you're doing, James."

"*Moi*?"

"Don't play that foreign language shit with me. You're trying to tell me to stop second guessing myself."

"*Are you* second guessing yourself, Alex?"

"I swear I'm gonna kick your ass the next time I see you."

"Hook the *MILF* up and haul her ass in, Alex. Give her an old fashioned Brooklyn North shakedown. At the very least you have a conspiracy charge. Maybe you'll get lucky and she will start talking, dig herself a nice hole that she can crawl in."

"You don't think it's too slim?"

"Fuck it," Maguire replied, "let her attorney argue that card. You have a deceased who was knocking the bottom out of her and videoing things he shouldn't have been. I'd make the case that they were working together. Kind of works out better that he's poking up daisies. At least this way they can't haul him in to contradict you."

"Thanks, James."

"I thought you wanted to kick my ass?"

"I'm still gonna kick your ass," she replied. "But thanks for being there for me."

"What are partners for, Alex?" he replied. "You need me to come up there and slap the bracelets on her too or do you think you can handle that on your own?"

"Bite me," Alex said.

"That's my girl. Call me if there's anything else you need."

"I will," she replied. "I'll call you back later."

Alex ended the call and laid the phone down on the desk. She took a sip of coffee. The cigarette had gone out in the ash tray and she lit another one.

She removed the security envelope from her jacket pocket and took a photo of the earring on her cell phone. When she was done she prepared an evidence receipt form, documenting exactly how the property had come into her possession and from where. When she was done, she stapled it to the security envelope. This would ensure a proper accounting of the chain of custody, for the evidence, should the case go to court.

Alex got up from the desk, and took the envelope, with the attached form, out to Abby.

"Hey, Abs, when you get a chance, can you assign a property control number to this and log it in for me?"

"Sure, Chief," she replied. "Is it from the accident this morning?"

"Yeah, Doc Bates found it in the car."

"Hutch said that you thought it was a homicide."

"Either that or he cut his throat shaving and was racing to get to the hospital."

"Only problem with that is that the hospital is on the other side of town."

"Well I didn't get the impression that Lou was really all that smart to begin with."

"What are you going to do next?" Abby asked.

It struck Alex as to how different things truly were around here. Back in New York City an event like this would have started the investigative ball rolling. Patrol would have secured the scene. The Crime Scene Unit would have handled all the forensic stuff and detectives from the Borough Homicide Unit would have begun putting the pieces together.

No one in the current Penobscot Police Department had ever handled a homicide investigation before, let alone two in as many weeks. In fact, the last recorded homicide had been in 1973 and was attributed to a drifter who had committed a similar crime in Alden, a little town about twenty miles northwest of Penobscot. Three days later he died in a gun battle, with the state police, who had caught him, at a vehicle checkpoint.

Now it seemed as if everyone in the department was watching to see what the *big city* cop was going to do next.

"Well," she said, "Now I guess I see if I can find someone else who's willing to talk to me."

Just then Hutch walked through the door.

"The Jeep is secured in the garage, boss," he said, laying his clip board and camera case on the nearest desk.

"Thanks, Hutch," Alex said. "Did you notice anything else after they removed the body?"

"I did a cursory examination of the interior to check for any weapons or other evidence, but I didn't see anything."

"Okay, well do the paperwork on the accident. I'll call the state police people and ask them to come in to do the forensic workup on it."

"Sounds like a plan," he replied.

Alex walked over to the coffee pot and poured a refill before heading back to her office. She sat down at the desk and picked up the phone.

"Major Crimes, Blackshear."

"Tom, Alex Taylor," she said.

"Hey, Alex, you must be clairvoyant," he replied. "I have you on my list to call this morning."

"After today you might just want to remove me from your rolodex."

"Why's that?"

"I got another body."

"Are you shitting me?"

"Nope, took a drive off the road and went head first into a tree."

"Accidental?"

"The body is over at the M.E.'s right now, but if the victim's slashed throat is a harbinger of things to come, I'd say my sleepy little town is in the middle of one helluva nightmare."

"*Jesus H. Christmas*," Blackshear said. "Well then you're going to love this news."

"What now?" asked Alex.

"Your floater isn't your missing."

Now it was Alex's turn to be shocked.

"Please tell me you're joking."

"Wish I could," he said. Your deceased is actually Hannah Kurtz, a nineteen year-old from Errol. She was reported missing when she didn't return home from school after her freshman year. She was enrolled at NNHU."

"*Outfuckingstanding*," Alex said, as she lit another cigarette. "So I still have a missing or another potential body that just hasn't turned up yet."

"You know what they say, *when it rains it pours*," Blackshear replied.

"I'm going to need more than an umbrella to weather this storm."

"Anything I can do for you?"

"Yeah, can you sweep the car I just had towed in? See if the killer left behind their business card or at least a potential DNA sample?"

"I'll get a team out first thing in the morning. You got a place to keep it secure until they arrive?"

"It's locked up in my garage. I also have an earring, which was recovered from the vehicles interior, locked away in evidence, as well."

"We'll do our best," he said. "Sorry about the other vic, but at least one family has closure."

"I wonder if they would have preferred not knowing, and just kept living in blissful ignorance?"

"I ask myself that same question a lot," Blackshear replied. "So now what are you going to do?"

"Well now I guess I see if I can make it rain on someone else's parade for a change."

"Let me know how that works out for you."

"I will," Alex said. "Talk to you soon, Tom."

She ended the call and hung the phone up. Alex took one last drag of the cigarette, crushing it out in the ashtray before getting up and heading for the door.

"Hutch, are you going to be here for a while?"

"Yes, ma'am," he replied.

"Do me a favor," she said. "When I was going through the storage unit the other day I remember seeing a video surveillance camera laying down there."

"Yeah, we got that under a grant a few years back, but Chief Parker said we had no use for it."

"Can you go get that and hook it up in the interview room?"

"You want me to setup the system to record?"

"No, not now," she said. "I just want you to mount the camera up on the ceiling in the corner."

"Sure thing, you want me to do that now?"

"Yeah," Alex said. "I'm going to go bring Rebecca Waltham in for a little chat."

"I'll have it done before you get back," Hutch replied.

Alex turned around to look at Abby Taylor.

"Suit up, Abs; it's your turn to baby-sit the boss."

"Yes, ma'am."

Alex walked back into her office and picked up the phone, dialing a number. It rang several times before she heard him answer.

"Nichols."

"Hey, Scott it's Alex Taylor again."

"Hi, Alex, what's going on?"

"I need a couple of subpoenas and a search warrant."

"That's funny, what do you really want?"

"I'm serious; I need a warrant to search for a piece of jewelry, a computer hard drive and possibly evidence related to the murder of Louis Jenkins."

There was silence on the other end of the line.

"I promise you this isn't a joke," she said. "And this is exigent circumstances so you're going to have to have to go to bat for me with Judge Garrett and do it for me. I need to get to the house to secure it."

"Okay, bring me back to square one and tell me what is going on."

"Alright, we executed that search warrant and uncovered a large scale, covert video setup at the hotel. Someone had already beaten us to it though, because the computer hard drive was removed. However, we located a back-up USB drive that contained numerous sex videos. We are still going through them all, at this time, but they were all recorded at the motel."

She could hear him writing notes on the other end.

"However, Mr. Jenkins made bail on us the other day. I was planning on talking with him today, but he met with an untimely demise."

"Accident?" he asked.

"Yep," she replied. "Unfortunately, the accident happened *after* his throat was slit open."

"Holy shit."

"What do you need the search warrant for?"

"Well, the person that bailed Jenkins out of jail was Rebecca Waltham, who did so surreptitiously under her maiden name. She is also the same person that is on the video tapes doing introductions between some of the men and young women. And if that wasn't enough she is also the same woman who was having an affair with Jenkins. It seems to me that she just might have had a lot to worry about with Lou and his little video collection. There was also an earring that was recovered from Lou's vehicle. It was a nicer piece and I think the companion might be in Waltham's jewelry box."

"So you think she snatched the hard drive and then killed him to make it all go away."

"It does make for an interesting bed time story, doesn't it?" Alex said. "I just want to bring her in and question her. See if I can shake anything loose. I need the search warrant to make sure I don't lose any evidence."

"And if she won't talk?"

"I'll arrest her for criminal conspiracy. Write it up that she was acting in concert with Jenkins to arrange and illegally record the sexual activities of others for a future gain. Hell, charge her for falsifying court papers by bailing out Jenkins under a false identity for all I care."

"What do you need the subpoenas for?"

"I want to grab Jenkins' phone and bank records, see if there is anything that will give us a clue as to who killed him or at least the reason why he was killed."

"Let me go talk to Judge Garrett and I'll call you back," Nichols said. "I'll need the name of the phone companies and the banks involved."

"I'll have my officer call you back with the information as soon as he gets it," Alex said. "I'm heading over to the Waltham house now. I don't want to lose a moment. Take down my cell phone number."

"Okay, give it to me."

Alex gave him the number.

"I'll call you back as soon as I can," Nichols said and hung up the phone.

Alex walked out of the office, "Hutch, when you get the details on Jenkins' phones and banking, give Nichols a call so he can do the subpoenas for us."

"Will do," Hutch replied.

"Are you ready to roll, Abs?"

"Yes, ma'am," Simpson replied as she finished putting on her gun belt.

They took two cars out to the house and parked just north of the driveway, with Abby Simpson's marked patrol car pulled in behind Alex's Charger. Abby had joined her in the car and the two women sat talking as they waited for the call back from Nichols.

"What's the plan?" Abby asked.

"Well, hopefully the judge signs off on the warrant. Then we ask Rebecca Waltham to come down to the office to discuss things with us."

"And what if she doesn't want to?"

"I'll ask her nicely at first, but if my charming personality doesn't work then she gets hooked up and you can haul her in while I do the search. Either way she's coming with us."

"I've never actually served a search warrant before," Abby said.

"I get the feeling you don't get out of the office too much."

"It's not for a lack of desire," she replied. "I got the impression that Chief Parker was never a big fan of females in law enforcement. To be honest I think he finally just got pressured from upstairs into hiring a woman."

"That's not something that is unique to Penobscot," Alex replied. "Believe it or not there are still many in the big cities that feel the same way."

"So how did you overcome it?"

"I'm not sure if I ever really did," Alex said. "I just never really concerned myself about it. I just let my work ethic and arrest record speak for itself. If that somehow managed to change a person's opinion of female cops, great. If it didn't, fuck 'em."

"I wish I had the opportunities you had in New York. Here I just feel like all I'm good for is answering phones and searching female prisoners."

Alex looked over at Abby.

She wondered to herself what she must have looked like when she first hit the streets. It seemed like only yesterday that she had first showed up, at the seven-three, looking more like a kid who had just stolen their parent's police uniform.

She had felt so out of place, as if everyone at roll call was staring at her. The truth was that they were.

Good looking female cops usually ended up somewhere far away from the mean streets of Brownsville. The other cops thought she must have some type of *defect* to have ended up there and did their best to avoid her. The funny thing was that some of her toughest critics were the other female cops in the command.

In Brooklyn North, respect was not easily earned.

She would show up for every tour feeling like the odd man out. For a long time she didn't have a steady partner. She just got passed around, from one cop to another, like a second place trophy. It took several months of proving herself on the street, before one of the veteran cops in her squad walked up to her at a *shot's fired* job and said the words she had been longing to hear.

"Good job, kid."

After that life had changed for. She had gone from *snot nosed rookie* to a cop. She felt as if she finally belonged and, more importantly, they began to treat her like one of their own.

Police work was like that. It was often a very brutal world and you either measured up to it or you didn't. You had to prove yourself before anyone was going to be willing to trust *you* with *their* life.

Still, Alex knew that the only way you could prove yourself worthy was if you were given the opportunity.

"That changes today, Abs," she said. "We'll start getting you out on patrol more. I'd like to see about hiring a civilian to run the office and answer the phones. I never understood why you would hire a cop and then keep them inside, anyway."

"I'd really appreciate that, Chief," Abby said.

Just then Alex's cell phone began to chime.

"What do you have for me, Scott?"

"Judge wasn't too happy about the way we requested it, but you've got your search warrant, Alex."

Alex signaled a thumbs up to Abby and motioned for her to head to her vehicle.

"He also wanted me to remind you not to make a habit of doing things this way and that you are *not in New York City anymore.*"

"Thanks, Scott," Alex said. "Do me a favor and fax me over a copy of the warrant to the office. I'll call you back when I am done here."

"Okay, I will," he replied. "Be safe and good luck."

Alex pulled the Charger into the driveway, Abby following close behind, and headed down the long gravel road. She made her way up the stairs, and was just about to knock, when the front door opened.

Rebecca Waltham stood in the doorway, her hair was wet and she was wearing sweatpants and a tee shirt that clung tightly to the damp skin beneath. It was a far cry from the well-dressed look Alex had previously experienced.

"Chief Taylor," she said. "What can I do for you?"

"I just thought I would stop by and ask you a couple more questions."

"I'm so sorry," she said. "This isn't really a good time. I have to go out of town for a few days. Maybe you could come back later."

"And when exactly would be a good time, Mrs. Waltham? Or are you just going by Becky Riggs these days?"

Rebecca Waltham stared at Alex for a moment longer, her facial expression quickly changing from confusion to anger.

"I'm sorry," she said, "I really do have to go."

Waltham succeeded in almost closing the door before Alex's hand slammed against it, pushing it back open forcefully.

She stepped into the house as Waltham stumbled backward, completely unprepared for what had just happened.

"I'm sorry too, but I really must insist."

"You need to get out now or I'm calling..."

"Calling who Rebecca? The cops?" Alex asked sarcastically. "We're already here, sweetheart."

"I'm calling my husband," she said angrily, turning to pick-up the phone sitting on the antique console table in the entryway.

"You really think that is the best choice in light of your recent activities?"

"What's that supposed to mean?"

"Well, think about that for a moment," Alex replied. "You're going to call your husband and tell him the police are here. Then he is going to wonder what the hell is going on and he'll want to talk to me. I'll get on the phone and he's going to ask why I'm at his house. I'm going to have to tell him that I came here to discuss why his wife is sucking some other guy's dick while he is away on business. I don't really see that ending too well for you. But hey, I'm not a marriage counselor so you knock your socks off, sweetheart. I'll wait."

Waltham slowly lowered the phone back onto the receiver cradle.

"That was probably a very smart idea."

"Why is my sex life any business of the Penobscot Police Department?"

"Under normal circumstances it wouldn't be," Alex replied. "But these aren't normal circumstances. But we can discuss that over coffee at the station."

"What if I don't want to go?" Rebecca asked cautiously.

Alex frowned and folded her arms in front of her, cocking her head to the side slightly and stared at the woman for a moment.

"Well, then that would be the part where you and I discuss new *jewelry* options."

Behind her, Abby removed her handcuffs from the pouch on her gun belt, slowly clicking them to drive home Alex's point.

Rebecca Waltham stared at the handcuffs, then back at Alex, as she internally weighed her dwindling options. She realized that it was fruitless to protest at this point. More importantly she really wanted to know exactly what she was up against.

"Okay," she replied. "I'll go, but I must insist that we do this as expeditiously as possible."

"Aw shucks," Alex said. "I'll do my best to accommodate you. Officer Simpson, would you be so kind as to provide Mrs. Waltham here with a ride to the station?"

"Yes, ma'am"

"I don't understand," Rebecca said. "Aren't you coming too?"

"Yeah, I'll be along in a little bit. Just as soon as I'm done executing the search warrant."

"What search warrant?"

"The one Officer Simpson is going to show you when you get back to the station," Alex said. "*Au revoir*, see you soon."

Abby ushered Waltham out of the house and toward the car. The woman didn't resist, but it was clear from her physical demeanor that she was not very happy.

Alex didn't really care. In fact she was counting on the woman to be angry. She would let her stew in the interview room, allowing the anger to build. People like Rebecca Waltham were used to being treated differently. This departure from the norm would eat away at her, only intensifying the anger that she felt inside.

The one thing Alex knew was that angry people often made mistakes.

As she watched the car pull away, she reached into her pocket and took out her cell phone.

"Hey, Hutch," she said, when he answered the phone, "Abs is on her way back with Rebecca Waltham. After she gets her into the interview room I want you to head over to the house and help me on this search."

"Will do, Chief," he said.

"Call in someone from the four to twelve shift and see if they can come on early to cover patrol."

"Okay, I'll start calling now."

Alex ended the call and walked up the stairs.

The second floor was divided into two wings on either side of the staircase.

From down the hallway, on the right side, she heard a loud, tumbling noise. She followed the noise until she found a laundry room. The sound she had heard was the dryer completing its cycle.

Alex opened the lid and looked inside. It was a mix of about a half dozen pieces of clothing. She sifted through them, drawing them out one at a time. There was a pair of jeans and a dark gray hoodie, underwear, bra, tee shirt, and socks.

Who wastes an entire load to wash only a few pieces of clothing, she wondered.

She headed back down the hall, past the staircase and Susan's room. She found what appeared to be the master bedroom and stepped inside. Alex donned a pair of latex gloves that she withdrew from her pocket.

The room was just as elegant and tastefully appointed as Susan Waltham's bedroom was. It was also just as devoid of any personal touches.

Alex made her way around the room and found the doorway that led into the master closet. It was a massive room that incorporated both his and her wardrobes. At the far end was another door which led into the en-suite bathroom.

It was easy to pick out Rebecca Waltham's side. The sheer volume of clothing and shoes stood out in stark contrast to the relatively few items that hung on Kevin Waltham's side. In the center of the room was an island that featured a number of drawers on each side. Alex began to go through them.

Most of the drawers featured under garments and socks for both of them. However, on one side, the drawers contained the Waltham's jewelry. The top drawer featured an assortment of cuff links and watches for him. The remaining three drawers contained her jewelry which consisted of a wide array of rings, necklaces, bracelets, and earrings. As Alex began to examine the pieces, it was clear to her that Rebecca Waltham's love of the finer things, definitely included jewelry.

Alex focused on the drawer that housed the collection of earrings. There had to be nearly a hundred different pairs ranging from diamond studs to intricate gold ornamental ones.

"I'm in the wrong line of work," Alex muttered.

In the back of the drawer she spotted the lone pearl earring wrapped in gold filigree.

"Gotcha," She said.

She removed a security envelope from her pocket and placed the earring inside, sealing it up. She withdrew a pen and entered the information on when and where the item had been located.

A voice cried out from the entry.

"Chief?"

"Up here, Hutch," she shouted back.

A moment later he walked inside the bedroom.

"Where are you?"

"I'm in the closet."

"Whatcha doing?"

"Remember that earring from this morning?"

"Yeah, the one Dr. Bates found?"

"It's not an orphan anymore," Alex said, holding up the envelope.

"You think Rebecca Waltham killed Lou Jenkins?"

"Not sure," she replied. "Right now we just have to gather up the evidence and see where it leads us."

"What do you need me to do?"

"The search warrant is for the earring, hard drive and potential murder weapon. We have to tread lightly on anything else we find. I want you to search the house, see if you can locate the missing hard drive from Jenkins' computer. I'm sure the kitchen cabinets are full of knives that might have done the job, but I doubt any are covered in blood. If it looks suspicious call me. I'll run it by Nichols and see if Judge Garrett will allow us to seize it."

"What are you going to do?"

"Oh I think it's time for me and Rebecca to have a little woman to woman chat."

"Have fun," he said.

"Oh, you know I will," she replied, "her, not so much. Call me if you find anything."

"Will do."

Alex walked out and headed down the hall. She stopped outside Susan Waltham's bedroom and stepped inside. Nothing had changed since the last time she had been in the room. It was all still perfectly spotless.

She walked over to the closet and opened the door, peering into the cluttered *normalcy*. It was the only place in this house that seemed to have been truly lived-in.

Where are you, Susan? Alex wondered.

She shut the closet door and made her way out of the house.

Rebecca Waltham was sitting impatiently in the interview room when Alex arrived back at the station. She had stopped to pick up coffee on the way back and had enjoyed a cigarette outside in the car before she came in. She wanted the woman to be as much on edge as she could possibly make her, before they had their chat.

The angrier a person was, the less likely that they would stop to think about what they were saying before it was too late.

"I'm so sorry to keep you waiting, Rebecca," Alex said as she walked into the room, closing the door behind her. "Traffic was brutal."

"I bet it was," Waltham said tersely. "Would you mind telling me what this is all about?"

Alex put the folder she was carrying on the table and sat down in the chair across from the woman. She opened up the lid on the coffee container and took a sip of the hot liquid.

"This is about Lou Jenkins."

"What do you want to know?"

"How long have you been seeing him?"

"That's none of your business."

"Does your husband know?"

"Again, that's really none of your business," Waltham replied. But, if you must know, Lou Jenkins is a business associate of mine. I meet him on a regular basis to negotiate hotel accommodations for the upcoming regatta."

"See, I knew there was a simple explanation," Alex said.

"Are we done?"

"Eh, in a little bit. I just have a few other questions to ask."

"Can we please make this quick."

"So, when you and Mr. Jenkins meet for your *regatta* business, do you meet at your home or the motel?"

"Mr. Jenkins is kind enough to respect my very busy schedule and accommodate me, by stopping by my home," she replied.

"Oh I bet he is very accommodating" Alex replied. "So when was the last time you saw him."

"I don't recall. I don't have my planner to reference."

"Give me a ballpark," she said. "A week, ten days, *last night*?"

"Just what is it that you are trying to get at, Chief Taylor?"

"I'm just curious as to when and where you saw Lou Jenkins last."

"Maybe you should ask him?" she said, her voice dripping with sarcasm.

"Maybe I will, but I'm asking you right now."

"Fuck you," Waltham replied.

"You know, you're not my usual type Rebecca, but then again it's been a little quiet on the romantic front lately. Maybe after our little chat here we can discuss it over drinks."

"I really think I've had enough *chatting* for today. I'd like to go home now."

Alex got up, walked over to the viewing window and closed the blinds. Next she reached up and pulled the wire from the video camera.

Rebecca Waltham watched as the little red light under the lens went dim.

"What are you doing?" the woman asked, her voice cracking slightly.

Alex smiled. She'd have to remember to thank Hutch later. Getting power to the unit was the perfect touch.

"I think you and I got off to the wrong start, Rebecca," Alex said. She walked back toward the table, resting her hands on top of it and stared down at the woman.

"You see I think you made the mistake of thinking you're some high and mighty socialite bitch that just can't help, but look down at everyone else around you, because they don't hold the same *station in life* that you do. I think you also made the mistake of thinking I'm some little Podunk cop who's so dumb that it takes me an hour and a half to watch *Sixty Minutes.* Well, I'm here to set the record straight."

Alex reached down and picked up the folder in her hands, then slammed it across the side of Rebecca Waltham's face hard enough that it nearly knocked her off her chair.

"That, Rebecca, is my *bullshit detector.* If it detects *any* bullshit coming from your mouth, that's what happens."

Waltham stared at her in shock, holding her reddened face in her hands.

"*Capiche*?"

"You're fucking insane!"

"Glad to see we have an understanding."

"I demand to see my attorney! I'll have your badge!"

Without hesitation Alex slapped the woman again with the folder.

"Really? You honestly think threatening me is the right thing to do under these circumstances?" Alex asked. "Here's a little news flash for you, sweetie. While you were having tea socials with your girlfriends and giving all the neighborhood boys blue balls, I was getting shot at and trying to save dying crack babies in some shit hole housing project in the ghetto. You'll have to excuse me if I don't pee my pants over your threats to *have my badge.*"

The woman sat motionless in her chair. She was on the verge of crying and her chin quivered ever so slightly.

Alex sat back down in her chair and lit up a cigarette.

"You're lying to me, Rebecca," Alex said. "You know it and I know it. Now, you can continue to play this game if you're still under the illusion that you are somehow smarter and tougher than I am, or you can save yourself another beat down of that skinny little uptight ass of yours. It's your choice, sister."

"What do you want?" she asked cautiously.

"I want to know why Lou Jenkins called *Becky Riggs* to bail him out of jail the other day."

The color drained from Rebecca Waltham's face.

"Let me guess, you didn't realize that they had cameras at the jail?"

"Lou called me and said he needed bail money. Said it was a big misunderstanding and that he would explain it to me later."

"Did he?"

"He said someone at the hotel had accused him of violating their privacy, but that it was all an honest mistake that would be cleared up in court."

"So if it was all honest, why did he need Becky Riggs to bail him out and not Rebecca Waltham?"

"We were right in the middle of negotiations dealing with the housing of attendees for the regatta. Until I knew the full story I didn't want the regatta to be impacted by anything *untoward.* I went to help Lou out as a friend, not as a business associate."

Alex took a drag on the cigarette an exhaled, blowing smoke at Waltham's face.

"I really should slap you again, *Becky*," she said. "You're not being honest with me. But I'm feeling benevolent at this moment so I'm going to give you another chance. There are only two types of business negotiations you had with Lou Jenkins. One revolved around what position the two of you were going to fuck in on that particular day. Personally, I for one don't give a rat's ass about what the two of you did behind closed doors. In fact, I'd really like to *not have* that mental image swimming around in my head. I'm more interested in the business negotiations the two of you were taking care of when *you* went to the motel."

Alex opened the folder and withdrew a photo of the screen grab showing Waltham in the motel room. She held it up for the woman to see.

Waltham's eyes grew wide. She opened her mouth to speak, but the words didn't come out.

"It looks to me like you're a pretty tough negotiator, Rebecca."

Waltham reached across the table and ripped the photo from Alex's hand. She stared at the image of her own face looking back at her.

"Wh...Wh....Where... did.... you get this?"

Alex smiled at her across the desk.

"I loved that thing you did with your tongue," she said. "Maybe you could teach that to me one day"

The woman's eyes darted back and forth between Alex and the photo; trying to process something she had no way of processing.

Alex reached over and removed the photo from her hands, tucking it back into the folder.

"You've got some decisions to make, Rebecca," Alex said. "Save yourself or save Lou Jenkins. But remember, the clock is ticking."

She had intentionally misled Waltham indicating to her that she believed Jenkins was alive. She wanted to gauge her reaction and response. Unfortunately, the moment was interrupted when the door suddenly opened up behind her.

Alex instinctively stood up and spun around aggressively to confront the interruption. A man in a three piece suit entered the room.

"We're done here," he said calmly.

"Who the hell are you?" Alex demanded.

Abby Simpson appeared in the doorway a second later, grabbing the man by the upper arm hard enough to elicit a grimace from him.

"I'm Alistair Sinclair," the man replied. "I'm Mrs. Waltham's attorney and she is not going to answer any more questions. Charge her or let her go."

Alex waved Abby off.

He was a distinguished looking man with salt and pepper hair. His chiseled facial features gave him a slightly *hawkish* appearance. She guessed that the man was probably in his late fifties. The suit he was wearing was not the typical off the rack style. This one had all the tell-tale signs of being a custom tailored one. Whatever kind of attorney Alistair Sinclair was, he was obviously paid very well to do it.

"Have it your way, Mr. Sinclair," Alex replied.

"Come with me, Rebecca," Sinclair said.

Waltham got up and started to walk out of the room when Alex grabbed her by the arm.

"Mrs. Waltham is being charged with Criminal Conspiracy," she said. "You can see her at court tomorrow."

"What?" the woman cried out.

Sinclair's eyes narrowed as he stared at Alex, who held the man's gaze until he blinked.

"Don't say another word, Rebecca," the man admonished her.

"Abby take Mrs. Waltham here and process her please," Alex said. "Mr. Sinclair, I do believe that it is time for you to leave my interview room."

"Yes, ma'am," Abby said, and led Rebecca Waltham out of the room.

Alex picked up her coffee cup and the folder. She waited until the man walked out, before following him into the squad room.

"In the future, Chief....."

"Taylor," Alex replied, taking a sip of coffee.

"In the future, Chief Taylor, I would politely warn you against speaking to my client outside of my presence," Sinclair said, a humorless smile on his face.

"In the future, Mr. Sinclair, I would warn you never to walk into this office again without being accompanied by one of my officers."

"Is that a threat, Chief Taylor?"

"Threat? Why no, Mr. Sinclair, I never threaten anyone. Merely a friendly warning considering all the weapons and testosterone we keep in ample supply here. My officers are always on alert for any security risks and a man barging into an interview room, even one as distinguished looking as you, could be viewed as aiding in an escape. We certainly wouldn't want any *accidents* to happen, now would we?"

Sinclair stared at her, gauging his response. In the end he thought better of it. He turned and walked out of the office.

Alex turned around and saw Abby going through Rebecca Waltham's personal effects.

"Chief Taylor," Waltham said. "Where did you get that photo?"

"Sorry, sweetheart, that train left the station when your attorney arrived. But don't worry; the answer to that question will come out in court."

"That's what I'm afraid of," she replied.

Alex walked into her office and closed the door. She pulled out the pack of cigarettes and lit one, inhaling deeply.

"Fuck!"

How the fuck did he know she was here? She wondered.

Just a few more minutes and she knew she would have gotten all the answers she needed. The photo had jarred her, but why? Was it because she already had the hard drive from the computer and had thought the secrets were now safe with her.

She picked up the phone and dialed the number.

"Nichols."

"Rebecca Waltham's lawyer, Alistair Sinclair, showed up and shut down the interview."

"How the hell did he find out she was there?"

"That's the million dollar question," Alex replied. "Not that it's going to do us any good."

"Did she cop to anything?"

"I had her on the ropes, Scott. Right before *Little Lord Fauntleroy* threw in the towel."

"Which, in legalese, means you've got nothing?"

"Pretty much," Alex said, blowing a smoke ring across the room. "I'm having her booked on Criminal Conspiracy."

"That won't last fifteen seconds with Sinclair," he said. "What about the search warrant?"

"One of my guys is combing the house now. Waltham seemed shocked when she saw the photo of her in the sack. That could mean she was either unaware she was being filmed or she has the hard drive and can't figure out where we got that picture from."

"All I'm hearing is a lot of *ifs* and *maybes*."

"I did locate the missing earring in her jewelry drawer."

"Yeah, but they are just going to say she lost it having sex in the car with him."

"I know it's slim, Scott, trust me. I did find some clothes in the wash when I was there. It was just one complete outfit. I doubt there is going to be any useable DNA, but I'd like to seize it and have it sent to the State Police Lab for a workup. If she did kill Jenkins maybe there is something they can pull from it"

"I'll talk to the judge and see if I can get an amended warrant for the clothing."

"Thank you."

"I'm going to need you here for court tomorrow."

"What time?"

"Be in my office by seven-thirty. If we have any shot at making something stick we are going to have to make sure all our ducks are in a row."

"I'll be there."

"Let me go talk to the judge and I'll get back to you."

CHAPTER NINETEEN

It was nearly six when Alex walked out of the office.

The remainder of the search at the Waltham home hadn't turned up anything useful. Hutch had bagged the clothing and put it into evidence. They would turn it over to the forensic guys in the morning, for testing.

As she drove home, she couldn't help but feel drained, both physically and emotionally. She had been running on adrenaline for the last few days now and it was beginning to take its toll.

How long had it been since they discovered the body in the lake? she wondered. *It had to be at least a week already.*

Despite her valiant attempts at working out, she knew she wasn't getting any younger. In fact it seemed to be getting harder and harder to bounce back under normal circumstances, let alone the rigors of burning the midnight oil doing an investigation like this. When this was all over, she'd need to see about sending her people out for additional investigative training. Not that she thought Penobscot was going to suddenly become a den of crime, but she would enjoy the opportunity to sit back and supervise while she let *them* run with the investigation.

It was quarter to seven when she finally walked through the door. The blast of cold air was like an answered prayer. She didn't know what she would have done if the landlord hadn't been able to fix it today.

Well, Lou Jenkins place is available now, she thought.

Alex changed into her sweats and poured herself a drink. She grabbed the takeout container before heading over to the couch. She had decided that it was time for a much needed break from everything. Tonight she just wanted to spend the evening curled up on the couch watching mindless television. Originally she had contemplated reading, but she didn't even know which of the boxes her books were packed away in. Plus, she didn't have the energy to look. The TV remote was a lot easier to deal with tonight.

As the news played in the background Alex ate her dinner. She picked up the drink and took a sip. She had cut back, opting to temper the whiskey with a Coke. It was her version of moderation. Truth was that the morning hangovers were becoming harder for her to handle and with everything going on she needed to have a clear head. It was bad enough that she was doing the lion's share of the work to begin with. She didn't want to blow this case because she missed something after drinking too much.

Moderation was her new catch phrase.

Unfortunately for her, the midweek prime time line-up left a lot to be desired. She ended up turning on one of the history stations and tried desperately to get caught up in a show about *Hatshepsut*, the Egyptian queen.

Despite her best intentions to take the night off, unconsciously she began to think about the direction the investigation had taken with Jenkins' death and the arrest of Rebecca Waltham. It was a fragile case at best right now.

With Lou Jenkins gone, there was no real way to pit them against each other. She wanted to talk to Nichols about getting a subpoena for Waltham's financial records. But she'd wait until after they had a look at Jenkins' records. It would be nice if you could make a case that there was a money trail between them.

Court was going to be tough. There was a ton of circumstantial evidence, but it was only bound together with very thin strands.

Who the hell tipped off her attorney? she thought.

The list was potentially pretty long. It wasn't even that someone could have done it with any actual malice. Penobscot was still a small town and gossip often traveled very fast, especially when a socialite like Rebecca Waltham is on the receiving end of a one way ride to the police station.

Regardless of how or why, the damage was already done. She'd lost the only opportunity she had to have a one on one with the woman. If only she had five more minutes with her. The look on her face, when she saw the photo, was the crucial turning point. Alex knew that cold hard reality had smacked Waltham harder than her little folder stunt and she had been poised to pounce on her. But Alistair Sinclair's *Hail Mary* had saved her and now she would have the opportunity to regroup. They would have ample time to come up with a well-rehearsed answer.

There was however a ton of videos to still go through as well as a number of document files. Tomorrow evening she and Hutch would have to pick back up reviewing them again. Hopefully they would be able to find something tangible to link Waltham with Jenkins. With Waltham now under legal representation, it was the last shot she had to make something stick.

Alex swirled the dark, caramel colored drink in her hand and took another sip. She had to admit that the Coke played well with the whiskey's rich, smoky flavor.

The cell phone on the table began to vibrate.

"Go ahead, admit it," she said, when she answered the phone. "You just can't get enough of me."

On the other end of the phone Maguire laughed.

"You've always been a handful."

"It's nice to see that all my hard work is finally being appreciated."

"I called to see how your interrogation went."

Alex lit a cigarette and propped her feet up on the edge of the coffee table.

"It was an Oscar worthy performance, James," she said. "I was in rare form. I led her right to where I wanted her and was just getting ready to drop the hammer when her friggen' attorney walked in and put an end to our little courtship."

"Are you kidding me?"

"I wish I was," Alex replied. "But that's what happened."

"What did he say?"

"He told me to charge her or let her go."

"What did you do?"

"I granted his wish. Kicked him out and sent her packing over to county."

"Good for you," Maguire said. "You might have lost that battle, but at least you let him know that he wasn't going to come in and push you around."

"Not sure how much future interaction I'll have with him. He's not your typical low life defense attorney. I'm pretty sure his retainer and my paycheck don't hang out in the same places."

"You don't have to win every game, Alex; you just have to enjoy playing it," he said. "Besides, at the very least you gave her a night in a decidedly non-affluent environment"

"I know," she replied. "But you also know how competitive I can be."

"Yeah, but remember not to take it personal like you did with Bernie Moskowitz."

"That little mother fucker had it coming," she yelled into the phone. "I should have jacked his punk ass one more time before they dragged me off of him."

Maguire laughed hysterically on the other end. He could still remember the day as clear as if it had happened yesterday.

The Seven-Three's softball team had been playing the One Hundred Precinct from Queens. It was a brutally hot day and as the boys and girls began drinking, things started getting a bit *colorful*. Members of both teams began to trade some rather disparaging remarks back and forth.

Bernie Moskowitz, the pitcher for the One Hundred Precinct, had begun to pitch inside, *brushing back* the hitters, and tempers began to flare.

When it was time for Alex to hit, she stepped into the box, crowding the plate. The first pitch went over the plate inside, followed by the second, Alex never budged. Bernie brought his mitt up to his face, making a snide comment to Alex, who politely told him to go fuck himself. The third pitch went high and tight, bushing right past her face and knocking her on her ass. Moskowitz threw his hands up as if to infer that it was an accident. At that point the umpire issued a warning to him.

Alex stood up, dusted herself off, and discretely flipped him the bird. The fourth pitch sent the message home, hitting her on the left side, just under her arm. Alex calmly chucked the bat back toward their dugout as the umpire ejected Moskowitz.

As the coach from the Hundredth went out to argue it, Moskowitz headed for the dugout, which took him right into Alex's path as she slowly jogged her way up to first base.

He had started to say something smart at her, but the words never came out. She had timed it perfectly and, without missing a beat, she lunged at him, knocking him to the ground where she began pummeling him. Alex managed to land a dozen blows before anyone had a chance to get to them.

For a moment everyone on the Seven-Three side broke into laughter at the sight of *little* Alex tuning up the dickhead until they realized that she was all alone on that side of the field and it became a bench clearing brawl.

Order was only restored when the local precinct cops showed up and the patrol sergeant had the two team's supervisors take control.

"Easy there, tiger," Maguire said.

"Fuck him," she said, her voice tinged with anger. "That raggedy-ass little fucker wanted to file charges against me. If he had any balls I'd have kicked them in as well."

"I think they excused Moskowitz from ever going to Brooklyn North, even on details."

"Ha," she laughed. "After I got promoted sergeant I ran into him at the New Year's Eve detail, in Times Square, one year. He was like a ground hog, one minute I saw him and then *poof* he was gone. Never saw him again."

"Probably a good thing," Maguire said. "Wouldn't have been good to turn on the TV to watch the ball drop and see you tossing Bernie another beating in the gutter."

Alex took a drag on her cigarette and smiled at the mental image. Those were the good old days and she missed them.

"So is this your version of a pep talk?"

"I guess," he replied. "I just wanted to see how you're making out up there, all alone."

"It's okay. The cops might not be as sharp as our old Brooklyn North crew, but they've got heart. As long as you have that, you can be taught the rest."

"Is that so?" Maguire said.

"Sure, look at what I managed to accomplish with you."

"*Touché.*"

"Speaking of you, how exactly are you doing?"

"I'm doing well," he said. "I met someone."

"You met *someone*?" Alex said, sitting up. "What the hell does that mean?"

"We met at a party a few months ago. Her name is Melody, she's a nice a lady, you'd like her."

She felt as if she had been sucker punched. As if her breath had been suddenly taken away and she physically struggled to get it back. The seconds ticked away slowly as she tried to regain her composure and formulate a response.

"Really?" Alex said. "I'm actually shocked."

"I see that," Maguire replied. "I guess I deserved it. Lord knows I haven't exactly been known as the settling down type."

"Well congratulations, I'm so happy for you, James," Alex said, knowing it was a lie.

"Thanks, Alex. Maybe when all the dust settles down we can all get together."

"That would be really great," she said. "Hey, I hate to cut you off, hotshot, but I have court in the morning and I really need my beauty sleep."

"Really? And here I always thought you were just naturally beautiful."

"That's because you never woke up with me at six a.m.," she said, cringing even as the words left her mouth.

Once again, silence filled the line between the two of them.

"Good luck at court tomorrow, Alex," Maguire said.

"Yeah, thanks. Keep the line free in case I need bail money."

"I will," he said. "Talk to you soon."

"Bye, James."

She ended the call and tossed the phone on the coffee table.

Alex felt numb inside. She wanted to feel happy for him, but she couldn't. It felt as if a part of her was dying inside.

Sure, she had known about the *other* women in his life, but they had never amounted to anything. It wasn't him, he didn't have a *settling-down* bone in his body. And yet somehow, just the way he said that he had *met* someone, she knew that this was different. He'd never offered to introduce her to anyone before.

Alex got up, grabbed her glass and headed to the kitchen. She dumped the remainder of her drink into the sink and poured a glass of straight whiskey. She needed it. More importantly she *wanted* it. She wanted to feel the numbness that came with it, to feel the pain drift away and be replaced with that peaceful sense of oblivion.

She raised the glass up to her lips and paused.

Every fiber in her body begged to taste the warmth of the drink on her lips. She looked down and gazed into the clear, golden liquid, watching it ripple on the surface as the hand that held the glass trembled ever so slightly.

Alex let out a scream and hurled the glass across the room. She watched it strike the wall, just to the left of the door, sending a spray of liquid and glass shards flying in every direction.

She closed her eyes tightly, as if to will away the tears. Nothing would keep them from flowing tonight. She felt the warm streaks as they slowly made their way down her cheeks.

Despite everything, she had always held onto something deep inside of her that believed there would one day be a chance for the two of them. All she had to do was to get her act together and show him that she could change. Now she was faced, once again, with the somber fact that she had let the opportunity pass her by.

She looked back down at the bottle that seemed to beckon to her.

It was true, it had never left her alone. It had always been there for her. Like a non-judgmental old friend who just allowed her to be herself.

Maybe that's your problem you dumbshit, she thought. *Maybe you need to find yourself a better class of friends.*

Alex capped the bottle, putting it back in the cabinet and went back to the couch. She picked up the pack of cigarettes and lit one. She felt completely drained. She closed her eyes, leaned back on the couch and inhaled deeply.

Exercising one demon was enough for one day.

CHAPTER TWENTY

No one really knows when the downfall of the justice system actually began. But somewhere along the line it had deteriorated into the *spectacle* that it had now become.

Since his creation, man has had an issue with following the rules. It started back in the Garden of Eve, progressed to Cain slaying his brother Able, and just went completely downhill from there.

In fact, society became so good at bad behavior that folks began quantifying crimes so that they could show how *their* crimes were not really as bad as the *other* persons.

From murder to assault, and from robbery to petit larceny, attorneys began to argue the merits of why their client's crimes were not as bad as the next persons. Degrees of crimes were soon established so as to distinguish between bad behavior and *really* bad behavior.

Under the New York State Penal Law there were no fewer than twenty-four different ways to commit the crime of assault or a similarly related crime.

If that was not bad enough, they then began treating victims differently. It wasn't bad enough to hurt someone, but if you hurt someone who was a *special* person, that made your crime even worse. Even judges had gotten in on the act. It was now considered to be a 'C' felony for anyone to cause serious physical injury to a judge and prevent him from doing his duties.

Of course this was all after the fact.

The truth was that a crime, which had most likely occurred in the span of a scant few seconds, would now be adjudicated in a court of law over a period of months or even years.

From the defense perspective, every minor detail would be critically examined, every nuance pursued, all in the hopes that some *technicality* could be unearthed that would allow damning evidence to be dismissed and a not guilty verdict to be returned.

On the prosecution side, convictions became the priority. Rather than put in the work, weaker cases were routinely plea bargained down. What criminal wouldn't love to have the felony tossed if they'd pled out to a misdemeanor with time served?

The criminal justice simply became nothing more than a revolving door system where criminals were routinely let back out on the street, even before the ink dried on the arrest paperwork.

For their part, cops became even more cynical. Attorneys, irregardless of what side of the aisle they sat on, where viewed the same. They generally believed that prosecutors were bottom of the rung attorneys, who didn't score high enough on the bar exam to merit a spot in private practice. They felt that they were simply doing their time in purgatory, padding their conviction rate and waiting until a slot opened up in a defense firm, where the real money was.

Their overall opinion of defense attorneys was significantly less kind.

Guilt and innocence became subjective.

A person's freedom, or incarceration, could often be determined based upon the amount of money they could come up with for the legal retainer.

Ultimately, this dysfunctional system caused them to reach the conclusion that the only real justice was what was meted out in the streets.

To borrow a quote from Judge Dredd: "There's no Justice, there's just Us."

In the end it all became just so much judicial theater.

Which was exactly where Alex found herself today, sitting at the prosecution table listening to the latest performance in the court room of Judge Preston Garrett.

As Yogi Berra famously said: "It's like *déjà vu*, all over again."

"Your Honor," Alistair Sinclair said. "My client pleads *not guilty* to the charges. The picture that Mr. Nichols has so eloquently painted here is simply, and factually, incorrect. In fact, we would argue that my client is herself a victim of the insidious activities of the late Louis Jenkins."

Scott Nichols stood up.

"Judge, the *fact* is Mrs. Waltham *was* engaged in an intimate extramarital relationship with Mr. Jenkins. She engaged in illegal activity when she bonded Mr. Jenkins out of the county jail using a misleading name."

"Yes, your Honor," Sinclair continued. "It is true, and Mrs. Waltham does not deny, that she had a relationship with Mr. Jenkins. However the nature of that relationship was a strictly platonic one, in which Mrs. Waltham simply was acting as a compassionate friend to Mr. Jenkins, with whom she had previously worked with. If the prosecution would like to provide evidence of another type of relationship we would certainly be eager to hear about it."

"Do you have such evidence, Mr. Nichols?" Judge Garrett asked.

"Your Honor, Mr. Jenkins vehicle was observed at the Waltham home, by Chief Taylor. Her earring was discovered in Mr. Jenkins vehicle, and he admitted to having an affair with the defendant. I think the state has established that the two had a relationship."

"Yes, a business one that required them to spend time together discussing business arrangements concerning the annual regatta and rental accommodations." Sinclair explained. "I find it rather convenient that the state is basing their case on the testimony of a dead man."

"Rebecca Waltham's business at the motel that Louis Jenkins managed was not limited to Mr. Jenkins," Nichols said. "The state contends that she and Louis Jenkins engaged in the operation of an illegal sex ring. The state also contends that the video, entered into evidence, shows Mrs. Waltham personally involved with a client of that ring."

"Who, if called to testify, would tell the court that they were simply friends who had engaged in consensual sex," Sinclair said.

"And the introduction in the other video?" asked Nichols.

"Mrs. Waltham happened to run into some mutual friends while she was at the motel. The fact that they were also the victims of Mr. Jenkins is reprehensible. Unless of course the state would like to provide the court with testimony to the contrary?"

Alex watched the two attorneys go back and forth at each other like she was at a ping pong match, and with the same level of enthusiasm. She didn't know who was more bored, her or Judge Garrett.

"Has the investigation thus far determined that there were any underage participants in these videos?" Garrett asked.

Nichols looked down at Alex, who stood up.

"Not at this time, your Honor. We are having some problems attempting to identify some of the individuals involved due to the quality of the video."

Garrett looked down at the paperwork before him.

"I am going to release the defendant on her own recognizance."

Garrett turned toward the clerk. "Do we have a date at the end of August for a preliminary hearing?"

"August 28th is open," the woman replied.

"Conflicts?" the judge asked the two attorneys.

Neither man objected to the date.

"Then I will see you all back here on the 28th."

Garrett got up and walked out of the courtroom, through a back door that led to his chambers, leaving the attorneys to gather up their folders.

Alex and Nichols were the first to leave and headed for the elevator.

"That was a huge fucking waste of time," Alex said.

"I expected that," Nichols said. "Right, wrong or indifferent, Rebecca Waltham is still a woman who has a lot of clout. It didn't matter whether Garrett OR'd her or set bail, she was walking out of that courtroom today."

They elevator began its slow descent to the first floor.

"Right now we need to identify everyone involved and see if any are underage. We don't have Jenkins to pit against Waltham."

"I need a subpoena for her phone and financial records."

"I'll get them for you," Nichols said. "The sex ring is one thing, Alex; Lou Jenkins' death is another matter entirely. Make sure whatever you have is airtight. Sinclair is a very competent attorney."

They walked out of the court house and stood on the steps, continuing to talk.

A few minutes later Rebecca Waltham walked past her with Alistair Sinclair in tow. Alex watched as they walked toward the curb. A large black Ford Expedition pulled up and Sinclair held the back door open for her.

As Waltham stepped up onto the running board, she paused for a moment and looked over at Alex. When the two women's eyes met Waltham smiled, waving at Alex and then blew her a kiss.

"I've got something for you to kiss, bitch," Alex muttered.

"What was that?" Nichols said.

"Sweet nothings," she replied.

She watched as the SUV pulled away and headed back in the direction of Penobscot.

"Get me that subpoena as quickly as you can. I'll call you when I know more."

"Okay, Alex, just don't do anything stupid will you?"

"*Moi*?" she said with a smile.

"Yes, you," Nichols replied. "Let's be honest, this case has a snowballs chance in hell of going forward. With Waltham's connections we are going to be on the shit end of the stick. Unless you can link her directly to Jenkins, and get me an underage minor, this case is going to dissolve really quick. No one will turn on Waltham, probably for fear they'll be identified as a client."

"So you're saying she's going to walk?"

"I'm a pragmatist. If we don't have more by the preliminary then it will all most likely go away. I'd even bet that Garrett has fielded a handful of calls already this morning."

"She becomes the victim and I become *persona non grata*."

"It's a fucked up world, Alex," he said. "But you already knew that. Just make sure you get the evidence to make this stick."

Nichols headed back into the court house while Alex made her way toward the parking lot across the street.

Inside the car she lit up a cigarette and checked her phone. There was a missed call from the office. She hit the speed dial button and waited for the call to connect.

"Penobscot Police Department, Officer Simpson."

"Hey, Abs, it's me."

"Hi, Chief, just wanted to let you know that Doc Bates called and asked you to get in touch with him when you got back."

"Okay, thanks."

"How'd court go?"

"They released her on her own recognizance," Alex replied. "Did the state ever show up?"

"Yep, they're down in the garage as we speak. Hutch is with them."

"Great, hopefully they can find something. I'm heading back to town now."

"Okay, see you when you get back."

Alex ended the call and pulled the car out of the parking lot.

Wonder what Bates wants to talk about? she thought.

As she headed toward Penobscot her mind went over the conversation that her and Nichols had.

Alex knew he was right. If they couldn't identify any of the girls as being underage, or come up with a financial trail between Waltham and Jenkins, then this case would get bounced. She knew it and, more importantly, Rebecca Waltham knew it.

Call it *coply* intuition, but Alex instinctively knew Rebecca Waltham was involved much more deeply than simply being a middle age housewife with an overactive sex drive. The video of her doing the introductions was all the proof she needed to know she was right. The only problem was that *coply* intuition wasn't admissible in court.

As she pulled into town she swung by Doc Bates office.

The doctor operated a private practice out of his home, a quaint old Victorian house that sat just on the edge of town. It was surrounded by massive trees and had a well-cared for garden in the front. As she pulled into the circular drive he stepped out onto the front porch.

"Afternoon, Chief Taylor," Bates said.

"Oh stop it, Peter," she replied, as she walked around the car and came up on the porch. "I've given you enough business lately that we should be on a first name basis."

"That you certainly have, Alex."

"What do you have for me?"

"I did the autopsy on Louis Jenkins," he replied. "But you didn't have to come all the way out here for that."

"Just coming back from court," she explained. "Besides I need some fresh air."

"Yes, I heard you arrested Rebecca Waltham. Do you really think she is involved with all this?"

"Do I think she is?" Alex asked. "Yes. Proving it is going to be the tough part."

"I'm not sure what you know, Alex, but be careful. The Waltham's have some very influential friends, not only in Penobscot, but down in Concorde as well."

"I appreciate your concern, Peter."

"Would you care for some coffee?" he asked?

"Sure, I'd love some."

"Grab a chair," Bates said, pointing to the wicker patio set. "I'll be right back."

Alex sat down and lit a cigarette, taking in the beauty of the property. It was so peaceful and quiet.

For the first time since she had come to Penobscot the weather was actually nice. The humidity had subsided and she could even hear the breeze blowing through the trees.

She really could get used to this type of living.

Bates returned a few minutes later with a tray containing two cups of coffee and a sugar and milk set.

"You do know those things will kill you," he said.

"I don't expect that any of us are going to make it out alive," she replied.

"Well, I just never saw the point of doing foolish things to help it along."

Alex laughed.

"Peter, I chase bad guys for a living and have already been in two shootouts. I figure smoking is the least foolish of the things I do."

She leaned over; picking up one of the coffee cups and took a sip.

"Well, have you ever thought of trying one of those electric cigarettes?"

"I'll think about it," she said. "Now what do you have for me?"

Bates knew he had hit a wall, at least for now. So he opened the folder he'd brought out with him and began to read.

"Well, Mr. Jenkins was the victim of a homicide. But you knew that already. Cause of death was a large incised wound on the right side of the neck, from the midline to the back. It had severed the sternocleidomastoid muscle, jugular vein, carotid sheath and artery, and everything down to the spine, trachea, and larynx. Jenkins died from exsanguination."

"*Exsanguination*?"

"Sorry," Bates replied. "He bled to death. The wound to his neck probably rendered him unconscious almost immediately. I estimate that he died in less than five minutes."

"Did you find any defensive wounds?"

"Nothing other than the damage sustained when he went through the windshield."

"So how did his throat get slashed?"

"From the angle and direction of the cut I would have to say that whoever did it was behind him."

"Behind him?" she asked.

"Yes, here let me show you."

Bates got up, grabbing his chair, which he placed behind Alex's, and sat down.

"Jenkins would have been driving down the road. Whoever did this to him would have had to have been behind him like this. Then they would have reached around him and pulled the knife backward like so."

He put his right two fingers in front of Alex's throat and slowly dragged them from the front, along the side, and partially around to the rear.

Just then a gentle breeze blew her hair back and he caught the light scent of the perfume she was wearing.

He shook his head to clear his thoughts. Hoping it hadn't seemed as awkward to her as it had felt to him. He got up, moved his chair back around and sat down.

Bates looked over and was relieved to see that she was still deep in thought.

Alex was trying to digest this latest information. Originally, she had thought that whoever it was, had been sitting next to Jenkins in the passenger seat. Now the evidence pointed to the assailant being in the back seat. It was possible that Jenkins may not even have been aware that they were back there, until it was too late.

"Are you absolutely sure, Peter?" Alex asked.

"People may lie, Alex; but bodies don't. The attack came from behind."

"*Unfuckingbelievable*," she said.

"What's wrong?"

"My prime suspect in Lou Jenkins death is left handed. She couldn't have killed him."

"I'm sorry to be the bearer of bad news," Bates said.

"Not your fault, Doc, it's just the way this day has been shaping up for me."

"I wish I had better news," he said. "I'll let you know what the toxicology reports say when I get them back"

"Thanks," Alex said. "And thanks for the coffee."

She got up from the chair and headed toward the stairs.

"Oh, by the way, you were right," Bates called out.

"About what?" she asked.

"He'd had sex recently. If you can get a sample, we can compare the DNA."

"Great, with my luck it'll turn out to be a friggen' ghost."

Peter watched as Alex got back into the unmarked car and headed down the driveway. He wished that there was a way the two of them could meet at something a bit more *social* than a crime scene.

CHAPTER TWENTY-ONE

It was just after ten o'clock when Alex pulled up in front of city hall. She had actually allowed herself the luxury of sleeping in a bit later this morning. Her body needed it.

She'd thought about stopping to get something to eat for breakfast, but she didn't really feel like eating anything. Nothing was sounding good to her. In fact, she realized that she was running on caffeine, nicotine and take-out. She'd have to begin making some changes soon, including getting on a healthier eating schedule.

As she walked into the office Abby greeted her.

"Sheldon Abbott wants to see you and he is not very happy."

Alex laughed.

She was wondering when he was going to finally poke his nose into things. Actually, she was surprised that it had taken as long as it had.

"Be careful, Abs," she replied. "I wouldn't stand to close to me. The way this day has been going you might just get struck by lightning."

"On a more positive note, the ammo came in."

"I'll take it," Alex said. "At this point beggars can't be choosers. What did you do with it?"

"Had Hutch haul it down to the property room and secure it."

"Good thinking. Do me a favor and put a notice up for the range. Choose two Saturdays in August and two in September. Make sure everyone signs up."

"I will take care of it," Abby said. "Oh and Bobby told me to tell you that he caught our little boxball perps."

"No kidding," Alex replied. "How'd he catch them?"

"He noticed that they had replaced all the busted up mail boxes earlier in the week. So he figured they'd come back around for the second inning. He started sitting up in Mr. Foery's driveway after dark and caught them when they came around."

"Was it the Kutcher kids again?"

"No, after old man Kutcher got a hold of them their boxball days were officially over. It was two kids that Bobby knows. He's friends with the parents. They're going to handle it. Restitution for the damage and the kids get a day of chores at each of the houses they hit."

"Street justice, the most effective kind there is," Alex said. "It's nice to finally see some parents taking their kid's bullshit seriously."

"Amen," Abby replied. "So what are you going to do about Abbott?"

"He'll have to wait a minute. I need coffee, a cigarette and a bathroom, not necessarily in that particular order."

"Close the blinds, shut the door and I'll cover for you."

"You're the best, Abs."

Fifteen minutes later she emerged from the office feeling a bit more relaxed.

"Alright, I'm heading upstairs," she said. "Call my cell if you need anything."

"Good luck, boss."

Alex made her way up to Sheldon Abbott's office and knocked on the door.

"Come in."

She opened the door and stepped inside.

"You wanted to speak with me?"

Abbott closed the folder on his desk and slipped it into the top drawer of his desk.

"Yes, Chief," he said. "Please have a seat."

She sat down in the same chair she had on the day she was sworn-in. But that was then and this was now.

Alex noticed the change in the man. Abbott's tone was a bit more formal and she knew there was more to come.

He wasn't his jovial, first name basis, self. His use of her title was not lost on her. She knew what was coming next. Management always liked to use your first name when things were going good and then they called you by your title when they were going to drop the hammer on you.

"I wanted to discuss the recent activities of the department."

"Oh," she said, "anything in particular?"

"Actually yes, I am a bit concerned about your recent investigations."

"And which one would that be exactly?"

Abbott didn't have a very good poker face. She could see by the growing redness of his ears that he had been fuming over this for most of the morning.

"The one in which you thought it would be a good idea to place handcuffs on one of the most respected woman in Penobscot!"

"Really?" Alex asked. "I would have thought Penobscot would have at least a few other women who were more respectable."

"What exactly is that supposed to mean?"

"I guess I am just not that overly impressed with what passes for respectability these days."

"Rebecca Waltham is a very fine woman," Abbott said, "and she is deeply involved with everything that goes on in this town. The very same town, might I remind you, that pay's the salary of both you and your officers."

"Oh, she is *deeply* involved in everything that goes on in here, I'll give you that."

"What the hell is that supposed to mean?"

"I'm sorry, I digressed," she replied. "What is the point you are trying to get at?"

"The point is that I'm beginning to wonder if hiring you wasn't such a good idea," he replied. "I'm not sure if you have the proper *appreciation* of the tight-knit relationship between the police and the citizens of small towns, like Penobscot."

She was done playing games. If he wanted to play tough guy with her then it was time for him to put all his cards on the table.

"I feel like we're dancing here without music," Alex said. "So what exactly is it that you want me to do, Sheldon?"

"What I want is for you to leave Rebecca Waltham and her family alone."

"That might be a bit difficult," she said. "I have no problem with her family, *per se*, but right now Rebecca Waltham is a prime suspect in my investigation."

"Even if costs you your job?"

"Justice is blind, Sheldon. It should be meted out objectively and impartially, without fear or favor, and regardless of one's identity, money, power, or weakness."

"That is a very romantic notion, Alex," Abbott replied, "But wholly unrealistic in the world we live in."

"Maybe it is in your world, Sheldon, but not in mind. Rebecca Waltham's position and prestige don't merit her any special behavior and treatment."

"You know I could fire you," he said bluntly.

Finally, she thought.

She'd wanted to see how far he would actually go, after the verbal jousting had hit the brick wall. Politicians rarely played all their cards, yet he'd just gone *all in*.

Alex stared at him, her face devoid of all emotions. She waited, watching for the right moment.

Abbott swallowed hard, his eyes blinking.

"You could," Alex said and stood up. "But you can't tell me how to do my job."

Abbott stared up at her trying to gauge what he should say next. He'd never been painted into a box before and he didn't like the way it felt, at all.

Everyone in Penobscot worked for *him* and they all knew it. Nothing got done without his approval, and nothing got started without his blessing.

That was until now.

He knew that he could fire her, but the blow-back would, in all likelihood, be much worse for him in the long run.

He had completely misjudged her abilities and character. He thought he had hired a 'last rung' candidate who would be happy to fill the seat as long as it didn't interfere with her drinking. He didn't expect her to actually be competent. He'd have to ride this out, weather the storm so to speak, and then launch her when things quieted down.

"I hope you know that wasn't a threat," Abbott said, his voice taking on a more empathetic tone. "I'm just worried about you, Alex. I don't want to see you get caught up in something that will potentially ruin your career. The people that Rebecca Waltham runs with are powerful and ruthless. They will be looking at every *I* and every *T* under a microscope. I just wanted to impress upon you how serious this really was."

"I truly do appreciate your concern, Sheldon," she replied. "Knowing that you have my back will allow me to sleep much easier at night."

"Of course you know that I will do whatever I can for you."

"Thank you so much for your support," she said.

She walked out of the office and headed back downstairs to the office.

"Are you still the chief?" Abby asked cautiously.

"For now," Alex said. "But I'll probably hold off on repainting the office till after the first of the year."

"By then you might not even want it."

"Right now I think I really need some fresh air," she replied. "I've got to attend a luncheon this afternoon at the Optimists Club."

"How special is that?" Abby said sarcastically. "What are you going to talk about?"

"Not sure, I guess I can talk about how lucky we should feel that we only have two homicides instead of three."

"You might want to work on that," she said. "By the way, I'm leaving at one o'clock today."

"Ok, call me if you need anything, otherwise I'll see you tomorrow."

"Not me, boss, it's the weekend," Abby replied.

"Shit, I really do need some fresh air. You have any plans this weekend?"

"Yeah, that's why I'm leaving early today. I have to go home and pack. I'm heading down to Dover for the Granite State Invitational. I'm hoping to place in the top three."

"No kidding? Good luck and I expect you to bring home a medal."

"I'll do my best, Chief."

"By the way, where is Hutch?"

"He's on patrol," she said.

"Did the state people finish up with the car yesterday?"

"Yeah, I don't think they found anything though."

"Did they get the clothing from Waltham's place?"

"Yeah, Hutch signed it out to them before they left."

"Great," Alex said. "Okay, Well I guess I will see you Monday then. Have a great weekend, Abs."

"You too, Chief."

CHAPTER TWENTY-TWO

Alex drove through the streets of Penobscot.

She'd thought about going back to the office after the luncheon, but she couldn't bear the thought of being cooped up. Besides, for the time being it was probably best to put some distance between Sheldon Abbott and herself. Not for her sake, but for his. She was starting to see growing similarities between him and Bernie Moskowitz.

Alex found that she actually missed being out on the streets. That was something very rewarding about having your office in a car. There was no monotony being on patrol. You never really knew what the next call was going to be or where it would take you.

One minute she could be handling a routine accident and the next she might be chasing a robbery suspect through the projects. You just learned to take everything in stride.

She loved that feeling.

Now as she rolled through town she felt those old feelings coming back to her. They might not have been the badlands of Brooklyn North, but every street had a rhythm. People either belonged there or they didn't and a cop intuitively knew the difference.

Alex pulled the pack of cigarettes out of her pocket and lit one. She had the air on and the windows rolled down. Listening to the sounds of the street. With each passing minute she felt the stress of the day dissipating. She just cruised around the town enjoying the sense of freedom.

Over at the park she turned right and headed out by the school, driving slowly through the tree lined streets. Up ahead a woman swept the curb in front of her house.

"Evening, ma'am," she said, as she came to a stop next to her.

"Good evening, officer," the woman replied.

"Is everything quiet?"

"Oh yes, it's very quiet. Nothing ever happens on this side of town."

"That's good to know," Alex replied.

"Are you new here?"

"Yes, ma'am, Alex Taylor. I'm the new chief of police."

"Really? A woman?"

"The times, they are a changing."

"I guess it was inevitable," she replied. "I'm Mildred, Mildred Parker. I believe you have my husband's old job."

"You're Charlie Parker's wife?" Alex asked.

"Widow I guess is the right title now. But yes, Charlie was my husband."

"I am so sorry for your loss."

"Thank you, sweetheart. That's very kind of you to say."

"If you don't mind my asking, how are you doing?"

"Besides being lonely?" she asked. "I get by alright. I try to stay busy."

She lifted up her broom, as if to emphasize the point.

"Does anyone stop by to check on you?"

"Oh in the beginning they did. But I suppose that the world doesn't stop because one person dies."

"Well, I guess we make time for the things that are important to us," Alex said. "You have a few minutes to visit?"

The woman suddenly perked up.

"Visit? Now? Why yes, I do have some free time before supper."

Alex pulled the car over to the curb and got out, walking around to where the woman stood.

"Sure is a hot one today," she said.

"Oh yes, this summer has been very hot. Do you like sweet tea, Alex?"

"Yes, ma'am."

"Well why don't you have a seat on the porch and I'll get us some."

"That would be fantastic."

A few minutes later Mildred Parker emerged from the house carrying two large glasses of tea. She handed one to Alex and took the seat across from her.

Alex took a sip of the cold drink.

"This is very good," she said. "Thank you."

"You're very welcome. You know you look much too pretty to be a police officer."

"Well thank you. That's very kind of you to say."

"You're not from around here, are you?"

"No, ma'am, I'm from New York City."

"I could tell. I can hear your accent."

"That's funny," Alex replied. "I thought everyone here had the accent."

Mildred laughed and took a sip of tea.

"So how exactly did you get stuck in Penobscot?"

"A friend of mine thought some fresh country air might be good for me and recommended me for the job."

"And how do you like it?"

"The air's great," Alex replied. "I'm reserving my opinion on the job till I have been here a bit longer."

"You seem like a very smart young woman. That will serve you well in that den of inequity they call city hall."

"Anyone I should be careful around?"

Mildred looked at Alex and smiled.

"All of them, sweetheart," she replied. "Starting with that egotistical little bastard up on the third floor."

"Sheldon Abbott."

"That man gives snake oil salesmen a bad name."

Alex took a sip of tea, gauging Mildred Parker's dislike of Abbott. There had to be more to the story and Alex guessed that it most likely involved her late husband.

"I'd gotten that impression myself," she said. "So how did your husband feel about working for him?"

"Charlie? Oh he and Sheldon were very close. In fact, it was Sheldon who had promoted Charlie to chief. But something changed between them. The last few years Charlie was so unhappy. He would never talk bad about Sheldon, but I knew that was where the problem was."

"Cops do have a tendency to hold stuff in."

"That is true," she replied. "Most of what I knew about the goings-on at the police department I learned by reading the newspaper."

Alex laughed.

It didn't matter where you were, cops were all the same.

"Anyway, after Charlie died, Sheldon came to the wake. He told me how sorry he was and that we were all family here in Penobscot. He had said that I would be taken care of. That was nearly two months ago and I haven't seen him since."

"Maybe with the summer, things have just been busy?"

"No, dear, Sheldon Abbott is nothing more than a politician. He lies so easily anymore that I don't even know if he realizes he is doing it. Don't trust a word that comes out of his mouth, especially when he is trying to convince you he's *concerned* about you. The only person that Sheldon Abbott has ever been concerned about is Sheldon Abbott."

Alex took another drink, suppressing a laugh.

"Well, he is married," Alex said. "He must at least have some concern for his wife."

"Ericka Abbott? Oh, honey, you have so much to learn. Sheldon married Ericka for one thing and one thing only."

"And what would that be?" Alex asked.

"Why, access to Conrad Kreutzmann, Ericka's father," she replied.

"Conrad Kreutzmann? As in the Kreutzmann Market chain?"

"One in the same," Mildred said.

"I think that when Sheldon came back from college with his degree in business he had very high aspirations. After he married Ericka, I think he believed that daddy Kreutzmann would just take him under his wing and give him the keys to the supermarket empire. He only made one mistake."

"What was that?"

"The only thing that Conrad Kreutzmann rewards is hard work."

"That's a pretty big mistake."

"For Sheldon it was," she replied. "I don't believe that man has ever worked hard a day in his life. He married Ericka looking for a payoff and what he got was an offer to be an assistant produce manager in one of the stores. Needless to say, that didn't go over well in Sheldon's little world."

"So what did he do?"

"He started his own financial investment company and began making friends, very wealthy friends. Once he had a good foundation he began running for office. Small things at first, but soon he was in the top seat and he's stayed there ever since.

"Whatever happened between him and Kreutzmann?"

"Have you ever heard of *Circus Cyaneus*?"

"Isn't that one of those weird acrobatic shows in Las Vegas?"

"I thought as much," Mildred said with a smile. "But don't feel bad, neither had Conrad. You see, he had spent years working out a deal for a parcel of land on the northern edge of town, just west of the lake. He wanted to turn it into a major distribution hub for his supermarkets. The land deal alone had cost him nearly a million dollars, not to mention what it took to then have it rezoned for commercial use."

"That's some serious money," Alex said.

"Conrad was always willing to take chances on good investments. But right after the rezoning went through; the zoning board commissioner suddenly stepped down and moved out of state. Early retirement is what they officially called it. Unfortunately for Conrad, at that time Sheldon was the deputy zoning board commissioner and he was appointed to fill the spot. Right before they were to do the ground breaking for the new building, someone placed an anonymous call to the state Fish and Wildlife Department."

"Anonymous? You mean as in Sheldon Abbott anonymous?"

"That's who I would put my money on. Anyway, it seemed as if *Circus Cyaneus*, also known as the Northern Harrier, had decided to take up residence on the property. Unfortunately for Conrad, the Northern Harrier is on the endangered species list in

New Hampshire. It seems that harming, harassing, injuring and killing is illegal and the operative word there is *harassing*."

"So it was Sheldon that had the whole thing shut down."

"Ah, that my dear is only *speculation*," she said with a wink and a nod. "Regardless of who made the call, what is known is that it cost Conrad Kreutzmann a ton of money."

"Very devious."

"Sheldon has the habit of coming across as a bit *peculiar* sometimes, but it is all an act. He actually has a very keen intellect and is not someone to be trifled with or underestimated."

"I bet that made holiday dinners at dear old daddies a bit uncomfortable."

"I don't think Sheldon cared too much to share holidays after what he perceived to be the snub from Conrad. Nor do I think there is any love lost between him and Ericka. I believe they both use each other for their respective needs. I would call it more of a business merger then an actual marriage."

"It's an odd feeling for me," Alex said. "I feel lost. You have feelings about certain things, but being an outsider, it's like I don't know who to trust or believe."

"I can't tell you how to do your job, Alex, but one thing I can tell you about, is the cast of characters that make up Penobscot," Mildred said. "Would you care for some supper, sweetheart?"

"Oh God, I would love it. I've been living on take-out food for so long I've almost forgotten what real food tastes like."

"Come in side and join me," she said. "I'll try and give you an idea of just where you have landed."

Alex took it all in over dinner.

Mildred Parker was like a walking encyclopedia of information on the folks in Penobscot. She was born and raised here and her family roots went back to the 1800's. She wasn't one of the rich and influential folks, so she managed to stay under the radar. But she belonged to a much more powerful group, the First Baptist Church, Ladies Auxiliary Coffee Club.

The group met every Saturday morning for coffee and a brief Bible lesson. Once that was done, they got down to the business of filling one another in on the latest goings-on. If it moved or breathed in Penobscot, they knew about it.

It was clear to her that Sheldon Abbott had made a critical mistake; he should have done everything in his power to keep on this woman's good side.

"I have to ask you Mildred, did Charlie ever keep any records on the police department? I feel as if I know the folks at the station, but there's something missing. All of the personnel folders just record the official stuff, but I wondered if Charlie didn't have his own records."

"I know that Charlie had some boxes in the basement. I wasn't really sure what to do with them. I'd thought about just burning what I could. We never had any children and I didn't want it ending up in the wrong hands. You're more than welcome to have them, Alex."

"I'd take anything that might help me do my job better."

There were four large cardboard boxes in all, most filled with files and miscellaneous paperwork. Mildred had also given Alex a large frame that contained all of the patches and badges that the Penobscot Police Department had used since their inception in 1923.

After she had loaded everything up in the car; her and Mildred sat on the front porch and had a cup of coffee.

"Alex, Charlie was not a saint," Mildred said. "The good Lord and I both knew he had his faults. But he was a decent man that tried hard to be a good cop. If you find anything to the contrary I'd appreciate it if you'd remember that those boxes were meant to be burned."

"Unlike Sheldon Abbott, my word means something, Mildred. Nothing you've shared with me will bring any discredit to your husband's legacy. I also come from a job where we actually do treat our own as family. Here is my cell phone number."

Alex wrote the number down and handed it to her.

"If you need anything at all, you call me, anytime."

"Thank you, sweetheart," she said. "And thank you for spending an evening with a lonely old woman."

"Thank you for opening your home to me. I'll check back with you in a few days."

"You do that," she said. "I'll make dinner for us again."

Alex kissed her on the cheek.

"That's a date," she said.

She got into the car and started it up, waving to the woman as she pulled away from the curb.

CHAPTER TWENTY-THREE

"Did you forget about me?"

"Yes," Alex said as she got out of the car.

"Well that doesn't make me feel very special," replied Hutch.

"Don't take it personal. I'd forget my own head lately if it wasn't attached."

Alex walked around to the back of the car and opened the trunk.

"Grab some boxes, junior, and I'll buy you a soda."

Hutch grabbed several of them and lifted them up in his arms.

"Let me guess, you've stolen more books."

"That's funny," Alex said as she grabbed the remaining box and frame, then closed the trunk.

"I thought you'd be excited about another evening of watching the sex lives of the rich and famous."

"It beats basic cable, I guess."

"I still can't believe that they let Rebecca Waltham walk."

"I didn't actually expect her to stay in jail. Her attorney is too good to allow that to happen."

She climbed the exterior staircase that led to the second floor.

"So now what?" he asked.

"Now we earn our paychecks."

Alex unlocked the front door and stepped inside.

"You can just stack them here," she said, setting her box down next to the entertainment center.

"You want your coke on the rocks or straight?"

"Ice please," he said, taking a seat at the table.

She put several ice cubes into a tall glass and poured the soda. When she was done she handed him the glass and made another for herself.

"You're not having whiskey tonight?"

"I came to the realization that I was only drinking to drown the pain," Alex said.

"So you're not in pain anymore?"

"No, I'm still in pain," she said. "I just found out that the pain could swim. So how did the crime scene search go?"

"Eh, it was okay," Hutch replied. "They didn't find anything major. Some fiber samples, hair. No murder weapon though."

"I didn't think they would," She replied. "Not that I think it matters. Rebecca Waltham just slid down several rungs on the suspect ladder."

"What makes you say that?"

Alex explained to him the conversation she'd had with Doc Bates and what his findings were.

"Well couldn't she have just been in the back seat?"

"Sure, but that still wouldn't make her a good suspect."

"Why not?" he asked.

"Remember when we were at her house the other day?"

"Yes."

"Well I watched her write down her cell phone number. Rebecca Waltham is left handed. There's no way she could have reached around that way to inflict the wound. She didn't kill Lou Jenkins."

"Are you serious?"

"Yes I am," Alex replied.

"So now what?"

"Now we get to do some old fashioned, honest to God, police work. Tonight we continue going through the videos and files. Tomorrow morning I want you to meet me over at Lou Jenkins apartment. We need to start doing some interviews of his neighbors. See if they noticed anyone who visited him frequently. Maybe we can jar some memories loose. We have to find something to connect the dots."

"And if that doesn't work?"

"I'm hoping that by Monday morning Nichols will have subpoenas for their phone and financial records."

"What if we are wrong?"

"You mean what if I'm wrong?"

"I don't think you're wrong, Chief," Hutch said. "But I heard about what happened with Sheldon Abbott."

Alex lit a cigarette, inhaling deeply.

She desperately wanted to open the cabinet and pour herself a real drink. She wanted to feel the comforting warmth of the whiskey as it went down her throat. But deep down inside she needed to fight this battle once and for all.

"Don't worry about me and Sheldon Abbott. I can handle him."

"Whatever you do, don't trust him," Hutch replied. "If he thinks you're going to get in his way, he'll move to get rid of you and no one on the town board will go against him."

"Next thing you're going to tell me is that you'll miss me."

"I would," he said. "The Department needs someone who is willing to be a leader."

Alex swirled the coke around in her glass.

"Thanks," she said.

"So where do we go next with this case?"

"We pursue the facts, Hutch," Alex said. "We know we have a dead girl in the lake. We know we have a missing girl. We know that there was a sex ring operating out of the motel that Lou Jenkins was the manager of and who was filming it. We know that Rebecca Waltham was actively involved in that ring and was also having an affair with Jenkins. And now we know that Jenkins is dead. We're not wrong, Hutch; we just haven't found the missing puzzle piece to connect everything yet."

"Doesn't it worry you that some of the people we have already identified are pretty wealthy and influential?"

"Not at all," Alex said, taking a drag on her cigarette. "What worries me is that there was a teenage girl floating in the lake, who'll never get a chance to grow up to be wealthy and influential. I'm also worried that I may not be able to find her killer. That's what worries me, not whether some horny old man, who has the hot's for young girls, is going to have my badge."

"I guess I just think about it more because I know a lot of the people in those videos. People, like Sheldon Abbott, who always seem to get away with things due to the fact of who they are or who they know."

"Remember one thing, Hutch; if you're more worried about keeping your job than you are of doing it, that's when you need to find a new line of work. Police work is a full contact sport and it is not for the faint of heart."

"I'll remember that," he said.

"And on that note it's time for us to once again foray into the wonderful world of vice and depravity that is Penobscot, U.S.A."

"You know I never would have thought that stuff like this went on here," he said, getting up from the chair and moving over to the couch.

"It goes on everywhere, Hutch. Didn't they teach you that sex is the oldest profession? The only thing that makes this any different is that people don't want to believe that it actually happens here."

Hutch opened the laptop and powered it up.

"I guess you're right. When this breaks there are going to be a lot of people shocked by all of this."

"Then we better find that damn missing puzzle piece quickly or this case is going to go the way of the *dodo* bird," Alex replied as she turned on her laptop.

"Do you think that whoever killed Lou Jenkins also killed the girl in the lake?"

"I'm not sure. Whoever killed Hannah Kurtz went through a lot of effort to keep her from being found. They didn't seem as concerned about Lou Jenkins being found."

"Maybe they had different reasons?"

"Interesting thought," Alex said. "Let me hear more."

"What if, whoever killed Hannah disposed of the body just to keep the pregnancy hidden. Then, when Lou got arrested, they realized that there might be evidence implicating them with the girl. So they stole the hard drive and got rid of Lou. You know what they say, *dead men tell no tales*."

Alex mulled it over in her mind. Something about Rebecca Waltham was still gnawing at her, but she wondered if she was allowing herself to get tunnel vision.

"It's plausible," she said. "We could be looking at a *john* trying to cover his tracks."

"Do you really think it's possible that someone would murder two people just to cover-up the fact they were having sex?"

"Oh, my little *padawan*," Alex said with a laugh. "People kill for just the thought of sex. Like you said, we are dealing with wealthy and influential folks. Having a pregnant nineteen year old mistress and a video tape of you doing the deed, can not only lead to a very costly divorce, but child support payments as well. It's time that you learn the fact that life is actually very cheap."

"Do you think Susan Waltham is dead?"

"The thought has crossed my mind."

"Do you think that she was involved in all of this?" he said, motioning toward the computer screen.

"Lou Jenkins certainly had a convincing line of shit. If he was able to get his hooks into her then anything is possible. Let's face it, her boyfriend just dumped her, she finds out her father is doing her friend, I'm thinking she's a poster child for fragile psyche. It wouldn't have taken much for Lou to seem like a knight in shining armor. But for now, all we can do is just keep digging and see where the clues lead us."

"Some days I just wish I could go back to traffic accidents and criminal mischief reports."

"Once you open *Pandora's Box*, you can never un-open it," Alex said. "Now let's get back to work. We have a long day ahead of us tomorrow."

CHAPTER TWENTY-FOUR

It was just after nine o'clock when Alex pulled up in front of Lou Jenkins apartment, just behind Hutch's patrol car.

"People are going to start talking," he said, as he watched her get out of the car.

"Fuck 'em," she replied, handing him a coffee container.

Hutch took the Styrofoam cup from her and took a sip.

"Thanks," he said. "So what exactly are we doing here on what used to be my day off?"

"Today we're going to shake the trees and see what falls out. Somebody had to see Jenkins with someone they recognized or something that just didn't seem right."

"And we need to do this on a Saturday?"

"Saturday morning is the best day to catch people at home."

"That's usually because it's their day off."

"Stop complaining, all you were going to do was work on your house. Think of all the pain and sweat I'm saving you from."

"True, he replied, "but I've never done an interview like this before."

"Stick with me and just take notes," she replied, handing him a note pad. "When you feel comfortable then you can start doing your own. Sound good?"

"That works for me."

"Okay, then let's go have some fun."

They started the interview with the tenants of the apartment directly across the hall from Jenkins' apartment.

"Good morning," Alex said to the middle aged man who answered the door. "I'm Chief Taylor, this is Officer Hutchinson, and we'd like to speak with you regarding your neighbor, Lou Jenkins."

"I'm Michael Moliska," the man said. "I'd heard that Lou was dead."

"Yes, he is," she replied. "We're investigating his death and trying to identify any friends or family that might have visited him here."

"I don't know," he said. "Lou was a pretty quiet guy. He kept to himself. I don't recall seeing too many people stopping by. Then again I work during the day so I usually don't get home till well after six most evenings."

"Do you know if he had any friends in the building?" Alex asked. "Anyone that you recall might have visited him on a regular basis?"

"I would see some men and women come and go in the past, but I don't recall it being very frequent," the man replied. "Lou kept to himself. Never any loud noises or parties, so I guess I just didn't pay very much attention."

"When you say men and women, are you saying his age group or older?"

"No one older that I recall, mostly college age kids, I would guess."

"And do you remember the last time you saw anyone come or go from the apartment?"

"It was probably a few weeks ago, at least," he replied.

"Is there anything else that sticks out in your mind?" Alex asked. "Anything unusual?"

"No, nothing at all really," he said. "He was just a great neighbor. Hope that whoever gets the apartment is just as quiet."

"Ok, well thank you for your time, Mister Moliska," she said. "If you don't mind me asking, is there a Mrs. Moliska that we might speak with?"

"No, I'm single."

"Okay, well if you do recall anything, no matter how trivial you think it might be, would you please call me at the Penobscot Police Department?"

"I sure will," the man said and closed the door.

The same conversation played out at the next three doors they knocked on. Most of the residents worked during the day. They all commented on what a good neighbor Jenkins had been, focusing on how quiet and respectful he was. No one noticed any *regular* visitors, although they did recall seeing people come and go on a fairly infrequent basis. Mostly they just recalled passing Jenkins in the hallway and saying hello.

One female resident thought that she had seen a woman visitor on a fairly regular basis, but that had been nearly a year ago. It only clicked with her because she thought that the woman was a lot older than Lou. She couldn't recall how many times she had seen the woman, only that she had dark brown hair and was probably in her mid to late thirties.

When the door closed Alex turned to look a Hutch.

"Okay, think you got the hang of it now?"

"I think so," he replied.

"If you're unsure about anything just give me a whistle," Alex said. "Go take the last two on the end and I'm going to grab that one over by the elevator."

As Hutch headed off down the hallway, Alex approached the door and knocked on it. As she listened she heard the sound of shuffling feet approaching the door. She saw the light change in the peephole and knew that someone was looking through it.

"Who is it?" an elderly woman's voice asked from the other side of the door.

"Police, ma'am," Alex answered.

The door opened slightly, a chain keeping it secure.

"What's this about?"

"I'm Chief Taylor of the Penobscot Police Department. I'm investigating the death of your neighbor, Lou Jenkins."

"Hold on a minute," the woman said, closing the door.

A moment later the door reopened all the way.

"Is it true?" the woman asked. "Is Louis really dead?"

"Yes, ma'am."

"Oh that's terrible. He was such a sweet young man."

"We're hoping someone might have noticed something that could help us."

"Oh where are my manners, please come in officer."

Alex walked inside the apartment, engaging the deadbolt so that the door didn't lock behind her. It was an old habit developed back in Brooklyn North. Back then, if you needed help, you didn't want a door standing between you and the cavalry.

The woman sat down at the small table beside the window, motioning for Alex to take the seat across from her.

"Could I get your name, ma'am?"

"Mrs. Lois Snyder," the woman replied.

"Mrs. Snyder, I was hoping you might have seen someone coming or going from Louis' apartment that you might recognize."

"No, Louis hardly ever had any company come over. Just that young girl who stayed with him for a little while. She was such a sweet thing."

"Girl?"

"Yes, she was a very nice girl, kept to herself mostly."

"Are you sure about that?" Alex asked. "No one else mentioned a girl."

"I wouldn't imagine they would. Everyone here works all the time, they never pay attention. I would hear her in the mornings, after Louis went to work. She wasn't noisy, but our living rooms share the same wall. Sometimes she would play music and I could hear her singing. She had a very beautiful voice. "

"What did she look like?"

"I don't really recall" she replied. "I don't think I would make a very good witness. I only saw her briefly a few times. She was young, maybe in her early twenties, I would say. She had brown hair that came down past her shoulders and she was petite."

"Do you recall when the last time that you saw her?"

"Oh it has to be a few weeks now at least. That's when I noticed that Louis was leaving in the evenings after dinner. He never did that when she was around."

"Did you ever hear her name mentioned?"

"No," Snyder said. "I wish I could help you more, but I can't remember anything else that would be useful."

"That's okay," Alex replied. "You've have actually been very helpful."

There was a knock at the door and Hutch stepped inside.

"Chief?"

"In here, Hutch."

Alex stood up as he walked into the room.

"Well, Mrs. Snyder, if you can think of anything else would you please contact me at the police station? Just ask for Chief Taylor."

"I will most certainly do that."

She and Hutch made their way to the front door.

"You have a great day, Mrs. Snyder," Alex said, stepping out into the hallway.

"You too, Chief Taylor," the woman replied as she closed the door.

Alex hit the elevator button.

"You get anything, Hutch?"

"Just a bunch of the same. No one really noticed him; he was a good neighbor, etc."

"It was worth a try."

The elevator doors opened and they stepped inside. As the doors began to close she heard a voice cry out in the hallway.

"Chief Taylor?"

Alex put her hand out and stopped the closing doors.

Lois Snyder suddenly appeared in front of her.

"I forgot to ask, but have you spoken to Hector Ortega?"

"No, who is that?"

"He's the super of the building. Mr. Ortega is a very dedicated person. He always makes sure that only the people, who are registered with him, stay here more than three days. He just might know the young woman's name."

"Thank you so much, Mrs. Snyder," Alex said. "You've really been a great help"

"My pleasure," she said, and headed back to her apartment.

Alex let the door close and looked at Hutch.

"Who knows, maybe this is our lucky day," she said.

They located Hector Ortega's apartment in the basement and Alex knocked on the door.

They waited for a moment, listening for a response.

Alex knocked again, louder this time.

"It is Saturday," Hutch said. "Maybe he's out enjoying his day off somewhere."

Alex looked back over her shoulder at him, raising her eyebrow.

"I'm just saying."

"When we close this case I'll come over and help you paint a room," she said. "Will that make you happy?"

"Do you do windows too?"

"Yeah, with a BB gun," Alex said and banged on the door with her fist.

"Painting will be just fine."

Alex turned from the door and looked at Hutch.

"Do you have a business card on you?" she asked.

"Yeah, here you go," he said, removing the card from his shirt pocket.

Alex wrote her name on the card and pressed into the door jamb, just above the lock, where she knew it would be seen.

They took the elevator up to the first floor and headed toward the front door, just as a man was walking through it, carrying two grocery bags.

"Can I help you?" he asked.

"I'm Chief Taylor, Penobscot Police," she said. "And you are?"

"Hector Ortega, I'm the building superintendent."

"Then you're just the man I want to speak to."

"What's this about?"

"Louis Jenkins."

"Oh yeah, I heard that Louis had died in a car accident."

"Yeah, something like that," Alex replied. "Actually, I'm more interested in whether you can help me find out who his recent female guest was."

"You mean Hannah?"

"You remember her?"

"Sure, she was a nice girl. Louis asked me if it would be alright if she stayed with him for a while. Until she found a place of her own."

Alex turned and looked at Hutch.

"Do you happen to remember when she left?"

"It was probably close to a month ago," the man replied. "Three weeks at the earliest."

"You wouldn't happen to know where she moved to?"

"Nah, I ran into Louis one day and he just said she was gone. I thought she had just found her own place so I didn't think anything more about it."

"Would you be able to describe her?"

"I can do you one better," the man said. "I have a copy of her driver's license."

"You do?" Alex asked.

"Sure, no one moves in without identification. I keep it all on file until after the primary tenant leaves, just in case. Not everyone is a good tenant."

"Thank God for conscientious supers like you," Alex said.

"Follow me," Ortega replied.

The three of them rode the elevator back down to the basement and went to his apartment.

Ortega removed the card from the jamb and offered it back to Alex.

"Keep it," she said. "Never know when you might need to get in touch with me."

The man opened the door and they stepped inside. He placed the grocery bags onto the kitchen counter.

"Please, have a seat," he said, motioning to the couch. "Let me go pull the folder.

Alex and Hutch sat down.

"Well this is certainly an interesting twist," Alex said. "Our dead girl was dating Lou Jenkins."

"Do you think Jenkins killed her?"

"Nothing shocks me anymore," Alex replied.

"But if he killed her, who killed him?"

"Small town secrets," she said. "Think of them as job security."

Ortega emerged out of the back office carrying a manila folder. He sat down in the chair across from them and began going through the folder's contents.

"How long has Jenkins lived here?" Alex asked.

Ortega glanced over at the cover of the folder.

"According to this he moved in on September 1st, 2011."

"So he lived here for just under two years?"

"Yep," he said, turning his attention back to the folder.

"Did you ever have any problems with him?"

"No, in fact he was probably one of my best tenants," Ortega replied. "No issues at all. Ah, here it is."

Ortega withdrew a piece of paper and handed it to Alex.

Alex took the paper and examined it as Hutch leaned in to get a better look.

It was a photocopy of a driver's license issued by the State of New Hampshire to a Hannah Marie Kurtz of 712 Virginia Ave, in Errol.

Alex stared down at the face of the girl looking back at her in the grainy photo. It was the face of Susan Waltham.

"*Sonofabitch!*"

CHAPTER TWENTY-FIVE

Alex and Hutch bolted through the front entrance door of the apartment building.

"You drive," Alex said, as the two of them made a beeline for Hutch's marked car.

"Do you really think its Susan Waltham?" Hutch asked as he got into the car.

"Can you give me another reason why her face would be on our dead woman's driver's license and why she lived under that assumed name at her former boyfriend's place?"

"I got nothing," Hutch said. "Where are we going?"

"To Rebecca Waltham's place."

"Do you think that's a good idea?" Hutch asked. "I thought her attorney didn't want you talking to her without him being present."

"Hutch, I don't want to talk to Rebecca Waltham, I want to warn her."

"About Susan? Why?"

"Because if my coply intuition is working right, I think Susan is settling old scores and her mother might be next on the list."

Hutch turned on the emergency lights as the car accelerated hard, racing toward the Waltham residence.

Alex picked up the radio.

"M-11-1 to Base, are you on the air?"

"Base, that's affirmative. Go with message."

"M-11-1, Base is M-11-7 there?"

"10-4, M-11-1. Go with message."

"Base, have M-11-7 respond, forthwith, to the Waltham residence. No sirens."

"10-4, message copied. M-11-7 is responding."

"So you think Susan is going after her mom?"

"Do the math, Hutch. Susan was living with Lou Jenkins and then suddenly left. The very same Lou Jenkins who was also doing Susan's mother. Yeah, I think she might have some *mommy issues* that she wants to resolve."

"So you think Susan killed Lou and Hannah?"

"I think she killed Lou, I'm not sure whether she is solely responsible for Hannah. Obviously she had an altered copy of Hannah's driver's license. Something our little *videophile* was more than capable of doing. He'd introduced her as Hannah so he had to be aware. I know that he was involved, the only question that I have is how big of a part did he play in her death."

As the car approached the residence, Alex turned off the lights.

"Roll in normal," she said. "I don't want to raise any suspicions, but be on the alert."

"Okay," Hutch replied.

They turned off the road slowly and pulled up the driveway.

Alex looked around as they reached the house. Nothing seemed out of place.

She got out of the car, walked up the stairs and rang the doorbell. She waited for Waltham to answer.

"Maybe she's not home," Hutch said.

"Maybe," Alex replied.

She rang the doorbell again and immediately followed it up by banging on the door with her fist.

Behind her, she heard the sound of tires on gravel. She turned to see Steve Harper's patrol car coming up the driveway.

"Go tell Steve to head around back and check things out."

Hutch headed down to the patrol car.

Alex walked over to the large front window and peeked inside. Nothing seemed out of place. Everything appeared to be as it should, and yet, Alex couldn't seem to shake the feeling that something wasn't right.

She banged on the door again, just as Hutch rejoined her.

"Steve's going to secure the back," he said. "Maybe she's out shopping. You know it is...."

"I know, Hutch, it's *Saturday*," she said. "You're starting to sound like that damn camel that keeps asking what day it is."

"What day is it?"

"Hump day."

"That's pretty funny," he replied.

Alex was just about to reply when they heard Harper's voice over the radio.

"Chief, get back here."

Alex and Hutch bolted around the side of the house until they found Harper standing at the rear door, gun drawn.

They immediately slowed down, withdrawing their own weapons as they cautiously approached.

"What do you have, Steve?" Alex asked.

"Back door is open," he replied.

Alex turned the corner and saw that the door was open about half way.

"Still think she's shopping?" she asked Hutch.

"Not so much," he replied.

"Steve, watch this door. If anyone, but us, comes out, they go on the ground, understand?"

"Yes, ma'am."

"We treat this like a burglary. Get on the radio, call for backup and get someone on the front door. Hutch, you come with me."

They entered the house cautiously.

There were three floors to search, the basement, first and second floor. As they walked through the kitchen Alex located a door to the basement. She grabbed a kitchen chair and forced it underneath the door knob, temporarily holding it in place. If anyone tried to force the door open they would hear it.

"We'll come back to that later," she said.

They searched the first floor, slowly and methodically, until they were certain it held no threats. They were aided by the fact that it was, for the most part, an open plan design. Once Alex was certain that they had cleared the entire floor, she and Hutch began their approach to the second floor.

"Okay, this is how we are going to do it," Alex said. "I'll go in and clear out each room. You've got my back, Hutch. You make sure nothing comes from behind me. Understand?"

"Yeah, Chief, crystal clear," he replied.

When they got to the second floor landing, Alex turned left and began clearing the rooms, one by one.

She started with Susan's room, which appeared to be untouched. As she cleared the room she stopped, noting that the closet door that she had closed the other day was now ajar. She pulled it open and peered inside.

Clearly someone had been through it recently. The room appeared to have been ransacked. Books were thrown all over the floor and the drawers of the desk were opened, their contents had been unceremoniously dumped out onto the floor.

Once she determined that nothing in the room posed a threat, she moved back out into the hallway and continued down to the next room.

Inside the master bedroom, she found it in disarray as well. The night table drawers were pulled out and tossed on the floor. Alex continued into the closet where she found more of the same. The jewelry drawers were completely empty along with the others in the unit, which had also been pulled out and dumped.

There were, what appeared to be, two other guest bedrooms on this side of the house. Both unoccupied and neither of these two rooms appeared to have been molested.

When she was sure that there were no threats, her and Hutch turned and made their way down the hall to the other side of the house.

The first door on the left held what appeared to be the remnants of an office. Again, she found that the drawers were pulled free from the desk and papers littered the floor. The door of a wall safe sat open. Whatever the contents were that it had previously held, were long gone.

Was it a burglary? she wondered. *Clearly someone was looking for something.*

Alex backed out and headed toward the end of the hall. She knew the door on the right contained the small laundry room so she turned her attention to the remaining door.

"I got this one," she said. "Take a look in there."

Hutch moved up to examine the laundry room as Alex reached down and opened the other door. She peered into a room that contained a small home gym.

"Fuck," she said, throwing the door open and scanning the room as she moved inside.

She made her way forward to where the body of Rebecca Waltham lay crumpled on the floor behind the still moving treadmill.

Alex reached down and felt for a pulse. It was feint and her breathing was shallow.

"Hutch, get an ambulance," she shouted. "She's unconscious."

"M-11-3, to Base, emergency transmission. Have an ambulance respond to the Waltham residence forthwith. We have an unconscious female."

"M-11-3, 10-4, dispatching ambulance and fire rescue to your location.

"They're on their way, Chief."

Alex scanned around the room, nothing seemed out of place. She stood up and looked at the treadmill. A pair of earbud headphones lay dangling from the music jack on the machine, a faint musical sound coming from them. On the top of the machine, where the controls for the treadmill were located, sat a large plastic water bottle, that was almost empty.

"Oh Christ, I think she's been poisoned," Alex said.

"What do we do?" Hutch asked.

"Nothing we can do, but hope they get here in time. Go downstairs and open the front door. Have whoever is out front, go around back and do the search of the basement with Steve."

Hutch headed out of the room.

Alex looked down at Waltham. The woman had to have been down for a while. That would have been the only way whoever had done this could have ransacked the house.

Had they interrupted it? She thought. *Was that why the back door was open?*

In the distance she could hear the wail of approaching sirens.

Alex reached into her pocket and removed a plastic envelope, which she slid the bottle into. She made sure the pop-up lid was secured and then sealed it.

She leaned down, taking Waltham's wrist in her hand and checked her pulse. It was there, faintly, but she wasn't sure how much longer the woman could hold on.

From downstairs she heard voices and the sound of heavy boots plodding up the stairs. A moment later several firemen came through the door.

"What do we have?"

"Female, mid forties, unconscious when we arrived on scene, pulse is very weak, possibility of poisoning," Alex replied.

"What makes you think that, Chief?" asked one of the firemen who wore a white shirt with gold lieutenant's bars on his collar.

"Call it a hunch, LT," she replied.

Two EMT's appeared in the doorway with a stretcher.

"Keep it outside," one of the fireman said. "We'll bring her to you."

"They'll transport her to Memorial Medical Center," the lieutenant said.

Alex watched as the men lifted Rebecca Waltham off the floor and carried her out the door, loading her up on the stretcher.

"Not looking good," someone said. "Let's get her loaded up quickly."

They strapped her in and the group began to navigate their way down the stairs, carrying the stretcher.

When they had left, Hutch reappeared.

"What did they say?"

"I think we better see if we can contact Kevin Waltham," Alex replied.

"You don't think she's going to make it, do you?"

"No, I don't," she said. "Did they search the basement?"

"Yeah, it was clear. Nothing seemed disturbed."

"Okay, come with me.

Alex and Hutch walked back down the hallway to the master bedroom and made their way into the closet.

"Looks like whoever did this knew what they were looking for. I want you to go grab your bag of tricks and dust this. See if you can lift any prints."

Alex handed him the plastic bag with the bottle inside.

"Start with this water bottle. Once you get whatever prints you can off it, have Steve run it over to the hospital so they can test it. Then you can work on this room."

"When I'm done here, where do you want me to dust next?"

"Once you're finished with this room check out the office. Maybe we will get lucky and find something to link Susan Waltham to this."

"Wouldn't her prints show up normally in the house?"

"Yeah, but it's a stronger argument if her prints are on a recently ransacked jewelry box or an office safe."

"What do you think she was looking for?"

"Jewelry, money, anything that would help her get away from here. I'd imagine that the Waltham's had an ample supply on hand to facilitate that."

"Okay, I'll get right on it," he said.

"I'm going to head back to the office. Call me if you get a hit on anything."

"Will do, Chief."

Alex made her way downstairs and stepped out onto the front porch where Steve Harper and one of the reserve officers, Mike Adams, stood.

"Think she's going to make it, boss?"

"She didn't look too good, Steve," Alex replied, lighting up her cigarette.

"What do you want us to do?"

"You hang out here till Hutch is done upstairs. He's going to need you to run a water bottle over to the hospital after he's done printing it. Mike I'm going to need you to give me a lift back to my car. Afterwards come back and hang out till Hutch is finished up with his crime scene investigation."

"What do you want me to tell anyone who shows up?" Harper asked.

"Tell them there was a medical emergency and she was taken to the hospital. No one goes into the house, unless it's Kevin Waltham. And before he does, you call me."

"Yes, ma'am."

"C'mon, Mike; let's go find my chariot."

CHAPTER TWENTY-SIX

"We're sorry. Your call cannot be completed at this time. The subscriber has either left the calling area or is unavailable. Please try your call again later."

Alex hung the phone up and leaned back in her chair.

She'd been trying to call Kevin Waltham's cell phone for the last three hours, but it wouldn't go through.

Alex had already contacted Scott Nichols, updating him on what had happened to Rebecca Waltham and to let him know what she had discovered about Susan Waltham.

A state wide alert had already been issued for her and Rebecca Waltham's Mercedes Benz, which they had discovered was missing from the garage. Now all that was left was a waiting game and the hope that she would surface somewhere.

Hutch had finished up an hour ago. He'd lifted a partial print off one of the drawers in the bedroom along with another from the safe door in the office. They would have to get comparison prints from both Kevin and Rebecca Waltham in order to rule them out.

She'd let him go off duty to enjoy what was left of his Saturday.

Now she sat in the office alone, listening to the monotonous sound of the second hand on the old clock above the door.

She crushed out the cigarette in the ash tray and got up. There was nothing left for her to do.

On the way home she swung by the hospital to check and see how Waltham was doing.

The Emergency Room at the Memorial Medical Center was a far cry from the war zone she had been accustomed to dealing with in Brooklyn.

As she walked through the sliding double doors, she was struck by just how quiet it seemed. There were no wailing patients, no screaming kids, no frantic shouts from doctors or nurses trying to stabilize a gunshot victim, prior to them being sent for surgery. It was all very peaceful.

Alex approached the nurse's desk.

"May I help you?" a young woman in pink scrubs asked.

"I'm Chief Taylor, Penobscot Police Department."

"Hi, Chief, I guess you're here for the Waltham woman?"

"Yeah, I was hoping to get an update on her condition."

"Sure, let me just page the doctor," the woman replied, picking up the phone.

"Dr. Jackson please call 104."

A few moments later the phone on the desk rang.

"Emergency Room, this is Marie," the woman said.

"Oh yes, Dr. Jay, I have the police chief in the ER, she'd like to speak with you regarding Rebecca Waltham."

She listened for a moment.

"Okay, I'll let her know," she said, and she hung up the phone.

"The doc is on her way down."

"Thank you," Alex replied. "Is it always so quiet here?"

"Oh it'll pick up a bit tonight. But overall it never really gets too bad."

"Where I come from it is standing room only."

"I don't think we have ever had all our beds in use at the same time," she replied. "We all wondered why they gave us ten treatment rooms when they redid the place, but I guess they just wanted to make sure they used up the allotted space."

"Better to have it and not need it," Alex said.

"I guess," the woman replied.

Off to the right she heard the elevator chime.

The doors opened and a woman wearing a white lab coat exited the elevator and approached the desk. She was a middle aged woman with graying hair, pulled back in a bun.

"I'm Dr. Lisa Jackson," she said, extending her hand toward Alex. "How can I help you?"

Alex shook the woman's hand.

"I'm Alex Taylor, the new police chief," she replied. "I just wanted to check on the condition of Rebecca Waltham."

"Well, we were able to stabilize her, but she is in a coma. The next twenty-four hours will tell us more, but right now I would say her prognosis is *guarded*."

"Which realistically means it could go either way."

"Exactly," she replied. "Have you had any luck reaching next of kin?"

"No. I tried calling several times already, but it won't go through."

"Could we get the number?"

"Sure," Alex replied.

The nurse handed Alex a piece of paper and she wrote Kevin Waltham's number down, along with hers.

"If you do happen to get through to him could you please call me and let me know. I really need to speak with him."

"Sure," Dr. Jackson replied. "By the way, good call on that water bottle. Toxicology came back and it tested positive for barbiturates. She had a massive dose in her system."

"If she comes out of it I am going to need to speak with her."

"I'll note it on her chart," Jackson replied. "But to be honest, I wouldn't plan on that being anytime soon."

"Gotcha," Alex said. "Well, thank you for your time, Doc."

"No problem," she said. "I just wish I had better news."

"She's alive," Alex replied. "It beats the alternative."

"That is very true."

Alex walked out of the ER and got back in her car.

She was hungry, but she didn't feel like takeout. She wanted comfort food. She pulled the car into the parking lot outside the

Dunkin' Donuts and went in. She emerged a few minutes later carrying a large coffee and a box of toasted coconut *Munchkin's* and headed home.

Alex set the coffee and donuts down on the kitchen table, then went to get changed.

Something has to give, she thought. *You can't spend the rest of your life sitting in this apartment drinking whiskey and eating crap.*

She wanted to blame the case she was working on, but she knew that was a lie. She had locked herself away back in New York as well, only leaving when it was time to work. After she had *retired*, she'd managed to get some side gigs doing security work. Basically it was just enough to cover her rent and the liquor store tab.

She reached over and plucked one of the *Munchkins* from the box, washing it down with the coffee.

Alex knew that this was all on her now. She had closed the other chapter of her life and had started a new one here in Penobscot. If she failed, she would have no one else to blame, but herself.

She got up and hauled the boxes, that she had gotten from Charlie Parker's widow, over to the couch and began sorting through them.

They contained all that remained of Parker's career.

There were manila envelopes that held the records of the arrests he had made, as a young cop. A number of pocket calendars that listed the shifts he had worked and when he was off. One folder contained photo copies of awards he had received along with certificates for courses he had attended. Yet another folder held a bunch of photos taken over the years with other officers, none of whom Alex knew.

One photo caught her eye. It was Charlie standing with another uniformed officer, their arms around one another's shoulders. Both men were young, maybe in their late twenties. She flipped it over and read the inscription: Charlie & Mike, May 1983.

Alex laid the photos to the side.

She took a sip of coffee and popped another donut into her mouth. As an afterthought, she reached over and picked up her cell phone. She positioned the coffee container and donut box next to each other and snapped a photo. She then sent it as a message on her cell phone.

Opening each box brought a renewed sense of pain that only another cop could understand. Boxes like this held everything for a cop. It was a glimpse into a career most would never know and fewer still could ever understand. It contained the accomplishments and the accolades, along with the memories and the misfortune.

She knew where the boxes were born from. They originated in the lockers of each and every man and woman who pinned a badge on their chest. It was their private sanctuary. The one place that was safe from the prying eyes of the world. It hid all the secrets, all the sins.

Then the day arrived when you took the badge off and left for the last time. On that day the locker opened for the last time and everything that was kept safe was relegated to the boxes. For most officers, like Charlie, the boxes would end up in a dark corner of the basement. Their secrets waiting to be discovered until after their owners had left the world.

The saddest part for any cop was the realization that most of it would just end up in the trash.

The cell phone began to vibrate.

She picked it up, pressing the icon for the text message and read the message from him.

Cop Food !! :-)

Alex smiled for a moment.

She looked over at the boxes stacked up next to the entertainment center. Those were her boxes.

Will you be the one going through my boxes one day, James? she wondered.

She pushed the thought from her mind and returned to the task at hand.

Alex opened the last box. This one held some old uniforms and equipment. There was a hat, gun belt, some uniform shirts and pants. She began to close the box back up and then decided against it.

She'd promised Mildred Parker that she wouldn't let anything that would tarnish his reputation get out. At least not from the boxes that she had been given. She didn't want to return them till she was certain there was nothing damaging in them.

Alex began to lift the items out. She set each of them down on the coffee table. She reached in to grab a folded uniformed shirt when her hand felt something stiff under the material.

She withdrew it, unfolding the shirt, and felt the envelope slip out into her lap.

The small manila envelope was addressed to Charlie at his home address and had a return address for M. Williams in Aptos, California. It was post marked May 7th, 2012.

She opened the envelope, pulling out the enclosed papers and began thumbing through them.

The top one was a letter from Williams to Parker.

She began to read it.

Chuck:

I'm sorry things had to happen the way they did partner, but I wasn't going to have a hand in allowing him to drag you and the Department through the mud.

You know what he is doing and it's going to blow up in your face or get someone killed. Maybe both, who the hell knows.

You're the chief and it's on your watch. I can't make you do the right thing, but I can give you the evidence that you need to make this right.

You know I would do anything for you, but I just couldn't stand around and do nothing.

He'll stop at nothing to advance himself. He has no allegiance to anyone or anything. He'll take you along for the ride, as long as things are going well. But when that ride finally comes to a stop, rest assured that he will throw your ass under the bus in a heartbeat.

Do the right thing partner.

Mike

Alex flipped through the rest of the papers. There were over thirty invoices for weapons and ammunition, from the mysterious Mountain View Sporting Goods in Belkin, totaling nearly a hundred and twenty thousand dollars.

As Alex sorted through the remaining papers she found several other invoices for assorted items ranging from office supplies to highway materials. All made out to different firms. At the end were several printouts from the New Hampshire Secretary of State's office. She examined them all, noting the same disposition on each. For all the business names on the invoices, there was no record in the Secretary of State database.

Alex bundled the papers back into the manila folder and set it down on the coffee table. She gathered up the rest of the items and returned them all to the boxes, stacking them back up by the door.

When she was done she opened the laptop and began running Williams' name through the different phone number search engines. It took a few minutes, but she located a listing for a Michael Williams in Aptos. Alex looked down at her watch. There was a three hour time difference between New Hampshire and California, which would make it just after six o'clock local time. She picked up the cell phone and dialed the number.

The phone rang several times before it connected.

"Hello?" a woman's voice said.

"Hi, I'm trying to each Michael Williams," Alex said.

There was a moment of silence on the other end.

"Who's calling?"

"My name is Alex Taylor. I'm the chief of police in Penobscot, New Hampshire."

"I'm sorry; Mike doesn't have this phone anymore."

"Well do you know where I could reach him at?" Alex asked. "It is really very important that I speak with him."

Again, there was another awkward moment of silence.

"Hello?" Alex asked.

"I'm sorry, Chief Taylor, Mike is dead."

"Dead? What happened?"

"I am terribly sorry," the woman replied. "But I really just don't want to talk about this. Please don't call back."

Alex heard the line go dead as the woman hung the phone up on the other end. She laid the phone down on the coffee table.

She leaned back, rubbing her eyes. She felt as if she was running up the down escalator. Every time she thought she was catching a break, she just found another wall in front of her.

Alex picked up the laptop, performing a search for the man's name and city. A moment later the results popped up on the screen. Alex selected the first entry which was from the online edition of the local newspaper.

May 13th, 2012 – Aptos Man Found Dead: An Aptos resident was found dead by authorities this morning of an apparent self-inflicted gunshot wound to the head. Officers responding to a call of shots being fired located the man, identified by police as Michael Duane Williams, in his garage. Williams, who was a former New Hampshire police officer, had recently moved to the area. No other details are being released at this time.

Alex typed in a new search and waited for the results. It only took a few seconds. She clicked on the link.

May 12th, 2012 – Heart Attack Claims Life of Local Police Chief: Chief Charles Parker died Saturday morning from an apparent heart attack while walking his dog.

She closed the laptop, staring at the manila envelope that Williams had sent.

Is that what caused Parker's heart attack? Had Williams thought that his letter had caused it? Had he taken his own life out of remorse over his friend's death?

Her intuition told her that she knew exactly who it was that Mike Williams had written about. The only problem was that her intuition, no matter how good it was, wasn't admissible in court.

If she was going to investigate him for embezzlement she would have to make sure that she did it right the first time. He was too smart to be underestimated.

Alex would only get one opportunity, because in this game, a second place finish would mean a trip back to the unemployment line for her.

She needed to focus her attention to the homicide investigation that was already on her plate and revisit this matter later. When she knew she would have the proper amount of time and energy to dedicate toward finding the link between him and the mystery firms.

Two men had already died as a result of Sheldon Abbott's greed and ambition. She was damn sure not going to add her name to that list as well.

CHAPTER TWENTY-SEVEN

Kevin Waltham looked down at his watch.

Thirty minutes till she gets here, he thought. *You had better get going.*

He logged off the lap top and got up from his desk.

The large, three bedroom and two bath apartment was working out well for him.

In the beginning he had questioned whether he'd really needed something this big, but when he saw the outside deck, that overlooked the scenic Merrimack River, he knew he couldn't pass it up. He decided to convert the third bedroom into an office which would allow him to handle the majority of his work from home.

The apartment building was in the trendy Riverfront section of Yardley, a quaint little city just north of Concord. Over several decades the city had experienced an overall decline in both population and property values. But this decline paved the way for the current gentrification that had taken hold.

Those seeking to escape the hustle and bustle of the state capital had flocked north, bringing an influx of cash along with them. As a result, Yardley had become a veritable Mecca for the upper middle class.

Waltham's apartment was situated in a newly developed complex. The neighborhood featured a full array of trendy restaurants, shopping, night clubs, and other entertainment venues. In fact, he had actually found the apartment while one of his construction companies was working on renovating a local restaurant. He and the restaurant's owner had become friends. The man had tipped him off that new units had just become available.

It wasn't exactly what he had grown accustomed to, living in the large house in Penobscot, but it would do for now. Maybe one day he would get another house, but for now he was enjoying this lifestyle to the fullest. Besides, he had always felt as if he were living in a museum, all these years, as opposed to a real home.

He doubted whether anyone even knew that he and Rebecca had separated. The only time they were ever together was during the summer, when they had to attend certain social events. She had gotten good at making excuses as to why he was out of town. Everyone knew that you went where the jobs were in the construction industry. Eventually they would have to deal with the divorce issues, but for now being separated was not much of a hardship on either of them. She had her *hobbies* and he had his.

He grabbed his wallet and car keys from the hutch in the entry way then walked out of the apartment, grabbing his sport coat as he left. It was a short ride on the elevator to the basement garage where his red Porsche Cayman was parked.

The sports car had been his *moving out* gift to himself.

The construction business in Yardley was proving to be quite lucrative for him. It afforded him the opportunity to splurge on himself, from time to time.

He drove the dozen blocks north to the River Front Baking Company. It was an upscale bakery and café, which served a thriving lunch and dinner crowd. Since moving to Yardley it had become one of his favorite places to eat.

It was just before the rush and he found a parking spot out front. He reached over to grab his coat and then opted to leave it. It was such a beautiful day out.

He located a table near the front and took a seat. With the sunny weather they had opened the large exterior doors, transforming the interior tables into an almost sidewalk café appearance.

He didn't have long to wait.

She walked in, scanning the room until she spotted him sitting in the booth waving at her.

Waltham watched as she approached him and stood up.

"I've missed you so much, baby," he said.

"I've missed you too," she said.

Kevin Waltham wasn't very big on public displays of affection, but he made an exception in this case, wrapping his arms around her and kissing her on the cheek.

"I've been counting the minutes till you were going to get here. I was so surprised when I got your text message."

"I know, I probably should have given you more info, but I figured that you'd want to see me."

"Oh you have no idea," he said. "I've been beside myself since you left."

"Good afternoon, Mr. Waltham," the waitress said. "Are you ready to order?"

Kevin Waltham looked up at the woman.

"Yes, Pam, I'll have my regular and a diet Coke."

"Okay, one Asian chicken noodle salad with ginger vinaigrette dressing, no peanuts, and a diet Coke," she replied. "And what would you like to have young lady?"

"I'll have the roasted turkey and avocado BLT along with a Coke.

"Great, I'll get this order in and be right back with your drinks."

Waltham watched as the waitress walked away, and then turned his attention back to her.

"How long did it take you to get down here?"

"Three hours, I only got lost once," she replied.

"That wasn't too bad."

"How long do you plan on being here?"

Before she could reply, the waitress returned and placed the two drinks down on the table.

"Your food will be up shortly."

"Thanks, Pam," Waltham replied.

"Looks like you've adjusted well to the new environment," she said with a laugh. "I thought I'd hang-out for a few days. I've never been here before and it looks like it might be fun."

"Well, my calendar just got cleared so I'll be more than happy to be your escort."

"Oh, I was hoping that you would do more than just escort me," she said with a mischievous grin.

From the pass through window in the kitchen, Susan Waltham stared out at the two; watching as the woman leaned across the table and kissed her father's lips.

"Paige, you little fucking whore," she muttered under her breath.

It had taken her weeks to track down where he had moved to. Lou had proven to be extremely helpful with that. It seemed the man had any number of skills, including computer hacking. He had managed to break into Kevin Waltham's cell phone account and located him through the phones internal GPS program.

Once she knew where he was at, she had spent several days watching him come and go. After she had established his patterns and habits, she focused on deciding what her best approach would be.

Getting a job here proved to be very easy. The growing population in this neighborhood seemed to be outpacing the ability of local businesses to keep up with demand, especially during the hectic lunch hour.

Kevin Waltham was a creature of habit and he ate lunch here almost every day. What made it even better was that he invariably ordered the same thing.

Poor daddy, you really should have been more careful, she thought.

It was just too bad she couldn't get a *twofer*. But she had something *special* planned for her former girlfriend and that would have to come later.

"Table five, order up," a man called out.

Susan walked by, picking up the plates and carried them over to the prep counter, placing them on trays. She added a side of bread and silverware, then she glanced around the room. When she as sure that no one was looking, she discretely removed the small container from her pocket and sprinkled the contents over the salad. When she was done, she laid the trays up on the pass through for the waitress.

"Hey, Joey," Susan said, to the manager standing at the other end of the kitchen. "Listen, I'm really not feeling too well. I might have eaten some bad food last night; I think I need to go home."

"Are you kidding me? It's lunch hour?"

"So what?" she asked. "You'd prefer me to just upchuck on the orders?"

"Alright, alright, go already," he replied. "But call me tonight and let me know if you're going to be a no-show tomorrow. I don't need to get fucked two days in a row."

"You wish you were that lucky."

Susan headed out the kitchen door and swiped her employee ID card in the scanner, ending her shift and her short culinary career.

She made her way out the back door of the restaurant. She quickly removed her smock and head-covering, dumping them in the nearest trash container. From her back pocket she pulled out a ball cap and put it on, tucking her hair up underneath.

The main thoroughfare of the Waterfront District was lined with park benches and trees, offering a tranquil respite for both shoppers as well as people watchers.

Susan crossed the street and sat down on one of the benches that afforded the best view of the restaurant. She could see them sitting there talking and laughing. She withdrew a pack of cigarettes from her pocket, and lit one.

"Let the show begin," Susan said.

The waitress came back, submitting another order and grabbed the two plates. She turned around, heading toward the table.

"Enjoy your lunch," she said, as she placed the plates down in front of them. "Is there anything else that you need?"

"No, I think we are good," Kevin replied.

"I'll bring you out some refills on the drinks."

Kevin Waltham looked over at Paige.

If there was any *little voice* in the back of his mind, telling him how this was all somehow wrong, it was drowned out by the one telling him how bad he wanted her. He found himself staring down at her breasts, which were accentuated nicely by the tight t-shirt she was wearing.

"My eyes are up here, you pervert," she said with a laugh.

Waltham looked up at her, smiling sheepishly.

"Sorry, my love," he said. "So what exactly did you have in mind?"

Paige looked around and then leaned in closer, speaking softly.

"I want you to take me back to your place, rip my clothes off and fuck me like a jackhammer for the next few days."

Waltham smiled, his face getting red. He squirmed in his seat as his mind replayed the last time he'd had her in the motel.

"Who's the pervert now?" he asked.

"Not a pervert at all, just telling you what you need to do to keep me happy."

"Then we'd better eat and get the hell out of here," he replied.

He pressed his fork into the bowl, taking a good helping of lettuce and sliced chicken.

"I thought you'd feel that way," she replied. "You better eat up; you're going to need your strength."

Waltham took a bite, savoring the chicken dish. He'd been amazed at how well they prepared it here and it had become his favorite. Maybe next time he might have to try something different. Paige's food looked really good. Then again Paige looked really good and he knew he'd be enjoying her shortly.

"When we take a break maybe you could show me around town," she said. "There's a lot of nice shops I wouldn't mind visiting."

"Absolutely," he replied, taking another bite. "Maybe after dinner tonight we can take a walk down by the water. They light up all the fountains and it really is quite beautiful."

"Are you sure it's alright if I stay with you?" she asked. "I'm not going to be imposing am I?"

"Imposing? Are you serious?" Waltham replied.

He reached into his pocket and then slid his hand over the table toward her.

"What's that?" she asked.

He opened his hand to reveal a key.

"You can even hang your clothes in the closet if it'll make you happy."

Paige smiled and reached down, removing the key which she then slipped into the back pocket of her jeans.

Waltham coughed, reaching out for the diet Coke.

"Are you going to let me leave my toothbrush there too?"

She laughed at the mental image and took another bite from her sandwich.

"Oh what, now you're not going to answer?" she asked.

She looked up at Waltham, realizing immediately that something was wrong.

"Kevin? Are you alright?"

The tickling sensation in his throat had changed to a feeling of constriction and it was tightening by the second. He tried to take another drink, feeling the liquid back-up in his mouth. His throat was swelling up and blocking his airway. Panic began to set in as he realized what was happening.

"Kevin!" Paige screamed.

Waltham stood up quickly, holding his throat. He tried to get out of the booth, but in his panic he found himself stuck. His mind was racing and he was having difficulty thinking.

Nearby diners suddenly looked up at the commotion, trying to make sense of what was going on.

"Help! Please!" Paige cried out.

Waltham managed to extricate himself from the table and stumbled toward the front door, managing to make it several feet before he collapsed to the ground.

"Oh my God," Paige said, rushing to his side. "Someone call 911."

As Paige held him in her arms, Kevin Waltham silently stared out at the car and the jacket that contained the *EpiPen* in it.

Across the street, Susan Waltham took a last drag on the cigarette, before crushing it out under her shoe.

"*Adios, Daddy-O,*" she said with a smile.

CHAPTER TWENTY-EIGHT

Alex popped one of the stale *Munchkins* in her mouth and washed it down with some hot coffee.

She was actually enjoying having a day off.

At first she had felt a bit guilty and had thought about reviewing more of the videos. But then she realized that she really needed a break. It would be better to attack it again tomorrow, when she was rested and had a clear head.

She'd spent the last several hours watching old movies on television and was wondering what she was going to do for dinner when her cell phone began to buzz.

She picked it up and looked at the display.

What the hell? she thought.

"Hello?"

"Chief Taylor?"

"Yes?"

"It's Officer Pat Miller, I'm one of the reserve officers."

"Yes, Pat, what can I do for you?"

"We just got a request from the Yardley Police Department for a death notification, ma'am."

"Okay and what's the problem?"

"Well, ma'am, we're not sure how to handle this."

"Spit it out, Pat."

"Well, Chief, the deceased is Kevin Waltham."

"Excuse me?" Alex said.

"Yeah, that's the problem. Who do we notify?"

"What happened?"

"Poor bastard apparently had an allergic reaction to some food he ate."

"They give you a contact name?"

"Yes, ma'am," Miller replied, repeating the name and number.

"Okay thanks," she said. "Put me down as notified. I'll take care of it."

"Thanks, Chief."

Alex ended the call and immediately dialed the number she had been given.

"Yardley Police, this is Detective Edwards."

"Detective, this is Chief Taylor from the Penobscot Police Department. I understand you have a death that you need a notification on."

"Yes we do, Chief," Edwards replied. "I certainly hope that they didn't ask you to do it."

"No, I was just calling to ask what happened."

"It was a freak accident. Guy had a severe allergic reaction to his lunch. He died at the hospital."

"Was he alone?"

"No, he was having lunch with a female," he said. "Let me check the paperwork."

Alex could hear the man shuffling papers on the other end of the phone.

"Uh, says here a Paige Wilson, also from Penobscot. Do you know her?"

"I know of her," Alex replied. "Listen Detective, there may be more to this than meets the eye."

"What do you mean?"

"Waltham's wife is lying in a coma in the hospital here and my prime suspect is their missing daughter."

"Are you shitting me?"

"I get asked that a lot lately," she replied, "and I wish I was. It looks like she ingested a water bottle loaded with barbiturates during her morning workout. If you don't mind, I'd like to take a ride down there and have a chat with the witnesses."

"No, don't mind at all," he said, "as long as you don't mind me sitting in."

"Not a problem. We can compare notes."

"Sounds good, Chief," Edwards replied. "I'll see you when you get here."

Alex ended the call and immediately placed another one.

"You miss me already?"

"That's right, hot shot," Alex said. "I miss you so much I want you to pick me up in a half hour."

"Are we getting dinner?"

"Not exactly, you're driving me down to Yardley."

"What the hell is in Yardley?"

"Kevin Waltham's corpse."

"That's not even funny," Hutch replied.

"I'm not laughing. See you in thirty minutes, and pick me up some coffee. It's going to be a long day."

Alex ended the call and headed for the shower.

I'm going to have to renegotiate my salary, she thought.

CHAPTER TWENTY-NINE

The nice thing about marked police cars is that they make getting from point 'A' to point 'B' a lot quicker. Not that traffic was particular egregious on a Sunday afternoon.

They pulled into the parking lot of the Yardley Police Department just after six o'clock. Inside they were directed up to the second floor where the Investigations Unit was located.

A man in a suit and tie met them at the second floor landing.

"Chief Taylor," the man said. "I'm Troy Edwards, nice to meet you."

"Same here, Detective," she replied. "This is Officer Chris Hutchinson."

Hutch shook the man's hand. "Hutch is fine."

"So, what can you tell me, Detective?" Alex asked.

"The victim was having lunch with a female companion when he suddenly clutched his throat and fell to the floor. He was transported to the hospital where he expired. Apparently he had a *severe* peanut allergy."

"What did he order?"

"That was the weird thing, he was a regular at the place and he always ordered the same thing," Edwards said, flipping through his notes. "Asian chicken noodle salad with ginger vinaigrette dressing, no peanuts, and a diet Coke. It was probably just a simple kitchen screw-up."

"It's possible," Alex said. "What happened to the girl who was with him?"

"Last I saw her, she was at the hospital. She was pretty shaken up. We took down her information, but there was nothing more we could do. She said she was just going to head back home."

"How many people witnessed this?" Alex asked.

"Probably about two dozen. It was just at the beginning of the lunch hour rush. No one knew him, except some of the restaurant staff."

"Is this place near here?"

"Sure," he replied. "It's only a few blocks away. I can take you over there."

A few minutes later the two vehicles arrived at the River Front Baking Company. Hutch pulled his car up behind Edwards' unmarked Chevy.

"Nice little place you got here," Alex said, as she stepped out of the car.

"Yeah, they've been pumping a ton of money into the Waterfront District," Edwards said. "Ten years ago you could have bought an entire city block for fifty thousand, now that same money is just a down payment on a one bedroom condo."

"I know that song," Alex replied. "The day my ship comes in, I'll be at the airport."

The three of them walked into the restaurant.

Most of the staff, that had been on duty at the time of the incident, had already gone home for the day, when they arrived. Only the manager, Josh Stevens, had been present.

Edwards introduced Alex to him.

"I was hoping that you might be able to tell me what you recall, Mr. Stevens," Alex asked.

"Not much to be honest," the man replied. "I was talking to my kitchen manager when I heard a scream. I actually thought we were getting robbed. I came out to the front and saw a group of people by the front and I rushed over. That's when I saw Mr. Waltham lying on the ground."

"Did he say anything?"

"No, I think he was unconscious at that point."

"You called him by name; did you know him pretty well?"

"Yeah, he was a regular. I'd see him several times a week. He was a really nice guy, always friendly. He once told me he was in construction and did a lot of the business renovations around here."

"Detective Edwards mentioned that he always ordered the same thing."

"Yes, and I checked it. The ticket that the waitress submitted went in with his regular order. It was marked in red *no peanuts* which is why I can't understand what happened."

"Anyone new in the kitchen?"

"No, we were actually shorthanded so the kitchen manager was working back there. He was the one who prepared Mr. Waltham's meal."

"What happens when the meal is ready?"

"They get picked up and put on the serving window."

"And he is positive he didn't use any peanuts?"

"Absolutely positive," Stevens replied. "He's been a kitchen manager for ten years. Eight years down at our place in Concord and the last two up here. Before that he worked the line for a dozen years. He wouldn't make a mistake like that. Now if it were one of the younger kids, then I could see it happening."

"You said you were talking to him right before the incident. What about?"

"What we always talk about this time of year, staffing issues. Every summer it is the same thing, sun comes out and the kids make excuses why they can't work."

"So you were shorthanded today?" Alex asked.

"Yeah and then we had one of our kitchen staff go home sick right before this happened."

"Well, thank you for your time, Mr. Stevens. I appreciate you talking to us. I can't think of anything else."

"My pleasure, Chief," Stevens replied. "I just wish there was more I could tell you."

"No, you did great, thanks."

Alex and Hutch followed Edwards out of the restaurant.

"Seems like a wasted trip for you, Chief," Edwards said.

"Eh, Hutch is always complaining how we don't spend enough quality time together," she replied. "By the way, did you guys check out the lunch?"

"Yeah, our crime guys did a cursory check. There were no peanuts in it that they could see. Still, I sent it to the lab anyway. I'll let you know when I get the results back."

"Alright, well thank you very much for your hospitality, Detective. I guess we'll make our way back north now."

"No problem, Chief. I'll get back to you as soon as I know more."

Alex and Hutch made their way over to the patrol car. Hutch put the key in the door and stopped, staring at Alex over the roof of the car.

"I complain that we *don't* spend enough time together?" Hutch asked. "Seriously?"

"It's not really the words you use, more like the vibe you put out."

"I'll work on that," he replied, unlocking the door.

"It's okay to admit that you want to be just like me," Alex said as she got in.

Hutch laughed and started the car. Alex watched the unmarked car in front of them pulled away.

"Do I at least get a dinner out of this?"

"Sure," she replied. "Just keep the car in park."

"Why? What did I miss?"

"Nothing," she said. "I'm just going to run in and get a recommendation."

"You're going to ask the manager of a restaurant to recommend a restaurant for you?"

"Hey, a guy died in there today. Do you want to eat in there?"

"You do have a point."

"While you're waiting, call the office and have someone take a ride over to Paige Wilson's residence. Tell her I want to speak with her first thing in the morning. Have them give it special attention while they are on patrol."

"You don't think this was just an accident?"

"Coincidence and I have a very rocky relationship. I'll be right back."

Alex got out of the car and walked back into the restaurant. She returned a few minutes later carrying a piece of paper.

"Where are we going?" Hutch asked.

"Joey Falcone's," She replied.

"Italian food?"

"No, he's the kitchen manger," Alex replied. "Make a left at the traffic light."

Hutch put the car in drive and pulled away from the curb.

"I knew that interview had gone way to easy."

"What can I say? I like to do my interviews in private."

"You're the boss."

CHAPTER THIRTY

Joey Falcone was sitting on his front stoop having a cigarette when they pulled up.

Judging from the growing pile of cigarette butts and beer bottles he wasn't having a good day.

"I'll handle this," she said to Hutch, and got out of the car.

"Mr. Falcone?"

"Yeah, that's me."

"Mind if I ask you a few questions about this afternoon?"

"I already spoke to the detectives this afternoon," he replied. "Is there something wrong?"

Alex walked up, removing the pack of cigarettes from her pocket and lighting one.

"No, I'm not from Yardley," she replied. "I'm Chief Taylor from Penobscot. Just wanted to see if you could give me some information about what happened today?"

"Do I need a lawyer?" the man asked.

"I don't know? Do you want one?"

"I didn't do anything wrong, officer, I swear. I don't know that man personally, but I do know the order and I didn't use any peanuts."

"I believe you, Mr. Falcone, I don't think you did anything wrong either."

"Then why are you here?"

"Josh said the two of you were talking, right before the incident with Mr. Waltham."

"Yeah, we were trying to figure out how to adjust the schedule because we were shorthanded."

"Did anyone not show up for work today?"

"Yeah, Josh had a waitress call in sick and I had one of my kitchen staff just not bother to show up."

"Really? Can you think of any reason why they would just not show up?"

"You've never worked in the food industry have you?"

"Nope, I did my time in supermarkets when I was younger," Alex replied.

"Then you'll understand, Chief. We hire kids; it's an entry level job. Some are in high school, some in college. But lately, you'd think they were doing you a favor by working. All they do is bitch and moan. They show up when they want and if a better offer comes along they leave without even the courtesy of a phone call."

"That's kids for you," Alex replied. "I guess nothing ever changes."

"Yeah, but when you try and hire someone older, all they ever do is complain about what it is that they *don't* get. They're not paid enough, they don't have vacations, or the health benefits are not good enough. I swear they think they should be the CEO after working for a week."

"So there really wasn't anything unusual about being short staffed today?"

"Not really," he replied. "My kitchen staff guy probably got drunk last night and was too hung over to work. He'll probably show up tomorrow and tell me how it will never happen again, till next week."

Alex shook her head.

"I wish you luck," she replied. "Thanks for your time."

"No problem," Falcone said, lighting up another cigarette. "Hey, you mind if I ask you a question?"

"No, go right ahead."

"You think I'm going to get sued?"

"I once had a guy rob a bank. As he was coming out he saw me and pointed a shotgun at me. I shot him and I got sued for wrongful death."

The man stared back at Alex, looking like he had the weight of the world on his shoulders.

"Yeah, Mr. Falcone, you're going to get sued."

"Fuck me," the man replied somberly.

"Don't take it personal, it's just the world we live in."

"If they want anything from me, they can get it from my ex-wife. Everything I have is hers anyway."

"That's the spirit," Alex replied.

Alex walked back to the car, stopping as she got to the sidewalk and looked back at the man.

"One other thing," she asked. "Josh mentioned something about one of your people leaving early today, before the incident."

"Yeah, she wasn't feeling good, said she felt like she was going to be sick. She left work a few minutes before he got sick"

"Any problems with her before?"

"Hannah? No, she's one of my better workers."

"What did you say?" Alex asked.

"She's one of my better workers."

"No, her name, what did you say her name was?"

"Hannah," Falcone replied. "Hannah Kurtz."

"*Sonofabitch!*"

CHAPTER THIRTY-ONE

Alex sat in the front seat of Troy Edwards unmarked car, watching the corner house on Palmer Street. Behind her, Hutch sat talking discretely on the phone to Pat Miller back in Penobscot.

It was still light outside and a group of kids were gathered around an ice cream truck, which sat in the middle of the street, its speaker blaring out the unmistakable tune.

As the last child walked away with their cone, the truck began making its way slowly up the street. Hoping to lure out a few more customers before it moved to the next block.

As soon as the street was clear Edwards picked up the radio mic.

"Yankee Seven to Hercules, you're clear for arrival."

A moment later two marked units converged on the scene, blocking off incoming traffic. As the uniformed officers exited their cars, they began motioning people back away from the corner. Moments later a large, black panel truck pulled up in front of the house.

Before it even came to a full stop, the back doors flew open and heavily armed members, of the Yardley Police Tactical Response Team, emerged. They headed up to the front door of the house and stacked outside.

Falcone had been eager to help them, especially when he surmised that he could get his ass out of the ringer by putting someone else's in it.

He had recently picked-up the young woman, whom he knew as Hannah, before work one day. He had given them the address, along with a sketch of the location as he had remembered it.

The house had been converted into multiple apartments and the one occupied by Hannah was up on the second floor facing the front.

As Alex watched, the entry team went through the front door. She began counting the seconds off in her head. She could almost envision them stacking outside the door to the apartment, preparing to breech the door.

At eleven seconds into her count, a brilliant flash of light appeared in the window followed a fraction of a second later by a thunderous explosion that blew out the window, sending shards of glass raining down onto the street below.

If there was anyone in the apartment, the flash-bang device would certainly have diminished their capacity to fight.

After what seemed like an eternity, a radio transmission broke the silence.

"Hercules Leader to Yankee Seven."

"Yankee Seven, go with your traffic," Edwards replied.

"Yankee Seven, the location is secure and unoccupied."

"*Fuck*," Alex muttered under her breath.

"She had too much time on us," Edwards replied.

They got out of the car and headed toward the house. The team was just coming out as they walked up the stairs.

"Sorry, Detective, apartments empty. But she left in a hurry," the TRT leader said to Edwards.

"What makes you say that?"

"Place looked tossed even before we started searching. Like someone rushed in and rushed out."

"Alright, thanks for the help," he said and stepped inside the room.

Alex looked around, the place was a mess. She couldn't decide whether Susan had actually left in a hurry, or if it was just the way she lived now that she was out from underneath her *neat-freak* mother's control.

"Let me know if you find anything," Edwards said. "I'll start in the living room."

Alex made her way into the bedroom.

The mattress and box spring were flipped off the frame, the result of the entry team's search, she surmised. The closet door was open and clothing littered the floor. She began going through the closet, hoping to find some clue as to where she might be heading. After a few minutes it was clear to her that the closet contained nothing more than the discarded clothes.

In the corner of the room was a cheap, fiberboard student's desk.

Alex examined it closer. A Cat 5 cord dangled from the back where a computer had once been hooked up to it.

Well, I guess you're managing to stay connected, Alex thought.

She walked over to the bedside table and opened the drawer.

It was empty.

"You find anything?" Edwards asked from the doorway.

"Nothing," Alex replied. "She's vanished."

"Well, at least we know who we're looking for," he said. "I found this in the kitchen."

Edwards held up two sealed plastic bags. On held a jar of peanuts and the other held a small food grater and a tan colored residue.

"It looks like she grated the peanuts into a powder. That would explain why no one saw anything in the dish."

"At least that locks down *your* case," she replied.

From the other room she heard Hutch's voice. He was having a conversation with someone on the phone.

"Boss?"

"In here, Hutch."

A moment later Hutch appeared in the bedroom doorway.

"What do you got?"

"Got a problem," he said. "I just got off the phone with Bobby Willis. He went by Paige Wilson's place. She's not home and no one has heard from her."

Alex looked over at Edwards.

"Did you guys happen to search Waltham's place?"

"No we just sealed up his personal effects and vouchered them. You don't think......."

"That you're body count is rising?" Alex asked. "Yeah, that thought just crossed my mind."

They raced down the stairs and out into the street. The entry team was already gone and all that remained were the two marked units.

"Snyder, secure that apartment" Edwards called out to one of the uniformed officers. "No one goes in."

"Yes, sir," the cop replied.

"Gaddis, you follow me."

The three of them got in the unmarked car and Edwards peeled away from the curb, activating the cars emergency lights.

"Yankee Seven to dispatch, emergency transmission."

"Yankee Seven go with traffic."

"Show me responding to 2321 Peregrine Landing with Yankee Thirty-Seven, in connection with the DOA from this afternoon. I need TRT to respond to that location forthwith. I also need you to broadcast an *attempt to locate* for two individuals. First one is a Paige Wilson, female white, eighteen years old. Second individual is a Susan Waltham, female white, eighteen years old. May also be using the name Hannah Kurtz. Waltham should be considered armed and dangerous."

"Yankee Seven, copy"

The cars raced along the darkening city streets. It had begun to rain and their emergency strobe lights reflected wildly off the glistening thoroughfares.

Moments later they arrived at Kevin Waltham's apartment building.

Inside the vestibule they located the buildings directory.

"1804!" Alex said.

The four cops rushed toward the elevator and made their way to the 18th floor. They located the apartment at the far end of the hallway.

Edwards checked the door and found it locked.

"We don't have time to wait for the entry team," Alex said.

"You sure about this?" asked Edwards.

"No," Alex replied. "But the only person who is going to complain is the guy on the slab in your hospital. And if I'm right, we don't have a second to spare."

"Ok step back."

Taking a door is never as easy as it looks on television and this one was no different. Modern doors are designed to protect their occupants from the evils of the world. It took eight hits to finally bust the door jamb, allowing them to gain entry inside the apartment. Neighbors began streaming out of their apartments to see what all the ruckus was about.

Guns drawn, they quickly spread out and began to search the apartment room by room. Alex found the office, it had been ransacked. Papers were strewn all over the floor and the desk drawers had all been pulled open and searched. It was a scene that she was becoming all too familiar with in this investigation.

She donned a pair of gloves and began examining the room. If there was anything missing it would be damned near impossible to tell.

It was Edwards, who had made his way to the back bedroom, who found the body of Paige Wilson on top of Waltham's bed. She'd been hog tied and her throat had been slit.

"Oh fuck," he said, as he stared at the grizzly scene. "Hey, Chief, you'd better come take a look at this."

Alex walked over and looked inside the room.

"Shit," she said.

"I should have taken her in to the station house," the man replied.

"Nothing you could have done about it, Troy," Alex replied. "There was no reason to think her safety was in danger at the time."

"You think this is the daughter's handiwork?"

"Oh yeah," Alex replied. "Girl has definitely got some issues."

"Hey, boss," Hutch called out. "I found something."

Alex and Edwards made their way to the living room where Hutch was.

"I found this under a half-eaten bowl of cereal on the back deck," he said, and held up an envelope.

Alex read the outside. It was addressed to her.

"You mind?" Alex said, looking at Edwards.

"Nah, someone's got to read it."

Alex took the envelope and sat down on one of the couches. She opened it and began reading.

Chief Taylor:

If you're reading this, congratulations, you're better than I thought.

I bet you're wondering why, aren't you?

I have to assume that you probably figured most of it out already, but maybe I can fill in some of the missing blanks for you.

First, I killed Hannah Kurtz.

Actually it was Lou's idea, but he didn't have the balls to do it. He was a nice enough guy, but he just couldn't keep his dick in his pants. Unfortunately for him she got pregnant and started talking about getting married. When he told her no, she began making noise about how it would be hard for him to see his kid from jail. Apparently she knew about Lou's little film hobby. I really didn't want to do it, but Lou had taken me in and I kinda figured I owed him. He said that he couldn't handle jail. I felt bad, so I did it. If you ply a girl with enough alcohol they'll do anything, even go out for a moonlight boat ride. The funny thing is that it really didn't bother me. After I killed her I knew I could never go back home, so I just assumed her identity and never looked back. It made my life a whole lot easier.

Things would have been just fine if Lou hadn't left me alone in his cabin one day. I was bored and began looking through his computer. It was bad enough to know dear old dad was doing it with my friend, but to see mommy dearest getting in on the action was a completely different story. I guess you could say that what I saw made me a little bitter. It was bad enough that I had been raised to be the perfect little daughter, to not bring any discredit to our perfect family, but to find out that the two people that had raised me to be this fucked-up, were both doing what they preached against, well I guess it pushed me over the edge. I felt angry, I felt betrayed.

I went to the house one day to have it out with her. When I got there I spotted Lou's Jeep parked outside. I slipped inside the house and, needless to say, I wasn't exactly ecstatic about what I saw.

I guess most would say I snapped. I actually think that I just had an epiphany. I'm done with people hurting me.

Lou thought I had just split town, I didn't. I was waiting for the perfect moment. He was right, he couldn't handle jail. The minute they started talking hard time he would have squealed like the little bitch that he was. I knew that I was going to get pinned for the one murder, so what's a few more going to hurt?

I slit Lou's throat for the same reason I did the whore in the other room. Cause they're both pigs and they deserved it. I wish I could have seen Lou's face, but I didn't have a whole lot of time on my hands. It was cute the way Paige looked at me, pleading with those big brown eyes. Why do people always think they are immune to the consequences of their actions? It's all fun and games until the crazy bitch with the knife shows up.

As for my parents, call it teenage angst. Truth is they both had it coming. Sorry to screw up your case. I tried to get to her earlier, but by the time I got there you had already arrested her. Still not sure how you figured it all out. I thought I had gotten everything I needed from Lou's cabin. There were some things missing from my closet, which I have been searching high and low for. Did you happen to find those as well?

Maybe you are a little better than the keystone cop you replaced. I'll have to keep that in mind.

In a way, I do feel kinda bad about Hannah, but, in retrospect, it was probably the best thing for her and the kid. Lou would have just fucked them both up.

I wish there was a happy ending for you. It has to suck as a cop to watch the bad guy, or girl in this matter, slip through your grasp. I feel for you, I really do. By the time you read this I'll be long gone.

Maybe the stars will align, the rest of society won't piss me off anymore and this will just be the end of it. But it's more likely that every time you pick up a paper and see another murder you'll ask yourself: is it her?

I gotta run, chief. You can tell Yardley's Finest that they can close the book on this case. I'm done here and I won't be back.

Catch me if you can….

Alex laid the letter on the table and slid it over to Edwards.

"God, I need a fucking drinking."

CHAPTER THIRTY-TWO

It was just after two o'clock in the morning when they arrived back in Penobscot. Hutch pulled the car up in front of Alex's apartment and put it in park.

"You want a drink?" Alex asked. "I'm buying."

"Yeah," he said. "I think I earned it today."

Inside the apartment Alex hung her jacket up and headed to the kitchen. She grabbed two glasses, filling them with ice and whiskey, then handed one to Hutch.

He set it down on the table and removed his gun belt, hooking it over the back of one of the chairs before taking a seat.

Alex walked over and took the seat opposite from him

"Here's to better luck next time," she said in a mock toast.

Hutch took a sip, coughing as the liquid went down his throat.

"How the hell do you drink this stuff?" he asked.

Alex took out a cigarette and lit it, inhaling deeply.

"It's an acquired taste," she replied.

"I think I'll keep my stomach lining and stick with coke."

"*Whaddya wanna live forever*?" she asked with an exaggerated Brooklyn accent.

"After today? No."

"Don't take it so hard, junior; the good guys don't always win in the end. Sometimes the bad guys do get away."

"How do you deal with that?"

Alex raised her glass and smiled.

"I guess I should be glad that I never worked in New York City."

"I was twenty-one when I graduated from the police academy, Hutch. I came out full of piss and vinegar thinking that I was going to save the world. It took me all of about six months to realize the world really doesn't want to be saved."

"How do you handle working like that every day?" he asked, sipping on his drink.

"Oh, in the beginning it's tough. The places I worked in aren't like Penobscot. Life's hard there, really hard. If you get hurt walking down the street in Penobscot a half dozen people will stop to help you. There are some places in New York City where if you get hurt, by the time the ambulance arrives someone's ripped off your wallet, jacket and sneakers."

"I can't even imagine."

"It's a tough life. After a while you begin to feel like you are part of some occupying army. They don't really want you there, but they know they need you and they resent you for that. You are like the last line of defense. It makes it very hard to work under those conditions, and it is very easy to grow bitter."

"You ever regret it? I mean becoming a cop?"

"Nah, I loved it," she said, tapping the cigarette into the ash tray and taking a drag. "Besides, before I became a cop I used to get these really awful friction burns from the stripper pole."

Hutch swallowed hard on the drink he had just taken, which resulted in a coughing fit.

"Just kidding," she said.

"That's not funny," he replied.

"No, it was pretty funny. You want a refill?"

"Sure, why not, you've already corrupted me."

Alex refilled the two glasses and brought them back to the table.

"So what do we do now?" he asked.

"Now? Nothing," Alex replied. "I doubt old Sheldon Abbott is going to want to pay us to track down Susan Waltham throughout the state of New Hampshire."

"But we know she killed those people. We have a confession."

"Sure, we do," Alex replied. "But we're not the feds. They can chase down leads wherever it takes them. We still have a job to do here. Unless Susan Waltham decides to take up residence on Main Street, the odds are we won't see her again."

"That's not right," he replied.

"There's no *justice,* Hutch, there's *just us*," she said. "Tomorrow I'll give Tom Blackshear a call and see what the state can do to help us. She's got four bodies under her belt right now so there should be some interest. Eventually something's got to give."

"To bad we don't know where she's going to go next."

"Yeah," Alex replied, taking a sip of her drink. "It would be nice if killers submitted lists of their intended victims in advance."

"That would certainly make our job easier."

"Yeah, it would, wouldn't it?" she said.

Alex swirled the tip of her cigarette around on the edge of the ashtray, lost in thought, before taking a drag on it.

Something gnawed at her, like she was missing something.

She got up and walked over to where her coat was hung up and removed the photocopies of Waltham's letter that Edwards had made for her.

"Is there something wrong?"

"I don't know," Alex replied.

She began to re-read the letter.

"Mind if I get a refill?" Hutch asked.

"Nah, hit me too," she replied, sliding her glass toward him.

A moment later Hutch came back and set the glass down in front of Alex.

"Find anything?"

"I keep feeling as if I am missing something in this letter," Alex replied. "Susan said she thought she had gotten everything she needed from Lou's place."

"Well, she did get the hard drive."

"Yeah, but if it were just the hard drive then why'd she trash the room?"

"Maybe she was making sure that there wasn't anything else," Hutch said. "I mean you did find that backup drive."

"It's possible."

"Or perhaps she was just looking for something to help her getaway, money maybe. We definitely know she took stuff from her house and most likely the father's apartment."

"She was looking for the photos," Alex said. "That I know for certain."

"Well Lou filmed her too," he said. "Maybe she was trying to protect herself."

"She also said that she was done in Yardley and wouldn't be back."

"So?"

"Why didn't she say that she was done in Penobscot? She'd already killed Paige."

"I don't know."

"This isn't over," Alex said. "She admitted as much in the letter."

"Which brings me back to my original point. It's too bad that we don't know where she's going to next."

Alex laid the photocopies down on the table and took a drink.

"Yeah, it would be nice," She replied. "You know what else would be nice?"

"What?"

"It would be nice to know what we missed in that cabin," Alex said as she lit another cigarette.

"It's too bad Lou didn't keep a carbon copy of everything hidden away, like that USB drive."

"What did you just say?"

"It's too bad Lou didn't keep a carbon copy of…"

"Fuck me," she said, getting up from the table.

"What did I miss?"

"Maybe nothing, but just maybe…"

She walked over to the boxes and pulled out the large folder, that she had been storing all the copies of the photos and journal entries in. She brought it over to the table and started removing the contents till she found what she was looking for.

"Isn't that…"

"The notepad from the cabin? Yes."

She reached over and picked up the pencil from atop the newspaper crossword puzzle she had been doing.

"What are you doing, Chief?"

Alex flipped through the pages of the notepad until she found a place where there was evidence that a piece of paper had been ripped out.

"Watch."

She took the pencil and slowly began rubbing the side of it gently over the empty page. As Hutch watched closely, letters began to appear on the once blank page. As Alex went wider with the pencil, the letters began to form into names.

Lisa Putnam

Paul Bollinger

Toni Meyer

Paige Wilson

As Alex continued five additional names appeared on the page.

Alex set the pencil down, then reached over, picking up her glass, and took a drink.

"Holy shit," Hutch exclaimed. "Is that what I think it is?"

"Susan Waltham's coming back to Penobscot," she said. "They're still more victims on her list.

EPILOGUE

Alex carried the last of the moving boxes into the living room and set them down onto the floor, before crashing on the couch.

After nearly six months in the apartment she had finally decided that she'd had enough and needed something a bit more substantive.

Hutch's sister, Emily, had found the house for her. It was nice having someone in the real estate business that wasn't trying to screw her over.

A month of dealing with bank loan officers, inspectors, and the title company, and she had finally gotten the keys to her new home.

At first Emily wasn't sure if it was something that she would be interested in. It was an old house. A *fixer-upper* as Hutch had called it. But to Alex it had character and that was all that mattered to her.

She'd make changes to it as she went along, but all that mattered was that it was hers and she finally had a place to call home.

If only everything else had gone as smoothly.

After twenty-three days in the Intensive Care Unit, Rebecca Waltham was declared brain dead and removed from the life support equipment that had kept her alive.

Her death effectively ended Alex's investigation into the sex ring and allowed a sizeable portion of the Penobscot male population to breathe a collective sigh of relief.

They'd done their best to back-track the financial and cell phone records for both Waltham and Lou Jenkins without any success.

In terms of following the *money trail* it was quite easy, there was none.

While Waltham had a sizeable bank account, it appeared as if Jenkins was living paycheck to paycheck. An examination of the accounts indicated that neither of them had any unusual transfers, deposits or withdrawals. If there had been money changing hands, it was most likely in cash and the whereabouts of that money had gone to the grave with the two of them.

The phone records were equally as bland. There were numerous calls between the two of them, but no calls to any of the persons in the videos which could potentially link them.

She knew that Waltham and Jenkins were intimately involved with one another. She also knew that Jenkins was behind the videoing and her gut told her that Waltham was more than just a participant in the sexual escapades.

Alex refused to believe that either of them was so good, that they had been able to cover their tracks that well. But with their two prime suspects buried underneath six feet of soil, their case was going nowhere fast.

Most likely there was a, as yet unidentified, third party running things. Someone who *was* that smart and could keep things separated.

It reminded her of the old Hell's Angels maxim: *Three can keep a secret, if two are dead.*

At Nichols urging they had done *discrete* interviews with those whom they had identified, all under the guise of investigating a potential blackmail scheme. Predictably, everyone involved admitted to engaging in consensual sex and were absolutely appalled that their privacy had been invaded by Louis Jenkins.

In the end Scott had convinced her to let it go.

"You run around here like you're chasing after some damn white whale," Nichols said, "and you'll find yourself lost at sea without a boat."

It was a bitter pill for Alex to swallow.

Maybe that was what Susan Waltham had been searching for. Maybe she found the money or the link to whoever was running things.

She'd never know until she had the chance to sit across from her in an interrogation room. But Susan had proven to be more resourceful than they had imagined.

They'd warned everyone that they had identified in the videos of the potential danger they were in. Alex had made sure that everyone in the Department was aware of those involved and maintained a list of the residences. No one was to respond to calls at any of the locations alone. Despite their valiant attempts to keep them safe, Susan Waltham had still managed to claim another victim.

Paul Bollinger was killed in November when the car he was driving had hit a patch of black ice and slammed into a tree. Originally they had classified it as an accident, but later changed it to a homicide when the toxicology report had found a massive dose of the date rape drug, *Gamma-Hydroxybutyric*, in his system.

It seemed if Susan Waltham had *fucked* him one last time.

After that, she had disappeared again.

Alex stared out the large bay window that over looked Lake Moriah. It was a beautiful view, especially now.

Winter had come to Penobscot.

The lake was frozen over and in the distance she could make out the silhouettes of people ice skating.

The trees and landscape were covered in a heavy blanket of snow. It was what she had always thought of when she heard the expression: *winter wonderland*.

It was so much different up here than in New York City. It was beautiful and pristine, not the gray, icy slush that she had grown accustomed to.

Here nothing seemed spoiled.

As she continued to gaze out the window, she could see the setting sun beginning to ease its way behind the trees on the other side of the lake. Streaks of red, orange and yellow added a warm, colorful splash to an otherwise cold and dreary day.

Over on the far wall of the living room a fire burned brightly in the fireplace, adding to the cozy feel of the place.

Alex got up and went into the kitchen, rummaging through the boxes until she found a glass. After a bit more searching she found the corkscrew opener and uncorked a bottle of wine. It had been six months since she had a *real* drink. She found that she much rather preferred the occasional glass of red wine as opposed to the hellacious hangovers that the whiskey had given her.

She'd even managed to cut back on her smoking, after a gym session with Abby Simpson had left her on her knees wishing for death to take her quickly.

Alex had always believed that she had kept herself in relatively good shape, but this woman was an absolute beast. For her part, Abby had seemed to be wholly unsympathetic to her plight.

All in all, it seemed as if the missing pieces of her personal life were beginning to fit back together.

Every piece that was, except for one.

It wasn't as if she hadn't tried.

After the case had gotten shelved, Scott Nichols had found every excuse he could, to visit her, hinting that they should do dinner and catch up on what was happening. Eventually she accepted.

Scott was a really nice guy. He had a lot of things going for him. He was young, came from a nice family, and wasn't exactly hard on the eyes. The only problem was, he just wasn't *him*.

Alex wished that she didn't feel this way. Wished she could let go of something that was never going to be, but she knew that every man who came into her life was going to be held to a standard they were never going to meet.

Was it wrong? Was she supposed to lower her standards just to have an active love life?

Alex just couldn't resolve her feelings toward him.

Happy Valentine's Day to me, she thought. *Maybe I should just get a dog.*

She took a sip of wine, watching as the sun finally dipped below the tree line. She'd taken the rest of the week off in order to get the house ready.

It felt good to be putting down some roots.

In all she had grown to like small town living. It was quaint and charming, not to mention that the people genuinely seemed to like her. It wasn't exactly how she had envisioned her life, but in a way maybe it was for the best.

She'd taken to visiting Mildred Parker every week or so, and had even spent Christmas day with her. The woman had taken her under her wing, and in a way it made Alex feel vaguely normal. She had even settled into a regular gym schedule with Abby, in spite of the fact that she could barely crawl out of bed after the first few times.

Alex had put her past behind her and was actually doing better than she had in a long time. Of course she still butted heads with Sheldon Abbott and the board from time to time, but they grudgingly admitted that she knew what she was doing. More importantly they knew she was not going to allow them to bully her the way they did the previous chiefs.

It didn't hurt to have the file from Mike Williams with all the invoices. She was still looking into that potential shit storm. Before she would dare take on Abbott face to face, she was going to make sure she had an ironclad case.

She swirled the wine around in the glass, taking another sip, and then cradled it in her hands as she watched the yellow flames dance over the logs in the fireplace.

It was mesmerizing.

Suddenly the cell phone on the coffee table began to vibrate.

She set the glass down and picked up the phone, seeing the name appear on the screen.

"Hey there, *Mister First Deputy Commissioner*," she said. "I thought you didn't have time for your old partner anymore."

"Alex, I need you to do me a favor and I need it done ASAP," Maguire replied.

Alex could hear the urgency in the man's voice, something was very wrong and it scared her. In all the years she had known him, she'd never heard this before. A sense of panic set in and she was acutely aware that her heart was racing.

She sat up in the seat.

"Whatever you need, James, just tell me."

About the Author

Andrew Nelson is a twenty-two year law enforcement veteran and a graduate of the State University of New York. He served twenty years with the New York City Police Department, achieving the rank of sergeant before retiring in 2005. He and his wife have four children and currently reside with their Irish Wolfhound in central Illinois.

He is also the author of Perfect Pawn and Queen's Gambit, the series featuring James Maguire.

For more information please visit:

http://andrewgnelson.blogspot.com/

Like us on Facebook:

https://www.facebook.com/pages/Andrew-Nelson/168310343376572